THE SECRET AND THE HIDDEN

Volume I of
Ibrahim's Eyes

THE SECRET AND THE HIDDEN

Volume I of
Ibrahim's Eyes

A NOVEL

Paul Hastings Wilson

BLUE ATLAS PRESS

ISBN-13: 979-8-9922110-0-9

Library of Congress Control Number: 2025900332

Published by Blue Atlas Press, Wallkill, New York.
blueatlaspress@gmail.com

This is a work of literary fiction. With the exception of certain historical events and personages referred to in the text, all characters appearing in or referred to in this book are fictitious, and any resemblance to real persons, living or dead, is entirely coincidental.

To Shirley,
With love

Acknowledgements

I would like to express my gratitude to Isabelle, my beautiful wife, for her unfailingly insightful remarks and for her love, faith, and indefatigable support throughout my work on this project.

My thanks also to Tom Gilbert and Lester Berman for their trenchant comments upon reading portions of an early draft of the manuscript.

The excerpt from the poem beginning, "Exile's hand has sown the seeds of mourning…," by Ibn el-Khatib that appears on page 47 is adapted from the translation appearing in *Alhambra,* by Michael Jacobs and Francisco Fernández (Rizzoli, 2000.)

*"The desert is not remote in southern tropics,
The desert is not only around the corner,
The desert is squeezed in the tube-train next to you.
The desert is in the heart of your brother."*

— T. S. Eliot, *The Rock*

"Those who dream by night in the dusty recesses of their minds wake in the day to find that all was vanity; but the dreamers of the day are dangerous men, for they may act their dream with open eyes, and make it possible."

—T. E. Lawrence, *Seven Pillars of Wisdom*

1.

"*Alhamdulillah*, my name is Hâfiz Amal Koraoun el-Mudharrisi, alias 'Samiel.' I was born…" he pauses and glances up at the Western prosecutor and other non-Arabic foreigners in the gallery, representatives of the World Court at the Hague and the U.N. who'd come to observe the trial, and explains, "My proper first name is Amal. Hâfiz is an honorific, meaning keeper of the faith, reciter of the *Qur'an*—I was able to recite the *Qur'an* from memory by the time I was nine." Returning to the papers in his hand, he continues, "I was born in the village of Mud-harris, on *Safar* 1, in the year 1351 of the Islamic calendar, which is to say, June 6th, 1932, Gregorian. I am seventy years old. I was my father's fifth son, but my older brothers all died in the womb—*aywá, Allah karim!* My father was Abd el-Mudharrisi, a direct descendant of the line of Hudhail bin Mudrika. My mother's name was Khalida. I have been known as Amal Koraoun el-Mudharrisi from birth until the time of the Revolution, between 1390 to 1397, Islamic, or 1970 and 1977, Gregorian, when—with the Court's per-mission," he says, interrupting his narrative to look up again from his prepared speech toward the magistrates' bench, "with the Court's permission, I thought I might omit the Islamic calendar conversions and use only the Gregorian dates, hereafter, in the interest of concision?"

"Permitted," the Chief Magistrate says, and glancing over to the court clerk, adds, "Let the record so note."

Samiel clears his throat and continues, "At the time of the Revolution, I took the nom de guerre of Samiel. After the fall of the QPR—the Qarmatian People's Republic—I was in exile under an assumed name in Moscow from 1977 until 1987.

"Returning to my youth, I completed my Qur'ânic studies under Wali Gemondabahn in 1948. I subsequently received my diploma at King Boualem University here in el-Rawi, and the following year, 1950 to 1951, I lived in Meena Yûsuf-as-Siddîq as a teacher. I was eighteen years old. I taught mathematics and history. In 1952 I joined the civil war to unite the Qarmatian tribes under King Boualem. After the war, in 1955, I was accepted at *École Normale Supérieure* in Paris and went there to pursue advanced studies in mathematics. I received my doctorate in number theory in 1958, and after two years of post-doctoral study I returned to Qarmat in 1960 to accept the position of associate professor at the University here in the Capital, where I taught and pursued research until 1968...."

He's speaking in his native Arabic, and he speaks slowly and clearly into the microphone, pausing frequently to allow the interpreters time to translate.

"I first met Mumi Malagawi el-Hawhza while I was teaching in Meena Yûsuf-as-Siddîq," he continues, flicking the fold out of the pages of the manuscript from which he's reading. "Mumi el-Hawhza was a Qur'ânic scholar of great renown and a profound student of international politics and European colonial history. He had studied these subjects at Cairo University and at Oxford University in England.

I considered Mumi el-Hawhza a great man. He explained many things to me about history and philosophy, things that had troubled me in my own youthful studies, and in this way, over time, he became my mentor. And as I left Qarmat to pursue my studies in France, I kept in mind Mumi el-Hawhza's words urging me to use the opportunity there to explore courses in world history and political theory. It was while I was in Paris that I...."

A signal beep heard over his earphones cues Samiel to pause to let the translators catch up. After a moment, he continues. "It was while I was in Paris that I encountered several young people from other parts of Europe and Asia with strong political views. I also met other students from the Maghreb, many of whom were on fellowships at the Sorbonne, and we began to meet occasionally at a mosque in Seine-Saint-Denis to discuss political theory and its place in the context of Islamic precepts. Then during the spring semester, I attended my first international mathematics conference, at Heidelberg University, where the brilliant and original Alexander Grothendieck was to present a lecture. I had been studying his research papers for some time. I admired his work and had initiated a correspondence with him while I was still at university in el-Rawi. I remember that Dr. Grothendieck lectured on his invention of the étale and l-adic cohomology theories, which explain an observation of André Weil's that there is a deep connection between the topological characteristics of a variety and its Diophantine properties. After the lecture, I took the opportunity of going up to meet him. I had already known something of Dr. Grothendieck's bold and independent political theories, which explored how the dissemination of Western ideas through the rapid spread of communication technologies triggered certain anomalies in Eastern and Third World cultural development—and projected how the reaction would inevitably come back to subvert Western civilization itself. But even so, I was not prepared for the depth of insight and breadth of vision he brought to these matters in our personal conversations. We met only three times—all during that conference—but we continued to correspond for many years, and there is no question that Dr. Alexander Grothendieck had as much, if not more, of an influence on my subsequent intellectual development as did Mumi el-Hawhza...."

It's strange, Samiel is thinking to himself as his voice drones on through his prepared statement to the Court, how he finds himself glancing up now and then toward the gallery to look for the familiar face of a boy he knows could not possibly be there.

...Was it only six months ago? It seemed to happen in another world. It was early in the morning, he remembers, and the air was still cool, with a vast clear vault of sky, pale silver in the east and shading into deep cobalt in the west. To the south, the mirage of the Hercules Mountains, which were actually too distant over the horizon to see, rose like a blue curtain over the desert, and closer by the great white dome of the Qubbah-el-Ismâ 'ili Shi'a was shining over the city like a lesser moon. But as he approached the souk, the illusion of serenity was soon shattered by the familiar noise of a gathering of gaunt, robed vendors stationed around the square crying their wares and raising a din that sounded like some harried host of prophets keening in el-Barzakh, the Qur'ânic boundary between Heaven and Hell. They were hawking carpets and cloths, brassware,

incense, candles, and intricate handicrafts in rosewood, cedar, and monkey wood inlaid with ivory, a rich sampling of local craftsmanship. There were, of course, the usual snake-charmers, acrobats, and contortionists—but there were also, unfortunately, others, the parasites, who despite the best efforts of the constabulary always managed to be there to give his people a bad name among the tourists: the pickpockets, the beggars, and especially the innumerable sly, spidery creatures who swept continually through the gathering crowd like a pestilence, their tone seductive and sibilant as they offered their skills as guides, pimps, and purveyors of all manner of licit and illicit goods.

One particularly large group of tourists standing quietly amid the rest caught his eye. The crowd was focusing its attention on a small boy making gestures as he spoke in the center of the circle. It was Ibrahim, of course....

Samiel moved closer.

The boy was one of those clever young street urchins who managed to pick up a certain rude fluency in half a dozen foreign languages merely from their brief interactions with tourists. Ibrahim was telling the crowd about the local wonders to be seen and touting his own talents as a guide. But he was going about it with his unique brand of imagination and verve, delivering a continuous stream of outrageous hyperbole tossed out in several languages alternately, retailing extraordinary things that lay hidden away in forbidden corners of the medina that he claimed to have exclusive access to but was willing to share with anyone who dared to accompany him—for a small consideration.

Working his way through the crowd to get a closer look at him, to see how Ibrahim was growing, how he might have changed, Samiel saw a boy of ten or eleven at most, barefoot but otherwise unusually neat and clean for the urchin he appeared to be. He performed little jigs, launched big, sweeping gestures, and sketched illustrative maps in the red clay with his toes as he garnished his fantastic claims with a grim sense of detail and rhapsodic fervor, making his pitch in a kaleidoscopic spin of pidgin German, French, English, Arabic, Italian, and Japanese. He deployed his range of linguistic phrases without pause even within the same sentences as he turned his eye on the various foreign nationals he spied among the crowd. From the looks on their faces, he held them in thrall. It was almost as if these people had journeyed from the ends of the earth to this small, out-of-the-way North African country for the sole purpose of putting themselves into the hands of this unscrupulous mini-magus, a small boy who, by virtue of nothing more than a precocious self-confidence and intensity, seemed somehow able to compress a world of exotic and forbidden experience into the few days allotted for their tour.

Unlike the dozens of other boys hustling tourists in the square, Ibrahim would often turn down the apparently richer or more cynical tourists who sought to hire him. He seemed almost impervious to the lure of their wallets. With his handsome young face and preternaturally intense almond eyes peering through a dark tussle of hair, he seemed to be sifting through his captive throng in search of something more intriguing than money. He appeared to be drawn to those in the crowd who looked the most sober and reserved, as if he were in the game for the sheer sport of it, bent on leading those who seemed the most resistant and morally impregnable into perdition. Keeping in the background so as to watch unobserved, Samiel saw the boy play one group of tourists against another, drawing them out until they were actually vying for his attention, while the boy focused not on those holding out fists full of dollars, euros, or yen, but on those who stood there awkwardly with their eyes cast down, eyeing him reluctantly with sidelong glances.

Finally, Ibrahim went over to a group of middle-aged to elderly American tourists, all of whom were wearing nametags and seemed to belong to some Christian church or society. Among them was a little girl of five or six dressed in white socks and red patent leather shoes. Taking her hand, Ibrahim whispered something in her ear that made her laugh and then playfully danced her around in the circle as he hummed a popular *chaabi* folk tune. After a moment, he turned toward the modestly dressed couple that had been standing beside the girl, and taking them for her grandparents, he complimented them on the little girl's dancing abilities, and then induced them to step forward. The couple he'd selected appeared awkward at the attention and looked like they were on their first vacation since their youthful honeymoon. The man, in cotton gabardine slacks, a short-sleeved plaid shirt open at the neck and a Panama, seemed ill at ease, as if not knowing what to expect, but he appeared to be the leader of the group, for the others seemed to defer to him as though he might have been their pastor. His wife sported a pair of quaint white lace gloves to match her frock. Ibrahim told them to follow him. But the man demurred. Ibrahim told him not to be concerned about paying, that he liked them so much he would guide them for nothing. (Samiel smiled to himself at hearing that old ploy.) Eventually, the man and his wife exchanged an embarrassed smile and a shrug of acquiescence. But as Ibrahim started to lead his latest quarry away, he suddenly hesitated and glanced back.

At the time, a procession had been approaching the square, its members chanting plaintively as they worked their way through the crowd toward the fountain at the center. Samiel remembered thinking at first that it was a funeral procession. But no, the wooden coffin they carried aloft seemed to ride lightly on their shoulders and was draped with a banner embroidered with the names of numerous victims in Arabic script. It was only symbolic then, meant for a demonstration. The "mourners" were chanting the names of the victims of a recent police raid and were carrying placards with religious and political slogans saying,

"Remember the Day of Shame!"

"Embrace the Messenger!"

"Down with (Prime Minister) Badat!"

"Piss on Badat!"

"Vote no!"

And so on. The participants, he realized, were protesting both a government crackdown on a previous demonstration and an upcoming constitutional referendum. As the demonstrators reached the fountain, they began to tear down a shrine that had already been placed there, meant to pay tribute to the victims of some earlier calamity. But as this latest group started tearing away the flowers, prayer beads, and finely embroidered garments on the earlier shrine, others rushed forward yelling in counter-protest, and a raucous altercation ensued. They soon got to shoving and cursing one another, as the tourists stood back and gawked.

Samiel then turned to go on his way, but happened to catch Ibrahim's eye. The boy seemed to be staring at him oddly. Then Ibrahim abruptly spun on his heel and started to run, leaving the elderly couple and their granddaughter whom he'd been about to lead away on his tour puzzled and gaping after him.

Suddenly there was a lot of shoving and yelling in the crowd, and Samiel found himself caught up in a churning mass of demonstrators and tourists who'd suddenly panicked for some reason and had begun screaming and trying to push past one another in the attempt to flee. And then all at once amid the clamor silence fell like a stone, and Samiel felt the wind sucked out of him. For an instant, the souk and everyone in it seemed to brighten and expand like figures on a painted balloon. And then, as though it came bursting out of a dream, he heard the muffled sound of the explosion.

———

"You have told the Court, Samiel," the prosecutor is saying, now in the second week of the trial, "that you've studied the classic military texts, Clausewitz, Jomini, Mahan, Foch, and Napoleon's campaigns, among others. Where did you read that a viable military strategy entailed crimes against humanity, including the mass murder, rape. and terrorism of the civilian population?"

"Objection! The prosecution is implying—"

"Your Honor, we are only trying to—"

"Overruled! The defendant will answer the question."

"But in fact," Samiel counters, "there were over a million fatalities in Napoleon's Russian campaign, alone—of which over a quarter million were civilians, and you may verify this yourself by consulting the historical records. Where was it written," he continues, "I should like to ask you, in return, that the bombing of forty thousand civilians in Dresden and two hundred thousand in Tokyo, or the irradiation of two hundred and thirty-seven thousand in Hiroshima and one hundred and eight thousand in Nagasaki should be the preferred course for a free democracy to pursue in order to triumph over a fascist or imperial state? As Chairman Mao once wrote, revolution is not a dinner party. A revolution is an insurrection, an act of violence by which one class overthrows another to advance the truth of its vision. But, as you mention Von Clausewitz, let us recall what he wrote about the fog of war: that the great uncertainty in war is of a peculiar difficulty because all action must, to a certain extent, be planned 'in a mere twilight,' which necessarily gives an exaggerated dimension to things.

"One makes plans, and sometimes they have unanticipated effects," he continues. "One fights a war with soldiers who are not automatons. They are human, and while they follow orders, they are also vulnerable to baser human distractions. Even Sun Tzu and the ancients understood that it is the nature of war to bring out the best and the worst in men. Notwithstanding, yes, I do not debate the fact that the responsibility for the shortcomings as well as for the successes of a campaign rests upon the shoulders of the general, no matter how ill-starred the times or how noble his intentions!"

"Yes, fine," the prosecutor says, dismissively. "However, what is more pertinent here is that the war you waged, the QPR Revolution, was a war of *choice*, a war—as you have said—a war the QPR initiated on its own to overthrow a legitimate government! And in the course of overthrowing that legitimate order—a constitutional monarchy—did it occur to you then, does it occur to you now, that the resulting disorder—chaos, rather—which wrought untold destruction and loss of life to so many *of your own countrymen*, might've been an evil far outweighing any possible good or truth you thought you were pursuing?"

"I would like to point out," Samiel responds, "that the 'constitutional monarchy' of King Saddahi el-Roweed was *not*, in fact, legitimate—certainly not according to the free democratic model underlying the rationale for this Court. Saddahi inherited the throne as the result of force during the civil wars preceding his reign, wars fought to consolidate the rival tribes of the country under the reign of his father, King Boualem, who *was* a great leader, but who died prematurely, unfortunately, and left the throne to Saddahi. All this happened a generation before the QPR Revolution. The 'Constitution' of which you speak was an arbitrary document drawn up by Saddahi and his appointed ministers as a cosmetic mask to satisfy the conscience of the French colonial government—without benefit of contribution or comment by any representative of the people. It merely clothed a tyranny in the garment of law!"

"Just a minute!" the prosecutor interjects, "the truth is the Constitution was—"

"I would also like to suggest," Samiel continues, overriding the interruption, "that the 'disorder' and 'chaos' you spoke of may simply be forms of complexity for which we don't yet know the rules. You spoke of truth. But Western science claims that what is considered true should be verifiable. And yet with moral truths there remains the enigma that the 'greater' the truth, the more difficult it seems to be to verify in ways we might all agree upon. 'Truths' we admire, such as liberty, fraternity, and equality, are rather like mirages we experience in the desert: the closer we approach one, the more the others recede from our grasp. These truths have proven to be elusive, mutually contradictory, and uncertain in the world we live in. It may even be that what you call disorder is, in fact, the new order. Just consider what we've witnessed over the recent span of years. Dissolution of the USSR and Yugoslavia, savage internecine wars in Cambodia, the Balkans, and Southern Africa!"

The prosecutor, impatient, tries to interrupt. "All right, I think that's enough!"

But Samiel, having only reached mid-stride, continues over him. "If your own vaunted Thomas Hobbes's argument for order had been held sacred—"

The prosecutor stands up, "If the Court please—"

"—neither the American nor the French Revolutions would have taken place. Revolutions are, by definition, 'unlawful' because they entail revolt against laws that are oppressive in order to replace them with laws that are just!"

The prosecutor, resolute, turns to the bench, "If the Court *please!* We would like to have the defendant limit his digressions and answer the questions he is asked!"

"Objection! The defendant is attempting to—"

"I am only trying to—"

"Your Honor—"

"Objection!"

"Order!" the Chief Magistrate says. "Come to order, please! Without ruling on the objection, specifically, the Court requests that the defendant curtail his responses to the requisite points raised by the prosecutor's questions. On the other hand, the Court requests that the prosecution refine its questions in order to elicit direct answers and discourage digressions. Defendant may proceed."

Samiel turns an inquiring glance from the bench to the prosecutor's desk and back. "With all due respect," he says, feigning an innocent lapse of memory, "would the prosecutor kindly repeat his question?"

The prosecuting attorney confers with his associates for a moment, then looks up and says, "Samiel, in one way or another, you have largely admitted to the nature and extent of the crimes of which—"

"Objection!"

"If the Court please, the defendant has not denied complicity in—"

"Sustained! The prosecution will please reword the question."

"Very well. The prosecution would like to ask the defendant whether, of those acts in which he has here not specifically denied complicity, he feels any guilt."

"I'm sorry," Samiel says, "I do not understand the question."

"Do you feel any guilt about what you have done?" the prosecutor asks, raising his voice in irritation. "You have stated your overriding goal as being to free your country from the rule of a tyrant and the exploitation of a foreign government, namely, France. Has it occurred to you…do you question, even now, whether those 'patriotic' ends you speak of justified the choice to wreak mass murder and the horrors of torture as a means?"

"Objection! The prosecution is making assumptions about connections between certain criminal acts and any personal political choices the defendant may have made.

Such connections have not yet been established—"

A long wail of anguish and frustration is heard from someone in the gallery.

"If the Court please, I am only—"

"Sustained! Prosecutor will please refrain from these assumptive leaps of logic and attempt to establish the facts in the necessary order."

"Do you, Samiel," the prosecutor begins again, "I repeat—do you feel any guilt about any choices you might have made with regard to the horrific outcome of acts with which you have, here, in your own testimony, admitted some complicity in?" The young American attorney then blushes and shakes his head, apparently appalled by his own muddled syntax, evidence of his increasing exasperation in the face of the defendant's evasions.

Samiel, meanwhile, who is fluent in English, French, German, and Russian, who reads Latin and Greek and is knowledgeable in a handful of other languages, and who certainly understands the implications of these questions immediately, nevertheless hesitates, as he finds himself distracted—possibly by a sound from the gallery?—and his mind flashes back to the day of the explosion in the souk, earlier that spring....

He remembers that he'd blacked out after the suicide bomber had detonated the explosives in the market square that day. He'd later awakened gasping for air with his eyes burning and swollen and feeling as though someone was dripping acid into them. The air was foul and full of smoke. Eventually, he started coughing and after a moment, he began to breathe more easily. There was little he could see through the thick smoke, except where jagged shafts of light shone through showing fleeting glimpses of wreckage. All he could make out at first was the crazy vision of a skinned goat dangling from a parapet above him with what looked like the disembodied arm of a woman in a long red evening glove draped over its flank. As his eyes began to focus again, he realized that what he'd thought was a goat was actually the naked and headless torso of a man. But it really seemed to be a woman's arm across the man's shoulder and what had looked like a long red glove was actually blood. The blood was dripping into his eyes. The gruesome coupling hung in the air suspended, he didn't know how, rotating slowly over his head in a ghastly dance.

Gradually, as the smoke cleared, he was able to see that the sun was still high, and he guessed he'd only been knocked out for a few minutes. But the square was nearly deserted after the explosion, the crowd having panicked and run. The dead and wounded lay scattered about with their torn-off limbs entangled and mired in gore. He thought he could hear people screaming, but he was still partially deafened by the blast and it all sounded very far away. He felt numb all over and couldn't immediately tell whether or not he, too, had suffered any serious injuries. For what seemed a long time, he couldn't move and simply hung there, wedged amid bolts of cloth into a niche in a building wall, and unable to do more than look down at the handful of those who'd remained below as they searched among the fallen looking for family or friends or offering help where they could.

By the time he was able to free himself and climb down from the wall, he'd counted at least eight or ten who were apparently dead and dozens more wounded. Except for torn clothes and a few scrapes, he seemed to have escaped injury. His hearing was gradually returning and he could now discern the voices of others crying out for help. Moving unsteadily, he made his way through the carnage toward the spot where the blast had occurred. Where the fountain had been, at the center of the market square, there was now only a crater in the earth some twenty feet wide and ten deep, and in it lay stone rubble, twisted piping, shreds of clothing, and a few body parts still visible above the water flooding up out of the burst pipes. Floating on the water was a straw Panama he recognized. It had belonged to the old preacher whom the boy, Ibrahim, had struck his bargain with, and resting on a burst pipe next to it, there was a small, red patent leather shoe, still neatly buckled around a child's foot that had been shorn off at the ankle.

So, it's starting again, he thought. It was the Seventh of March, il Yawm 'Aar, the Day of Shame. We've come full circle!

But by then, he could hear the long mournful wail of sirens approaching in the distance. He realized that under the circumstances it would have been inadvisable for him to be discovered there. He turned and quickly left the souk....

Speaking aloud in Court, in answer to the prosecutor's last contorted question about whether he felt any guilt for what he'd done, Samiel says, "There is always a price to pay for freedom. The alternative is slavery and resentment. At some point, every people in history has had to come to terms with this fact. I have no hope of clearing my conscience. The things I found it necessary to do for the sake of freeing my country from the oppression of a ruthless despot and the exploitation of a colonial power are so terrible that no legal argument or political posturing will save my soul. I can say that I'm sorry, and at the same time I know that to say so does nothing to resurrect the dead or to heal the suffering in the hearts of the survivors. I can only say that I'm sorry—but that it was necessary!"

This last statement is met with a hush in the courtroom. For the first time, there are no immediate challenging questions from the attorneys. No one calls out from the gallery. No one even coughs. The silence continues for so long that Samiel glances around the courtroom to see what the matter is. They are all staring at him. Their expressions seem frozen: expectation, puzzlement, surprise, confusion, anger. It's as if they've all been listening for something—and are still listening, because what they just heard makes no sense, as if they've suddenly lost the ability to grasp the meaning of simple words. They all know that the murdered victims of the QPR are still being unearthed, even now, twenty-five years after the fact, still being identified through DNA and dental records, and their information entered into a central database, so that their kin might be notified and their fates permanently recorded and memorialized. But many of those sitting in the gallery at Samiel's trial on this day and who heard what he has just said, are the families of these victims. And every year, since the government began restorations of the *Qubbah-el-Ismâ 'ili Shi'a*—which had been destroyed by fire during the Revolution—and rededicated the building as a mausoleum and monument to the victims, every year these families had made the Memorial Day pilgrimage by foot up the steep, winding road of the mountain overlooking the city, passed busloads of gaping tourists, to that white-domed shrine of the saint who was the City of el-Rawi's heavenly intercessor. They had followed Mumi Ahmed el-Hawhza (son of Samiel's early mentor and now Qarmat's Minister of Islamic Affairs), as he led them in the *salât el-janâzah,* the funeral prayer to commemorate the dead. They had murmured, after him, the names he'd read aloud from a list of the first two hundred victims whose skeletal remains were known to be laid to rest there, a portion in each of the four *iwans,* the great halls spaced around the plaza. They had followed Mumi Ahmed into the first hall and had seen with their own eyes the remains stored there, each one tagged with an inventory number in the form of a BAR Code indicating when and where the body had been found and by which forensic team, approximately when and how the person had been killed, and finally, the victim's name, sex, age, and family, or as much of that as had been determined. This coding system was necessary because only certain of the QPR officers had kept reliable records, and victims had often been transferred several times from one prison camp to another, where they had been tortured and interrogated by different officers before being eventually executed, so that even after more than a quarter of a century, remains were still being discovered in many different mass graves around the country. The families had seen these skeletal remains, 600,000 of them, each one laid out next to the other, on tier after tier of plexiglas shelves stretching from wall to wall, front to back, and stacked from the floor right up to the forty-foot-high ceiling. And they knew, because they had seen it in the newspapers and on television and heard it on the radio, that by the time the victims had all been recovered and cataloged and all four halls filled, it was estimated that the mausoleum would house the remains of close to two-and-a-half million of their countrymen.

And so, it would seem that the words Samiel had just uttered constituted the admission of guilt that they'd all come together after so long to hear. But the clarification and emotional release they'd apparently anticipated upon hearing that admission seems, now, to have been stolen away from them. They exchange glances with their neighbors and turn back to stare at him again as if they find his words so plain, so simple, and so breathtakingly out of proportion to the monstrous events to which they referred that it leaves them reeling and wondering what it all could mean.

2.

"Samiel," the prosecutor begins dryly, resuming his arguments later that afternoon, "you said, before the recess, that you were sorry. My question is, do you feel any *guilt* for your actions? Do you have any *remorse?* Do you feel your actions were *morally wrong?*"

"The question of morality is interesting," Samiel says, tilting his head in thought, "but honestly, I think it is of a class that is essentially undecidable. Morality is culture-specific. Morality isn't a science, possibly it isn't even an art, although, as an artifact of political expediency it has been artfully manipulated."

"Uhh, excuse me!" the prosecutor raises a hand to interrupt. "Let's skip the *artful* philosophy, if you don't mind. I'll rephrase the question—"

"With the Court's permission," Samiel interjects. "I feel the prosecuting attorney's question is pertinent and I'm trying to explain—"

"Your Honor," the prosecutor interposes, "in keeping with the rules set down—and reiterated during the course of these proceedings—for the conduct of this trial, the prosecution wishes to curtail irrelevant and rambling obfuscations of the points in question, and so, we would like to rephrase—"

"Objection!" the defense counselor calls out again, rising to his feet. He is a Bengali in his late fifties, appointed from an international roster by the Court, and while Samiel has found him capable thus far, the man was previously unknown to him. The counselor continues now in his crisp, accented English: "The charges against the defendant hang upon assumptions of intent, whether the defendant *intended* to order, encourage or actually commit acts of mass murder, torture, and crimes against humanity. The defendant is a professional scientist and university scholar, and the level of his thought, most especially in matters of morality, is by nature philosophical. The defense therefore deems it essential to its case that the defendant be allowed to explain to the Court his philosophical attitude at the time of the crimes in question!"

"Objection sustained," the Chief Magistrate, says. "The prosecution may reiterate, or rephrase its question, but the defendant will be allowed to answer in full. Counsel?"

But the young prosecuting attorney briefly turns his head aside, as if to hide an involuntary expression of anger and exasperation, before turning back to fix his eyes on a point on the far wall above Samiel's head. "The prosecution would like to know," he says, at last, "whether the defendant feels any guilt for his actions? Does he have any remorse?"

Samiel absently traces the line of his jaw with a finger as he considers the question again. After a moment, he says, "You have asked me, just before, whether the ends justified the choice of the means to accomplish them. But I think it is important to appreciate the fact that there is a difference between choosing and deciding. I did not *choose* murder and torture. I chose *freedom*. I made that choice as an individual person. Every man must make that choice for himself. As it happens, I am of a culture in which every man—every man, every woman, and every child—is interconnected with every other in the community in a profound way, a way that is very difficult to explain to one from a different culture.

"Let me try and illustrate with an example or two. In Islam, where community responsibility is paramount, it is moral for a man to take as many wives as he can support. It is immoral not to give alms to the poor. In America," he adds, looking squarely at the young American prosecutor, "the heartland of independence, where bigamy is immoral, the poor are expected to fend for themselves. In America, individualism is encouraged. But in my culture, individualism is not a trait to be admired. One may be exceptional in any of a number of ways—but these ways must all be reflected in the culture's self-image—in religious insight, for example, or moral rectitude—but to be individualistic is to be antithetical to our mores.

"But let me give another example. In 1918, in the aftermath of the great carnage of the First World War, the American President, Woodrow Wilson—who was well known to hate war and crimes against humanity and who had worked very hard to help create the League of Nations—this same person, whom the world respected then as a great humanitarian and archetype of morality on the international political plane, rejected the notion of a universal principle of justice to determine whether to prosecute crimes against humanity *within a state's national borders*. His secretary of state, Robert Lansing, was quoted as saying, 'the essence of sovereignty is the absence of responsibility.' *The absence of responsibility!*

"But it seems to me," he continues, "that there can be no morality where there is no responsibility. America did not protest when Pakistani troops killed between one and two million Bengalis and raped some two hundred thousand women—possibly because, at the time, in 1971, President Nixon was using Pakistan as an intermediary in his attempt to establish a trading rapprochement with China. It was a choice that may have made political sense, then—and may have addressed what the President perceived as his moral duty of putting the commercial advantage of his own country first—but in the court of public opinion—certainly on the Indian Subcontinent, it seemed a fault!"

Samiel glances briefly across the room to see whether his defense counselor has any reaction to what he's just said. Bangladesh, originally part of the historic region of Bengal, had suffered two long and bloody wars with India and Pakistan after the fall of the British Raj, before finally being declared an independent country. But the defense attorney, maintaining a professional demeanor, lets slip only the merest hint of a smile to acknowledge the reference, while keeping his eyes lowered to his desk, where he scribbles a note.

"And then, of course," Samiel goes on, turning back toward the judges, "within the last decade, there were the horrors of Bosnia and Rwanda, from which America also chose to remain aloof.

"But excuse me," he adds quickly, "please do not misunderstand! I'm not presuming to accuse America of any wrongdoing here. That would be beyond my competence in any case. I'm not even trying to suggest that America is any more immoral than any other country—or even more hypocritical, for that matter—although it may be said, hypocrisy is *not* culture-specific, it may be found almost anywhere.

I'm really struggling to answer the question, which I think is a very important question. But it is a very complicated question, and I think that in the realm of international law and justice, it serves no purpose to confuse morality with self-righteousness. If morality and responsibility can be circumscribed by national boundaries, then it seems that they might be understood to be circumscribed and differentiated among different cultures, as well. But in that case, who is qualified to judge the actions of the rest of us?

"It would seem that in each culture, the reasonable man should adhere to the mores of the society in which he was reared. Yes, of course, we may all agree that certain acts, like war and genocide, are horrific and tragic. But whether they are the result of unavoidable circumstance or criminal intent must be examined on a case-by-case basis.

"Notwithstanding this, there are times when reason might fall short of what is just and good, when a new and more vital truth seems to lie just beyond the general community's line of sight. Habits of mind, outlasting the original contexts that once gave them value, might blind a society to some impending confrontation with fate. To one able to see beyond that horizon, one with a vision of such a long-range truth, the impulse to press ahead to try and grasp it—and to communicate that vision to others—might entail great risks, personal, social, and political. Such a choice could lead to a great upheaval—despite the fact that one might prefer to *avoid* such an upheaval. It would be a difficult decision. It would seem unreasonable to pursue such a course. And yet, history provides many examples of moments when the fate of a society hung upon its ability to adapt to a sea change— despite the resistance of the majority to giving up the old ways. For the one standing on that cusp, would it be moral to choose to forge ahead, or to turn back?

"I would like to remind you of something the great Irish author George Bernard Shaw once wrote. Shaw said, 'The reasonable man adapts himself to the world. The unreasonable one persists in trying to adapt the world to himself. Therefore, all progress depends on the unreasonable man.' Among such 'unreasonable' men of history, one might number Socrates, Copernicus, Galileo, and the signers of the American Declaration of Independence.

"But as we know, these things happen in cycles, when the tide of discontent surges to a crest and one with the right talents at the right time is thrown to the surface. Had it not been me in this case it would have been someone else. And so when I considered choosing freedom for myself, it necessarily meant that I had to take into account how my freedom would affect my country—it was a question, you see, of what we in Islam call *akhlâq,* a question of responsibility to the community, whether, in fact, my personal freedom could amount to anything more than a selfish abstraction if it did not engage every other man, woman, and child in Qarmat. So, I chose freedom. Once I'd made that choice, I had then to decide how to achieve it. In Qarmat, at the time, there was only one option. There was no choice. The decision was to seek freedom by the only means available, or to return to study in Europe, cutting myself off from my own country, a country I loved, and leaving my people to continue in slavery!"

But as he waits for the interpreters to translate his words, a curious quotation from the *Qur'an* surfaces of its own accord in Samiel's mind:

"Fighting is prescribed for you, and ye dislike it.
But it is possible that ye dislike a thing that is good for you,
and that ye love a thing that is bad for you.
But Allah knoweth, and ye know not!"

3.

Picking at his dinner as he sat in his cell one evening during a recess in the trial, Samiel finds himself mulling over the events that followed the suicide-bombing in the souk. Ibrahim had escaped unharmed, but someone had brought him word, when he'd returned to his home in Mud-harris, that the boy had subsequently been attacked. And so he'd returned to el-Rawi and made his way to the hammam, arriving a quarter-hour before closing. He'd purposely arrived at the end of the day in hope of being the last patron there. The bathhouse was located on a quiet street in an out-of-the-way corner of the old Jewish quarter, and the cannon at the city center would soon go off, signaling the end of the day's fast and prompting devout Muslims throughout the city who were observing the Ramadan fast to rush home for the evening meal.

He entered the small, shabby building just as the last tourists were leaving.

"*Salaam aleikem.*"

"*Aleikem salaam.*"

Musheikhi "el-Aqrab" el-Barzan, the masseur and owner of the hammam, a short, sullen, barrel-chested man in his sixties, met him at the door with an odd, piercing look, but after a moment, bowed obsequiously and led him down the hall toward the dressing room. He provided Samiel with a robe, towel, bar of soap, and a *kese*. But as he turned away, there was an awkward moment when the two men found themselves tugging at the robe, a loose thread of which had caught on a ring the masseur was wearing. El-Aqrab's broad, blunt Houdaq features betrayed no emotion as he extricated the thread from the prong of the ring, a gold signet ring with a scorpion incised in a large jade stone. He turned again, without a word, and walked away.

Moments later, Samiel, having removed his clothes and hung his robe on a hook on the wall, was making his way through a thick cloud of steam to take a place on the tiled bathing floor.

As he went about soaping the *kese*, a coarse woolen mitt, or washcloth, that felt like steel wool in his hand but was useful for scrubbing and massage, he was surprised by the sound of a voice addressing him. He turned and could just make out the form of another bather, also naked, sitting on the floor nearby. He hadn't noticed him when he'd entered.

"*Salaam aleikem*," the man said.

"*Aleikem salaam.*"

"*Alhamdulillah. Kullisana winta tayyib!*" the man said, and smiled, the stained ivory of his uneven teeth the only feature clearly visible through the mist.

"*Winta tayyib,*" Samiel replied, courteously, suppressing his annoyance and returning the man's wishes for a good Ramadan. He'd expected to be alone there.

Continuing in Arabic, the man said he was a medical doctor, now retired from practice in a small village in the interior. This was his first visit to the Capital in many years, he said, adding in a hoarse whisper that he'd heard this was the best hammam in el-Rawi.

As the man leaned closer to share this confidence, Samiel made an excuse and shifted away. He didn't care to chat. He intended to dispatch his business privately and as discreetly as possible.

But the man only drew closer and gestured with his own washcloth, a customary offer, politely made, to scrub another bather's back. He was elderly too, but seemed more fragile than Samiel. His manner seemed straightforward and friendly, but Samiel waved him off.

The man nevertheless leapt up and went to stand behind him and began chatting idly about his family, his disappointment in his son, and his hopes for his grandson, as he set about scrubbing Samiel's back with a purposeful vigor.

As Samiel rose to dissuade him, the electric light suddenly went out, and he turned to find, in the dim shaft of daylight coming through a window, the husky form of el-Aqrab crouched before him. Out of the corner of his eye, he glimpsed the silhouette of the other man slipping out of the room.

"*Allahu akbar!*" the masseur cried, and lunged, swinging his arm. Samiel, dodging, caught the glint of a dagger flashing past in the man's hand. El-Aqrab swung again, cutting Samiel across the bridge of his nose as he jerked away, and then came at him a third time. The wet tiles of the floor were slick with soap under his bare feet, and Samiel found it difficult to see clearly through the haze of steam. As el-Aqrab feinted and rushed him, Samiel dodged again, but slipped and fell, jarring his knee on the hard floor. He cursed inwardly at his own folly. He'd planned to settle this business somewhat differently. He hadn't wanted to leave a trail. He hadn't even brought a weapon—but he didn't need a weapon to deal with this lumbering brute. On the other hand, he realized he should've expected the possibility of a hostile reception. He'd come to exact retribution—there'd been a witness—but rumors flew both ways between his home in Mudharris and the Capital, and the Houdaq had apparently been forewarned.

As el-Aqrab swung the knife downward, Samiel ducked under and came up with the masseurs' arm captured in the loop of his own and threw him down, knocking the knife from his hand. For several minutes, they grappled on the wet floor fighting for possession of the weapon. Then el-Aqrab kneed Samiel in the groin, knocking the wind out of him, got one strong hand around his throat, and began to strangle him. Samiel grabbed el-Aqrab's thumb and began to bend it backward. At the same time, he squirmed around on the floor and locked his legs around the other man's waist. After a moment, he managed to roll the masseur over, wedge his heel in his throat, and shove him away. But el-Aqrab came up with the knife and lunged at him again. Samiel feinted and, stepping to one side, snatched his robe from where he'd hung it on the wall. As the masseur swung the knife, Samiel caught his hand in the robe, and cupping his elbow, bent the masseur's arm around behind his back. El-Aqrab only grunted, but there was an audible *thunk* as his shoulder popped out of its socket. In the same moment, Samiel eased the long blade of the knife, which was protruding from the folds of the robe, into el-Aqrab's spleen and cut upward into the lung. With a final groan, the masseur slumped aside and lay still.

Samiel took hold of the carved jade hilt of the knife, pulled it free from between the masseur's ribs and methodically slid the blade across the man's stomach and then up to his sternum, effectively disemboweling him. He then reached down and felt for the signet ring on his hand. It was snugged behind the knuckle and difficult to work off. He pulled the knife out of the man's gut and severed the finger.

"Allah yirhammuh" ("May God rest his soul") he muttered, toeing the bloodstained robe over the dead man. And as the boom of the cannon came from the city square to mark the end of the day's fast, he turned and went to retrieve his clothes.

4.

"...**D**jellaba! Burqaa! Caftan! Haik! Gandoura! Finest cotton! Silk trim! Gold trim! Ten dollar, ten dollar! Here, *ya beyh*, I give you this one for nine dollar, nine dollar!"

A few days after his visit to the hammam, Samiel had returned to the market to look for Ibrahim. He hadn't found the boy, and had come instead upon the old cloth merchant with a face like bruised mahogany—and Ibrahim's eyes. The old man was squatting before the doorway of his shop with his elbows propped on his knees and calling out his wares to the tourists as they passed. He wore a dusty haik and big yellow slippers, and held a piece of hand-embroidered cloth like a sunshade over the *kaffiyeh* wound around his head. The cloth was stretched out like a fragrant lintel between the spindly posts of his arms. Behind him and to the right steps led up past a high, curved wall separating the building in front from an inner courtyard. The courtyard was coursed with windows and doorways, but they were all closed and dark.

"*Sakaakeen!* Knives! *Khanaajir!* Daggers! All made by master blacksmiths in Fez!"

Samiel hadn't come there to shop, he'd come to see Ibrahim. He knew the boy might often be found in this back alley of the souk bartering with the tradesmen—or stealing from them. On this occasion, however, he'd found no sign of Ibrahim and he was concerned. As far as he knew, the boy had no regular address. Meanwhile, when the wizened old cloth merchant glanced up and spied Samiel, he quickly began packing up his goods. But Samiel, who normally avoided the old man, decided to approach him this time.

"*Salaam Aleichem*," Samiel said.

"*Aleichem salaam*," the man replied automatically over his shoulder, without pausing to look around as he proceeded to gather his things.

"*Alhamdulillah, ya Hajj*," Samiel said, pressing him with formalities as he came up behind him.

The old man dropped his stack of cloth, and whirling around, shied back in alarm. He stood up against the doorjamb of his shop regarding Samiel warily for a moment, before stammering the formal response: "*Alhamdu…Alhamdulillah!*"

They stared at one another in silence for a long moment, until the color drained from the old man's face.

Finally, Samiel said, "So, we see that Allah has spared you to count the leaves of many summers."

The old man didn't answer. He glanced about nervously, as if hoping for someone to pass by, anyone he might call upon to intervene, but there was no one.

"And *blessed you*," Samiel added, with bitter irony, as he took in the size and contents of the old man's shop and inwardly compared their value to the little bundle the merchant had once carried around on his back, hawking his soft goods about the village where they'd met so many years ago, "blessed you with good fortune, as well!"

The old cloth merchant gave a non-committal shrug—more like a shiver—and his lips moved silently, mouthing a proverb, "Blessed be He who gave Muhammad a mansion."

Samiel forced a smile, then, to try and put him at ease, and gestured for him to unpack his goods again so that he could look them over, "I came to buy something," he said, "as a gift."

The old man stared at him for a moment, confused and frightened, as if not sure whether he'd heard correctly. But as Samiel continued to hover there, like a menacing stone blocking the light, and gestured again at the goods heaped on the ground at his feet, the old man reluctantly stooped and spread them out.

Giving the items a cursory glance, Samiel said, "Do you have something better? Something special—*for the boy?*"

The old man gaped at him, astonishment now added to his fear. But he didn't need to ask which boy Samiel was referring to, because he knew. He rose slowly, as if mesmerized, turned and stepped back into his shop. He returned in a moment with a gandoura, which he held out for Samiel to take. It was made of the softest fine-spun black cotton cloth. It had a narrow orphrey of gold leaf over a deep orange backing along the edge of the neckline. Samiel took it from him and unfolded it, examining it appreciatively. A sleeveless, floor-length man's house robe cut as full as a chasuble, it weighed barely a couple of ounces. The hand-sewn stitching was nearly invisible to the naked eye. One felt a cooling comfort, despite the growing heat of the day, simply to hold it in one's hand and look upon it. It was exquisite.

"*Kamm?*" Samiel said, finally.

The old man nervously cleared his throat before hesitantly naming a price.

The amount was absurdly high, Samiel thought, even

for such a jewel of workmanship, but he only pursed his lips. There was no question in his mind that he'd buy it, for the robe was the means to an end. But to accomplish that end, despite—or, rather, even because—of the antipathy between them, he knew he would have to bargain for it, so he named a much lower price. The old man simply repeated his initial price, and Samiel countered, barely raising his. The first few exchanges appeared to be impossibly far apart, and the cloth merchant seemed stiff and wooden in his manner, his responses almost mechanical. But as the bargaining proceeded and the game heated up, the merchant seemed to find his footing. He began to put some feeling into his side of the business, scowling, grimacing, sneering, gesticulating, becoming almost defiant. Samiel persisted, bearing down—while thinking wryly to himself, that if this had been an exercise between two Westerners in New York, Paris or Heidelberg, one might've been tempted to try to skip the arduous bargaining process and cut to the bottom line. But Western ways are very different from ours, he thought, which might explain why so many attempts at negotiation between us came to grief. Because here at home, there was no bottom line. For the old merchant—and for himself, as well—the robe was merely a token in the game. The game was a contest of wills, and the game was everything.

But the conclusion was foregone, and as the bargaining drew to its end, the old cloth merchant's demeanor became more and more dejected, his responses increasingly fatalistic, until he finally sagged back in the doorway of his shop and reluctantly handed over the robe. And Samiel, seeing him staring at the ground, clearly beaten down in spirit, for a moment almost pitied him.

Their business done, Samiel nodded, and the old man rose without another word and led the way into the courtyard behind the store and up a set of winding stairs to a long dark corridor within the building on the next level. After the first turning, the corridor split into two, the main part continuing toward the parlor landing, and the other, the one they followed, branching off to slope curiously downward again. The old man proved surprisingly nimble and Samiel, despite knowing the district well, had to step lively to keep him in sight, for along the roughly paved serpentine path other tunnels branched off in different directions and the walls themselves were barely visible in the gloom. A gray half-light filtered in from a tier of stone jalis above them that formed a sort of clearstory between the tops of the supporting columns and the arched stone ceiling lost in shadows overhead. When they eventually came into a subterranean chamber scoured out of the bedrock beneath the foundation of another building—some two hundred meters from the original one they'd entered—Samiel began to sense he knew where he was. He'd come this way before, years ago. A woman was sitting there on a low stool carding wool by the light flooding in through an archway on the other side. She never looked up when they entered, but kept her eyes on her work, her hand swinging the wire-toothed brush in a steady, mechanical rhythm. As they approached, Samiel could see a small child kneeling on a carpet on the bare ground beside the woman and babbling to itself as it toyed with a shuttle from a loom.

The light through the arch was dazzling at first after the gloom of the passageway, but as they advanced, Samiel soon made out a hedge of blue and yellow myrtle he recognized at the head of a cobblestone path sloping steeply upward again from the underground chamber.

Once beyond the hedge, when his eyes adjusted to the light, he found himself in the elegantly appointed *sahn* of a house he knew well. Such inner courtyards, or cloisters, were typical of the fine houses of the rich that were hidden away in unexpected corners behind the drab and dingy exterior walls of the medina. The city's maze of narrow streets often turned back upon themselves or tunneled under the hodge-podge of stone buildings huddled together against the desert winds to offer cover to the wealthier members of the population, who tended to veil their good fortune under a cloak of austerity. But in this case, the courtyard exhibited none of the ornate stone scrollwork or painted effusions common to so many others. A plain yellow plaster colonnade enclosed the space and supported an overhanging upper story on one side. The cobblestoned courtyard was largely bare, save for two stone benches and a large central fountain of gray marble, at the base of which a pair of lions, guardant, were carved in bas-relief. They, and the ancient, striated stones of the pavement, etched with time and wear, seemed to gain a certain weight, an added dimension of intrigue and complexity, against the deceptively simple background. There was only one stairway leading up to the balcony beyond the fountain. No one was there. As he looked about him, he realized that the old cloth merchant was gone, too, having probably returned the way he'd come. The place had the feeling of being unoccupied for a long time. And yet Samiel knew it was occupied, even then. It was the home of his old friend, Abul-Abbas. He'd been there numerous times in years past to visit with the jurist for long, open-ended conversations about mathematics, law, and morality, in which they'd exchanged their respective interpretations of passages from the *Qur'an* and such other topics as Averroes' interpretation of Aristotle's notion of the soul, of Leibniz's monads, Spinoza's attributes of God, and Augustine of Hippo's torturous, heroic, intellectual wrestling with the nature of faith and the paradoxes of time. It had been a favorite spot, Samiel reflected ironically now, in which he and Abul-Abbas, a rising young attorney then and an amateur mathematician besides, would sit in the evening over glasses of sweetened mint tea, as the cobblestones cooled and the shadows crept up the walls, to meditate on the vanities of life.

He went over and leaned against the stone lip of the fountain to wait, thinking that if this was where Ibrahim was living now, then the boy must be playing the part of a juvenile thief and con artist out of sheer boredom and mischief, for he'd clearly managed to work out a much better option.

The fountain, which Abul-Abbas had found and brought back from Andalusia, had a yellow enamel basin with oxidized iron stains that legend said were traces of the blood of the Abencerrages, the ancient lords of the Alhambra. There was an inscription at the bottom in blue Arabic characters. It was a passage Samiel knew from a poem by Ibn el-Khatib, who was a minister to Muhammad V at the court of Fez after the Christian defeat of the Islamic forces at Rio Salado. It was the outcome of that battle that had precipitated the Moorish withdrawal from Spain in 1492. But as Samiel perused the lines, now, they seemed to strike a personal chord. Given the events of the last several days, his main reason for coming was to put his mind at rest about the boy's wellbeing. But the poem evoked the memory of someone else, and for an uncomfortable moment, Samiel was overcome with feelings he'd thought he'd buried long ago.

The passage, in translation, read:

"Exile's hand has sown the seeds of mourning,
And fires of anguish have forged a chain about our hearts;
We knelt one evening by the river's sweet waters
And wept as the waters turned to salt...."

A young dark face appeared floating on the water, obscuring the inscription.

Samiel waited, not looking up.

"Salaam aleikem," the boy said, perfunctorily.

"Aleikem salaam," Samiel replied, not raising his eyes from the fountain. He was watching the boy, in reflection, taking this rare opportunity to study him up close.

The boy simply stared back at him for a moment, then suddenly blurted out, "I'm not afraid of you!" But when Samiel didn't look up or respond, Ibrahim, using an imperious tone unbecoming of a child addressing an adult, demanded, "Why'd you come back! What do you want!"

Samiel didn't answer. He remained still, simply watching, as the boy's reflection in the fountain gathered clarity and definition out of the ebbing tide of his own feelings.

"I'm not afraid of you!" Ibrahim repeated, adding, "Why'd you come back? Why are you wearing those Western clothes and pretending to be someone else? Everybody here knows who you are!"

Yes, Samiel said to himself, they know me as Samiel, but—unfortunately—that goes for you, too, Ibrahim—and that is all you know! Then he raised his eyes to look at the boy directly. "What you say is true. And since they *do* know who I am, they'll keep my secret. Don't you think so?"

The boy's eyes wavered for a moment, before he said, "You came to see the old judge?"

"No. I came to see you."

"Me? Why? Why do you want to see me?"

Samiel held his gaze and asked his own question. "Abul-Abbas treating you well?" It was a rhetorical question, because the jurist's kind and generous nature was well known.

The boy's lips twitched, briefly, into a patronizing smile, but he didn't speak.

"How long have you been staying here?"

The boy made a vague gesture. "Two, maybe three years, on and off. He said I could, uhm—" he broke off as another thought crossed his mind, and then raising his voice, as if defensively, he repeated his earlier demand, "What do you want, now! What do you want with me!"

Samiel studied Ibrahim abstractly for a moment. He was relived to see that the boy had recovered from his attack. He's resilient, he thought to himself with a certain satisfaction, and intelligent, after all. "I brought you something," he said, lightly, "—well, a couple of things, actually, as a token. I thought you might like to have them."

The boy stared at the folded gandoura Samiel held out to him, but didn't move.

Samiel gestured for him to take it.

Ibrahim simply stared at it with a guarded expression and then shrugged dismissively, "Tsk, I don't need that."

"The gandoura's just the wrapping," Samiel said. "There's something inside."

"I don't want it."

"It's a sort of a surprise. Take it. Open it. You'll see."

The boy shook his head, no, and took a step back, but his eyes remained fixed on the parcel.

"Tsk-tsk, come, Ibrahim. There's nothing in it you need to be afraid of now. Come, take it. I think you'll be very pleased when you see what it is. No, really and truly. Hmn?" Samiel placed the parcel on the lip of the fountain and pushed it toward him.

Ibrahim took another step back, hesitating again, before finally reaching forward to pick it up and weigh it gingerly in his hand. "What is it," he demanded.

"It's yours. Open it and see."

"I don't want it!" the boy said again, and turning, flung the parcel defiantly across the courtyard. As it tumbled in the air, the gandoura unfolded, spilling its contents, which fell to the stone walkway with a metallic clatter.

Samiel, seeing the knife had caught the boy's eye, merely pursed his lips, unperturbed.

"Why would you give me anything?" Ibrahim said, and then with a gesture toward the house behind him, he added, "I'm here, now, with *him*. You can't do anything! What do you want from me?"

"When the time comes," Samiel said, rising and starting back toward the myrtle hedge and the dark passage beyond, "When the time comes, perhaps you'll know, *inshallah*."

But when he reached the mouth of the tunnel Samiel stopped, and hidden by the myrtle hedge, he turned to watch as Ibrahim, thinking he'd gone, ran across the court-yard and squatted on his heels to pick up the knife. He handled it delicately, almost as if it were a live animal that might bite him, and turned it over and over, admiring it. It was a handmade Tuareg dagger with a hilt of carved jade and a handsome, curved, chased-steel blade. For a moment he knitted his brow, apparently made curious when he saw that the runnel was stained with blood. Then his face lit up, and Samiel realized that Ibrahim had recognized the knife. The boy weighed the blade and tested its sharpness, pulling a hair from his head and letting it float down over the upturned cutting edge, where it parted with the ends drifting away even before they could droop. Ignoring the gandoura, Ibrahim turned and picked up the other object that had fallen out of it. It was an emerald signet ring, but he noticed it was stuck on a curious holder of some sort. As he looked more closely, his expression changed, first to astonishment, then to anger, and finally to elation, as he realized that the ring was stuck on a bloody finger, and he understood, finally, the significance of what he had before him.

As Samiel watched, he imagined the thoughts that might be running through the boy's mind:

Why should this man have avenged him with el-Aqrab and then brought these things to show him? The man was Samiel, he knew that, but Samiel didn't know him. He'd heard all about Samiel from his grandfather. His grandfather Bâbâ Wâswâs, the old cloth merchant, had told him that Samiel was a murderer, that Samiel had murdered a lot of innocent people! Samiel was a monster! Everybody knew about Samiel! But nobody would touch him. He didn't understand why everybody was afraid of Samiel. Nobody would even look him in the eye. But he *wasn't afraid of Samiel! If Samiel had killed el-Aqrab, that was fine with him! Good riddance to that motherfucker! And if Samiel had brought him el-Aqrab's knife and finger to prove it, it was probably only because he was trying to make nice with him.*

Samiel was qatal! (a murderer)—yes, and maybe xawal sakhif wi luti! (a fucking faggot and a pedophile, too!) Who knows, maybe one day, when I grow up, I'll get even with Samiel for killing all those people! Maybe one day!

Samiel saw that the boy's hand was trembling as he picked up the knife again. And as he turned to go, it flashed through his mind what the boy must have gone through:

"…Des fossils, Messieurs? Des fossils?"
"Non, non, merci."
"Des fossils?"
"Vas t'en! Vas t'en!" ("Go away! Go away!")
"Commes des moucherons, merde alors! Vas t'en!" ("They're like gnats, for shit's sake! Scram!")
"Des fossils?"

It was just the week before. Ibrahim had apparently been on the steps of the hammam trying to sell fossils to the tourists as they came and went. From what Samiel had heard, it had happened like this:

As three Frenchmen came out of the locker room the boy approached them and held up the stones for them to see. They said no, and the first two managed to slip past him. But he managed to catch the attention of the third, who took the two stones he held out and looked them over shrewdly.

Ibrahim took another large one out of the cloth bag he had hanging by a cord around his neck and showed it as well, "Regardez celui-ci, Monsieur. Magnifique, n'est-ce pas? Il n'est pas faux, Monsieur. C'est du vrai!"

The man raised his eyebrows in mock astonishment, "Ah,

mais non! C'est du vrai?" ("No joke, are they really real?")

He realized that the man was putting him on and must have known that the fossils of el-Rawi were cheap and plentiful, abounding in the matrix of the rocky outcroppings among the dunes at the edge of the city. Nevertheless, the fact that the man had stopped to look meant he might be willing to buy a souvenir in return for a little entertainment. Also, Ibrahim thought, giving the three men a sidelong glance, maybe they're xawalaat (faggots.) So he pouted his lips and turned his head to give the man a sly, coquettish glance, as if to let it be known that he was aware the Frenchman was only humoring him, but he nevertheless intended to turn the game around to his own advantage.

"Ils ne sont pas comme les autres, Monsieur," he said, with mock seriousness. ("These fossils are not like the others.") "Ils arrachent les mamelons de leurs soeurs avec des tenailles!"

The Frenchman snorted and fell back against the doorway, almost choking with laughter. "Ecoutez!" he said, calling out to his friends to share the joke. "Listen, did you hear what this little devil just said? He said his fossils are real. The other boys make their fake ones by tearing out their sisters' nipples with red hot pincers!"

The Frenchmen all cackled like hens at that.

"Oh!" said the first one, still giggling and reaching into his pocket at last for some change, "Il est méchant, celui-ci!"("A little devil, this one!")

But at that moment, el-Aqrab charged out of the locker-room cursing at Ibrahim and trying to shoo him away.

"What're you doing here! I told you not to bother my clients! Get out of here, you dirty little urchin!"

But Ibrahim ignored the masseur and pressed his advantage with the tourist. "Well, Monsieur," he continued, in French, "so don't you want to buy a real fossil and save our women from this shame?"

El-Aqrab reached for him, but Ibrahim dodged away and kept looking at the Frenchman with mock-pathos. "Monsieur?"

"It's all right," the Frenchman told the masseur, and turning back to Ibrahim, said, "Very well, I will buy one—but only one." And leaning close to the boy added, "Parce qu' un peu de honte me purifie!" ("Because a little shame purifies one!")

"You have a very delicate taste, Monsieur," Ibrahim said facetiously in French.

And as he reached for the handful of crumpled euros, the masseur swung his arm and the money went flying, leaving his hand stinging from a cut where the masseur's big scorpion ring had struck him.

"I told you to get outta here!"

"Telhas Teeze!" Ibrahim yelled, reverting to Arabic, "yaatak Darba fi 'albak!" ("Kiss my ass! Drop dead!") "Leave me alone!" he went on. "Mind your own business! Monsieur—" he added, turning toward the tourist for support. But the Frenchman only waved at him over his shoulder and sashayed off laughing with his friends.

El-Aqrab reached for him again. "Come here, you little piece of shit! I'm gonna teach you to show some respect!"

"You couldn't teach your ass to wipe itself!" Ibrahim retorted. "Who are you calling a piece of shit? You're a shit! You owe me money yourself! Those last two tourists in there right now are mine! I brought them here! I want my tip!"

"Tip, my ass! Get it from them, like you're supposed to!"

"What I get from them is none of your business! When I bring them to your hammam, you're supposed to pay me, too!"

"Bullshit! I told you, you bring in enough business, and

then maybe I'll let you have something at the end of the week. Now, Get your skinny ass outta here!"

The masseur reached for him again, but again Ibrahim evaded him. "That's what you told me last week, but you didn't pay! Gimme my money! Three dirham! That's what you owe me! Two from last week and one today! Three dirham—or I don't bring nobody back here!"

"Go fuck yourself, you little weasel!"

"Fuck you, you fat tampon!"

But it had been getting late by then, and the two of them had apparently been alone there in the darkening entryway. Ibrahim had probably realized that he should've left. But instead, he'd stayed there arguing with the man and insulting him, determined to get his money for the sake of his self-respect, determined not to be ripped off. El-Aqrab was old, fat, and short, but quick for his age, and in that narrow space it hadn't been smart to go on taunting him like that. And sure enough, the man had caught him and started beating him up. He was bleeding from his nose and mouth by the time el-Aqrab had dragged him into the building and down the hall into a dark room. When he had the boy there, el-Aqrab had pulled out that long knife and threatened him with it. Then he'd cut off the boy's clothes and thrown him face down on the massage table. But the last client had still been there. El-Aqrab had seen him out of the corner of his eye and turning, had threatened him with the knife. The man had later said he'd simply run out the door with Ibrahim's voice ringing in his ears, crying out for help. But the man said he'd stopped and hidden himself at the side of the building, trying to decide where to go for help. Moments later, he'd seen Ibrahim coming out of the hammam, gagging on his own vomit, with blood running down his legs as he stumbled away, bent over and hugging his stomach as if he'd had his insides gouged out with a poker.

5.

*akdhib! Buraaz al 'anta! Yatabawwal al 'anta!
Assassin!"*

Samiel, who has been answering a question just put to him by the prosecution, pauses at the disturbance. The trial has been going on, now, for six months. He is well used to the outcries by this time. Almost every day, since he'd first been called upon to give testimony, there'd been some outburst, someone in the gallery would jump up and start yelling insults. The defense attorney had told him that the trial was being conducted as an official proceeding largely closed to the public, in order to prevent provoking old resentments and possible belated reprisals in the community. Even the press had been excluded from the courtroom and was merely handed brief daily statements—with all names redacted—by the court clerk at the end of each session. No word got out even about Samiel's real name—which Samiel found ironic, because his real name would probably mean very little to anyone in Qarmat now living. His old QPR comrades-in-arms were all dead or in hiding in Qarmat or abroad, as far as he knew—and most of them had known him only as Samiel. His family had all passed on, and to preserve the honor of his forebears, he had ceased to use his family name since the fall of the Revolution—except for the few mathematical papers he'd published in foreign journals.

And when he'd returned from exile, he'd had no desire to hide behind another alias. It probably would have served no purpose, because his face would have been easily recognizable from old posters by anyone old enough to remember the Revolution. There was also, he admitted, the possible unconscious desire on his part to be called to account, to have the opportunity, after so many years, to state his case publicly. It was, he supposed, a vestige of his old instinct to teach, to enlighten others, whether it be in the mysteries of mathematics or of the dynamics of social and political forces. But as it happened, no one had sought him out, no one had seemed to care, the world had moved on. And in all that time, those who had recognized him on the street had merely cast down their eyes and stepped aside as he'd passed. Until now.

There were only two exceptions, it seems to him, two people remaining in Qarmat to whom his birth name would be meaningful. One was his old friend, Abul-Abbas el-Irewat, the Chief Magistrate now presiding over his trial. Abul-Abbas certainly did know him—or knew him *once*, perhaps all too well—and yet Abul-Abbas has managed to avoid his eyes throughout these proceedings. Samiel turns now to look at the judge as the question occurs to him again—considering the fact that Abul-Abbas, a widely respected scholar of international jurisprudence and constitutional law, is unquestionably a man of good conscience and a jurist of the highest ethical standards—why has he not recused himself? The other exception was the Prime Minister, Marwan Badat. Badat, whose tendency for self-promotion would lead one to expect him to make a show of himself here, urging on the prosecutor, had not made a single appearance at the trial.

On the other hand, Samiel muses, Badat does have good reason for making himself scarce here. But that's another story entirely.

Meanwhile, for the same reason—that is, to keep the names of all perpetrators and victims that might come up in testimony from leaking to the public—observers in the gallery, other than the international representatives of the U.N. and the World Court at the Hague, had been restricted to a couple dozen family members of deceased victims. But even these, like the few surviving victims who were to be called as witnesses, had all been drawn from little villages and hamlets hundreds of miles away across the desert to the south and east of the Capital, and were sequestered during their stay in el-Rawi for the duration of the trial. And once the trial was over, they would all be bused back again to their homes—because, it was feared, the aggressive press in the Capital might manage to interview them and publish names, dates, and places mentioned in the trial for all to see. And yet, for twenty-five years, Samiel reflects, and for whatever reasons, nobody had ever talked about the Revolution. For twenty-five years it had almost seemed as if the Revolution had never happened. He'd been told that the purpose of the trial was to bring the guilty to justice and provide closure to the victims. But then they had imposed all these rules of secrecy. It would seem a strange miscalculation, Samiel thought, because the truth of history would be denied to present and future generations and the vast majority of surviving victims would be left in the dark and without any sense of closure to the end. But as he had come to realize early on, the trial wasn't about justice and closure at all. Not that he had really expected it to be. He wasn't even sure himself, at this remove, what form justice could actually take. But he had hoped that by making this last gesture, by sacrificing himself at the end of his life to the charade, he might still offer the surviving victims some final resolution. He had even hoped—he was almost embarrassed at his own naiveté in admitting this to himself—but he had even had some hope of provoking a serious prosecutorial investigation into the complex historical causes of the Revolution, why it had been inevitable and why such revolutions take the bloody course that they do. But it seems it's not to be. The prosecution continually resists following his lead, and in the end, the trial will be another whitewash. He is to be sacrificed, while others in power, whose abuses had laid the groundwork for the Revolution, or who had conspired with him, are to be passed over, their reputations unsullied.

But periodically, one of the poor souls in the gallery would erupt in emotion, and given that much of the testimony was rehashing torments they or their loved ones had experienced, he supposes that's to be expected. He reaches into his pocket and takes out a small vial of opium, and as the court officers rush forward to restrain the excited person and eject him from the courtroom, Samiel taps a little into his mouth from the dispenser in the cap.

"...So, that was—ahem—excuse me," he resumes, taking up where he left off when order was restored, "that was in the early days of the QPR, the Qarmatian People's Republic. When I returned to Qarmat, I went home to Mudharris to visit with my parents, because I had heard that my father was very ill at the time."

"Excuse me, Your Honor!" the prosecutor says, rising. "With the Court's permission, the prosecution would like to call the Court's attention to page 3,012, paragraph III,1(j) of document QPC-dash-13b, and to ask the defendant to repeat exactly when, what year and when exactly, it was that he returned to Qarmat—and whether his return had, in fact, *not* been prompted by his father's illness, but instead possibly by some connection with the Karalim uprising that occurred a month before he went home, as he says, to Mudharris, and that precipitated the organized QPR assaults on government outposts, when nearly a hundred—well, to be exact," the attorney added, pausing to refer to his own notes, "when 87 people were killed by—"

"Objection!"

"One moment, please, one moment!" the Chief Magistrate says. He is a man of advancing age with a noticeable tremor. He hunches over to glance through a sheaf of court papers on the bench before him, and after a moment, looks up again, and speaking slowly for the translators, says, "The objection is sustained. Preliminary investigation has already established the year and date of the defendant's return to Qarmat. If the prosecution merely wishes to confirm the date for the record, prosecution may do so later, during cross-examination. At this time, the defendant is to be provided the opportunity to answer the question in full. If the prosecuting attorney wishes to insert an additional point or to bring to light other information pertinent to the trial that was not already documented in the pretrial investigation, please indicate the relevancy of that line of questioning now, before we proceed—"

"The prosecution's purpose, Your Honor, is to—"

"—And...*and!*" the Chief Magistrate continues, holding up his hand for patience, "in that latter case, will the prosecution be so kind as to articulate its questions succinctly, one at a time, to facilitate the Court's following the testimony clearly through the translators."

"Uh, yes, certainly, Your Honor. Excuse me."

———

"…With the Court's permission," the prosecutor is saying, now, a few weeks later, "while it's likely that many documents pertinent to this case that might have been submitted as evidence of the guilt of the defendant—and possibly of others—were apparently lost when the *Qubbah-el-Is—*" he paused, having stumbled in attempting to pronounce the name….

(The *Qubbah* was originally the repository of the country's most precious religious and governmental documents, but the building was destroyed by a fire during the Revolution.)

"…When the *Qubbah-el-Ismâ 'ili Shi'a* burned down," the prosecutor says finally, and continues, "despite this destruction, ongoing investigation has unearthed numerous other documents that do serve to incriminate the defendant. I refer to document QPC-dash-17a, pages 291 through…" he shuffles through his own copy of the document for verification, and continues, "Yes, pages 291 through 372. The contents of these documents are such that they might cast doubt on Samiel's protestations of initial naiveté and innocence of the methods of the QPR. It has already been established through prior testimony that the QPR were widely referred to among the population at the time, as *el-Jaysh Damm*, 'The Blood Army.' That nickname alone would seem to have suggested much about their methods, even without further inquiry! But it bears repeating here that the defendant's own admitted nom de guerre was Samiel. 'Samiel,' which may be translated from the Arabic as 'poisonous wind,' usually refers to the simoom, the harsh southern wind that blows across the Sahara in the summer. But 'Samiel' also happens to be an alternate local nickname for the Devil, and it would not seem unreasonable to suppose—"

"Objection! The prosecution is making baseless inferences!"

"Sustained." The Chief Magistrate strikes the bench with his gavel, "The Court must remind the prosecutor—"

"Ah, yes, Your Honor. Sorry, of course," he said, but the faint blush on his cheeks betrayed his satisfaction in having scored a point in the minds of the judges.

"We will keep strict order in these proceedings, and the Court warns the attorneys—all parties, in fact—that penalties will be imposed should these irregularities continue!"

The prosecutor nods in acquiescence. "Yes, Your Honor. I apologize. With the Court's permission, let us continue. The prosecution wishes to ascertain the defendant's true memory of the sequence of events indicated in these documents, as it will affect certain aspects of cross-examination later."

"I see," the Chief Magistrate says. He then glances at his watch and adds, "It is now twenty minutes to four. The Court deems it a good time to recess for the evening and to take up this new line of questioning in the morning. The attendants will please prepare these new documents for distribution to the Court and for presentation on the computer screens at least a half-hour prior to the opening of session tomorrow. *Alhamdulillah,* Court is adjourned."

The bailiff rings a chime, and the court rises. Everyone waits respectfully as the Chief Magistrate pushes back his chair and stands to lead his associates out of the courtroom.

Samiel, watching him go, is thinking that Abul-Abbas is of the tribe of el-Irewat, as he also is, as well as second cousin to the present young King Essid. Abul-Abbas's family originally came from the same settlement in the northern reaches of the Qarmatian desert where Samiel grew up. The jurist is a tall and imposing man still, though aged before his time, walking with a cane, and stooped with Parkinson's disease. Samiel had known him since they were boys in school, and as he proceeds toward the door leading to the judges' chambers now, Samiel tries to read the expression behind the solemn mask of his face. But the Chief Magistrate is an enigma to him now.

6.

"*Bismi-llahi-r-rahmani-r-rahim!*"
         "*Allahu akbar!*"
         "*Bismi-llahi-r-rahmani-r-rahim!*"
"*Allahu akbar!*"

Abul-Abbas mounted the steep, winding path with some difficulty, steadying his cane against frequent deflections by loose stones along the way. With each step the stones seemed to seethe and rattle around his feet like the gnashing of teeth. It was brutally hot and he was having some trouble catching his breath. Here, on the mountain, the air was thin, and where he stood now, at the height of the plateau, there seemed to be a fine mist in the air, like fog. But it wasn't fog, of course, for this was the desert, and the air was dry as bone. The mist was a haze of dust raised by a feint updraft one couldn't feel, a current of air that lifted the sand and dust and made it difficult to breathe without offering any relief from the heat of the day. But the fine granules of silica tumbling about in the air seemed to reflect the light, rather than obscure it, as if the very air was scintillating. It had an illusive reflectivity, as if you were peering through a nimbus, and the world far below, the town amidst the crisscrossing oueds, synclines, troughs and dunes of the surrounding erg, a world he knew so intimately, seemed to him now, as he gazed down upon it, like a parchment with indecipherable characters written in an alien hand. The impression of writing was tantalizing, because it seemed to hold some fateful message the sense of which eluded him. The house walls and streets of el-Rawi coiled back upon themselves in ways that seemed random, but taken in context with the topography of the enveloping desert, it all seemed suddenly suggestive, like pseudo-kufic calligraphy, as if a decorative but essentially meaningless Arabic script had been brushed in by the ironic hand of Fate *on purpose*—as it sometimes was by human artists—to hide the underlying sacred text from the eyes of the uninitiated.

Still, he was trying to keep his attention focused on the plain white cotton shroud over the bier before him. His eyes were on the bier, but his mind was elsewhere—everywhere, it seemed, to his annoyance, but where it should have been. And yet he knew in his heart that he was trying to avoid dwelling on the troubling circumstances of the trial he was overseeing, which had been postponed for two days while the defendant, Samiel, underwent psychological evaluations. He'd thought the postponement would be a respite, giving him time to mull over the facts of the case—while distancing himself from his personal history with Samiel. But it wasn't to be. First thing the morning after postponement, he'd gotten the news that his father had passed during the night.

With a sigh, he turned away now from the cloudless sky and the magnificent desert vistas falling away to either side of the mountain, and climbed on toward the burial field, still higher up, where the graves were arrayed by family within rectangular plots set off by low stone walls. Even the *salāt el-janāzah,* the funerary prayers, which had been led by the sonorous voice of Mumi Ahmed el-Hawhza at the *musalla*, the outdoor area of worship they had just left, at the gateway to the cemetery, and the soft, intermittent crying of the women, muffled behind their hands and barely audible above the shuffling of their feet, all seemed to be coming to him from far away....

"...In the name of Allah the Merciful, the Compassionate,
Praise be to God!
The Cherisher and Sustainer of the Worlds,
Most Gracious, Most Merciful;
Master of the Day of Judgment,
Thee do we worship, and Thine aid we seek!"

...Dostoevsky had a name for it, remember?
...The voices around him, his own among them, intoning the prayers in response to Mumi el-Hawhza, clashed in his mind with the echoes of the cries of exasperation from the survivors observing the trial the day before when Samiel once again seemed to be sparring with the prosecution, as if he found the spectacle of his own trial merely an opportunity for verbal one-upmanship. But their cries merged too in his imagination with the wild cries of the millions tortured and murdered during the Revolution, cries that had followed him since the opening of the trial, as if reverberating now from the desert below, where imaginary hoards of murdered souls roved over the barren ground chasing after unattainable justice after so many years. And yet all of it came to him only as background, for in the moment, the firm, mellifluous voice of his old friend and adversary, Amal Koraoun el-Mudharrisi, intruded to claim his attention. It was Amal—now known at trial as Samiel, of course, but for him it will always be Amal—whose voice he heard most closely in his inner ear,

calling his attention now to connections hidden among all these events and back to the bare, windswept golden dunes stretching away to the horizon, which in his mind's eye were teeming with the comings and goings of hostile tribes called up by the vivid rhetoric of his old friend—or, rather, one who had once been his friend.

Conversations with Amal had often left him feeling a little exhilarated, as though he'd been breathing in a purer air. But that was so long ago, and yet the seductive rhythms of that voice kept echoing back in his mind, drawing him toward another lapse into nostalgia—the end of which he knew would only leave him once again wretched and in shock. The experience returned with unabated intensity each time he thought of it—stepping out into the hall, so many years ago at the very beginning of the Revolution, to bid his dear old friend goodbye—knowing it was possibly the last time they might see each other alive—only to find that Amal had gone—departed without a word—except for leaving that subtle sign, on purpose, to warn him. He'd taken the warning and had fled that night to join his family in Rabat. He had no doubt that had he not done so, Amal—whom he only later came to realize was the same Samiel, the leader of the QPR—would have had him tortured and probably killed, as he had so many others. But how was that possible? How could he have known Amal, a close friend, so well and so long—from the time they'd first met in preparatory school—and never even imagined that dark, Satanic side of his nature? Was he so blind? He'd always thought he was a shrewd judge of character, sensitive to others' weaknesses—as well as his own—and to their strengths, but clear-sighted and able to put any faults into perspective. He was a trained jurist of considerable experience, Chief Magistrate of the Royal High Court of Qarmat after all. Or was it that Amal had simply been so masterful at fooling him—and not only him, but everyone—all those years? Was it possible that human nature could be so divided within the same individual? Was it even possible that Amal was so divided that even he himself was not aware of the evil that crouched within him until something happened to call it forth, some transformative experience? But what could that have been? He'd known Amal's parents, they were good, decent Muslims, his mother a paragon of quiet strength and compassion who'd suffered the loss of several children, and his father a Sufi, a man of peace and culture, who'd almost never been seen without a book of poetry under his arm, and who'd made a small fortune in the spice trade by virtue of his singular, open-handed honesty and self-effacing, personal magnetism. Amal had always been known for his exceptional calm, intelligence, and tolerance, his ability to see reason in all sides of an argument while cleaving to the underlying ethical principles. In fact, he'd been an idealist. By the time they'd graduated school, and believing he was the more practical of the two, he'd teased Amal for being *too* idealistic, despite his fine-tuned sensitivity to the shifting of political winds, too willing to turn his back on real-world considerations for the sake of the higher good. What had happened? What could have happened to change him?

Just as baffling was the reversal of fortune that had brought Samiel into his courtroom now to have his fate determined by the same old adversary he'd apparently considered to have tortured and killed thirty years before—

"*...It's probably for the best,*" he'd said, "*that you sent your family away!*"

As if, although they had welcomed him into their family as one of their own for so many years, had they still been within his reach, he would have coldly and casually slaughtered them all! What kind of monster had Amal turned into? And then, what was he supposed to think about that business of Amal's leaving that warning? Was he supposed to be *grateful?* Had the self-effacing Amal Koraoun el-Mudharrisi become so infatuated with his own ascendance to power that he thought he'd be exhibiting grandiosity with such a gesture, that his old, befuddled friend, Abul-Abbas, would think him so great a personage that he might feel gratitude in being granted amnesty by so grand a figure—while, at the same time, absorbing the implication that he and his family owed their lives to his whim? What arrogance! No, insanity!

The cortege had come to a stop. They'd reached the wide, low wall marking the burial site of the clan of Acheron el-Irewat. The pallbearers lowered his father's bier to the ground, and the mourners arrayed themselves to the left and right of where Abul-Abbas stood, at the edge of the grave. Further back, he could hear the susurrus of the women, arranging themselves behind the men, trying to stifle their sobbing, because the *Qur'an* forbade such lamentations. Why should one lament? Isn't the deceased going home to his reward in Allah's garden? And shouldn't we then rejoice?

Youssef Acheron, fifty-five years old, tall, and robust, with the trimmed beard and haughty bearing of a prince of the realm, strode up to take his place opposite Abul-Abbas, his father. Youssef was accompanied by his younger brother,

Omar, and his son, Yaqub. Omar, tall and strongly built like Youssef, was also, Abul-Abbas thought, just as handsome in his own way, despite an old scar crossing his left cheek from his days as a football center-back at university. Recently promoted to major in His Majesty's Elite Royal Honor Guards, Omar stood erect and resplendent in his new uniform. Yaqub, stood beside him looking somewhat abashed, as if embarrassed by the modesty of his own plain white djellaba and kaffiyeh, next to his dazzling uncle. Abul-Abbas had been in the habit of calling Yaqub by a pet name, "Fanakee" (my little fox), from the time he was a child. The boy had been small for his age, but he had big ears—and keen hearing—and he was very quick as an infant, scampering about on all fours almost faster than you could keep up with him, much like the tiny fox of the desert for which the judge had named him. But Yaqub had sprouted up into a tall, slender young man now, more reserved than his father, but with perhaps a more subtle intelligence. He'd been advancing rapidly in the family's mining business since graduating university and Youssef was grooming him to take his place one day at the head of the firm. The family had high hopes for Yaqub.

At that moment, Youssef turned to face Abul-Abbas across the open grave, and the older man suddenly felt himself flush in anger. He glanced away, toward the gravestones around him, where four generations of their family were buried. He looked for the wit of his old uncle Anwar; for his aunt Nadya's smile; for the bright eyes and beautiful hair of Dahlia his sister who'd died of tuberculosis at fifteen, on the eve of her wedding day; his brother Jamal's mischievous grin; his mother's sweet caress, and Khalid his baby, his youngest—and his favorite—son, bright, sweet Khalid with his ruby-throated laughter!

Allah yirhamuh! Allah yirhamuh! Allah yirhamuh!

They were all there, under the stones, but the stones, like the cold, impassive mask on the face of his eldest living son, Youssef, gave back no light and left him inwardly reeling at the edge of the grave, a darkness before him.

The mourners finished the service by making *taslim* (a gesture of willing acceptance) to either side.

"Oh, my dear," Abul-Abbas said, speaking mutely to the shrouded body of Sheikh Nizar ben Khalid Acheron el-Irewat, his beloved father, as the earth was thrown upon him, *"we're sending you down to a cold reunion! Allah karim! Allah karim! But I'll be joining you there soon enough, inshallah!"*

Meanwhile, the other part of his mind was taunting him: Here he was, theoretically retired, but having to reassert whatever authority he could muster at this late stage to try and curb his own son's avariciousness—*and* sit in judgment over his own old friend, a fallen monster! Samiel had been all too ready to have him slaughtered once, but now he was sitting on the bench and about to pronounce judgment over *him!* How strange life is! Who could have imagined such a turn of events? But it was up to him now to be the arbiter, to determine whether Samiel was to spend the rest of his natural life in prison for his sins—because there was no question about his guilt and responsibility!

And yet, the trial was a sham! Is a sham trial better than none? He had been torturing himself over that question ever since his cousin Badat, the Prime Minister, had broached the subject. But what other opportunity would there be, he wondered? It seemed so crucial to try and understand the mind that could wreak such havoc....

"...Dostoevsky had a name for it, remember?" Amal was saying all those years ago, making that little gesture in which he joined his extended fingertips and reaching out, dipped them into the air, as if to pluck out a rhetorical plum. It was an unconscious, habitual gesture, but as it came back to him now, the judge was thinking that old, unconscious gesture of reaching and plucking seemed more sinister, more impersonal, almost machine-like, even surgical. Amal's whole air of serenity, the semblance of a purity that implied not innocence but wisdom, appeared now to be owing not to a deeper humanity, as it had seemed once, but to an utter lack of humanity, a want of compassion. It wasn't a sign of one at peace with his emotions, but rather a dissimulating mask for one who could wage bloody destruction out of a process of warped reasoning, without apparent recourse to any human emotion at all.

"...What the Scriptures called 'the river of living water,'" Amal had continued, "Dostoevsky, in *The Possessed*, had called the subliminal 'aesthetic of the soul!'"

He'd brought a gift. They hadn't seen each other in almost two years—in fact, the last time was when Amal had come to Khalid's funeral. (Khalid had been killed by an accident during a visit with his grandfather at one of the family's phosphate mines in the south. He was just short of his eighteenth birthday. He'd slipped from the moving elevator when the gate latch failed and had fallen sixty-five feet into the mineshaft.) The judge hadn't seen Amal since then. Amal and Khalid had been very fond of each other.

But it was a long absence, after having been so close. Amal lived about a hundred kilometers away in the little country village of Mudharris—an area Abul-Abbas knew well, for he'd grown up not far from there—but Amal used to come to el-Rawi often, for he had business in the Capital, and when he came he usually stayed with them as a house guest. Abul-Abbas had been busy too in the interim, occupied with court affairs, and the time had flown by almost before he knew it. But to all intents and purposes, Amal was part of the family, and he'd missed him, missed his intellect as well as his personal presence, his bright, youthful smile. So, when he'd called to say he was coming to town and would it be all right if he stopped by, Abul-Abbas had been delighted— at the same time, he was a little puzzled. His friend had sounded somewhat distant on the phone, almost formal, his voice seeming to carry a forced casualness. They'd been very close for most of their lives, and Amal often used to drop in unannounced. As it happened, although he didn't real- ize it at the time, it was to be the last conversation he and Amal were to have as friends before the Revolution would unleash its reign of terror—and Amal, then operating under the nom de guerre of Samiel, would appear like a dark angel at his door, to measure him for a coffin! But before that, when he did appear at that previous—and last—"friendly" visit, when he was still just "Amal," he'd entered with his usual grace, his stride exhibiting a natural, athletic vigor— he'd been a very competitive footballer in his youth—and he smiled as they embraced. But it wasn't his usual smile. Abul-Abbas used to tease him about his handsome baby face, but now his face was marked with lines that the judge didn't recall, and his manner seemed strained, as if there was something—something unpleasant—he'd come to say. Their first polite exchanges were rather awkward, until Amal said,

"Oh, by the way, I hope you don't mind, I brought you something."

"Mind?"

He smiled, "I found it only a few weeks ago, on my last dig." He was an amateur archeologist, in addition to his other accomplishments, and periodically he would go on expeditions to explore the sites of old Roman ruins in the desert. The area had been an important trading outpost of the African Proconsularis from the conquest of Carthage to the fall of the Empire, and had been prized at the time for its extensive orchards of native olives and vineyards of Phoenician wine grapes and its medicinal clay and fine red pottery. Over the centuries since then, the climate had grown more arid and the once-fertile soil had turned largely to sand. Occasionally, Amal would bring him a small clay pot or figurine for his collection over the years, but what he'd brought that day was quite unusual.

"Oh, my!" Abul-Abbas said, getting his first glimpse of it as he opened the package. "It's magnificent!" He hesitated before lifting it out of its elaborate tissue paper and cotton wrapping, almost afraid to intrude upon its delicate antiquity. "It's quite different from anything you've shown me before. Where did you find it?"

"At a new site in the hills just a few kilometers south of Mudharris. A friend, an itinerant Berber trader, told me some ruins had been uncovered by recent windstorms. We've only started excavations, but it seems to have been a major site for producing pottery on an industrial scale. We found several buildings constructed of mud brick, with potter's wheels, numerous implements, and well over a thousand pots and fragments. The most remarkable finds, however, were two huge kilns, one almost intact! There may even be a third yet to be unearthed, because the area is large. The kilns are rectangular, stone-built structures over eleven meters deep, six wide and nearly seven meters high."

"But that's extraordinary!"

"The inside of the one we excavated was apparently divisible into nine stories, but the shelving was probably dismantled after each firing."

"How old do you suppose the site is?"

"I'm still awaiting the carbon test results from the lab, but given the depth at which we found the artifacts and the known age of previously excavated sites in the vicinity, I'm guessing late first century. It's probably one of the first—if not *the* first—operation of its size in Roman North Africa!"

"This platter is really quite beautiful! But it's hard to imagine the technology at the time allowing them to work with such a huge kiln. How could they control the heat?"

"It shows very clever engineering. Each level of the kiln was formed of a removable tile floor, and vertical columns of clay pipes distributed the heat from a cavernous oven at the base. I'd guess they were capable of maintaining a temperature of close to a thousand degrees centigrade. They could probably fire thirty or forty thousand vessels at a time."

"Allah be praised! And this platter is perfectly preserved, it hasn't a chip, not even a crack! Did all the pieces you found there look like this? It's so different from what I've seen before."

"That's the most interesting part, Abul-Abbas. Of over

a thousand pieces we found, most were the usual red *terre sigillée*—"

"*Terre sigillée*, yes, 'sealed earth.' But this is very different, both in color and pattern. It's a black slip over the usual yellow ocher."

"The platter is actually also *terre sigillée*—the black slip is unusual here, but not unknown. Nevertheless, I'd say it's a unique find—for a number of reasons. There were fewer than a hundred like this one—if you were to put all the fragments together into whole pieces—and by the way," he added, with a conspiratorial wink, "a good many of these black and yellow pots were in near-perfect condition, so I thought the museum wouldn't really miss this one."

Abul-Abbas grinned, happily complicit.

"If you look at these rosettes," Amal said, pointing to the barbotine border along the inside edge of the platter, "they were probably piped onto the unfired clay through an antelope horn—that's not common in the local pottery, either."

"But, unless I'm mistaken, I think I've seen something like this before."

"In books or catalogs, probably. But not likely in North African pottery. It shows up in some Ancient Egyptian clays. We believe the motif originated in Babylon and this is strikingly similar to that. It could be a fluke, but for me, this was an especially significant find for another reason."

The judge examined the artifact more closely as Amal continued. It was a most beautiful specimen, a large, round yellow platter, or shallow bowl, some sixty centimeters wide with a rolled, flaring edge, an intriguing black pattern, and an over-all brilliant luster. He was particularly taken with the geometric design inside. It consisted of a stylized gazelle with long, graceful horns, whose legs and body, drawn together, formed an upside-down pyramid—all in black—and perforated, like lace, with tiny yellow ocher triangles. The point of the pyramid rested on the point of a perforated rhomboid. The pattern was symmetrical, repeated four times around the interior of the bowl, with the rhomboid in the center. What he found perhaps most remarkable was an effect of the pattern to trick the eye, giving the illusion it was whirling like a wheel, although it stood quite still. And yet the design was deceptively simple on the whole, as delicate as filigree, much more pleasing visually than one might imagine just from hearing it described.

"…The difference between 'red' and 'black' slipware," Amal was saying, "was thought to be due to the presence or absence of reducing gases from the kiln acting on the iron oxides. If reducing gases were present, they produced a black coating; if they were absent, one got a red coating. And while it's true that North African kilns were generally constructed to prevent the reducing gases from the fuel from coming into contact with the pottery, for some reason I was never satisfied with that. I've had a hunch about the black color, but this was the first time I had examples of my own in hand to test. Well, as it happens, I just received confirmation from the lab as I was on my way here. It now appears that I was right. The color depends on the size of the crystals in the hematite."

As he continued to speak of the technical details, bringing to mind his old role as a university lecturer, Abul-Abbas recalled more consciously this time the impression he'd had, only moments before, when Amal had entered the house. It had been a very strange impression. He'd no sooner stepped into the vestibule, when the air had somehow changed, as if suddenly tinged with ozone. But it wasn't an odor. In fact, hardly even a feeling. It was more of a visual sensation, as if the light had changed and everything in the house—his, Abul-Abbas's house—the Persian carpets on the walls, the teak and rosewood furniture, the tenth century jade Yakshini from India, the ivory and alabaster objets d'art, it all seemed oddly different—just as familiar—but as if, for a moment, he were seeing them with someone else's eyes—someone indifferent to the aesthetic value of the pieces and merely taking stock of the wealth squandered on them that might have been put to better use in some socially constructive cause, like feeding the poor or building a road. As strange and even silly as that may sound, now, it was so sharp a sensation at the time that he can still remember it.

"…But the form of iron oxide found throughout much of North Africa," Amal was saying, "is of the small-crystal type, which is why the clay here is so red."

"Congratulations! Are you publishing your results?"

"I've sent preliminary notes off to a colleague in France, Michel Bonifay of Aix-Marseille University. I'm not an accredited archeologist myself, as you know, but as a field assistant to accredited scholars, my contributions have appeared in journals from time to time. In fact, I'm hoping Professor Bonifay will find it interesting enough to come down and supervise further excavation of the site in person."

"But now, here's another question, if the black hematite used in these plates is so rare in North Africa, where did it come from?"

"From Elba, I'm fairly sure. Some of it could have been

brought by the Phoenicians early on, but I suspect most of it was brought by the Romans themselves. My reason for thinking so is what else we found." He hesitated, as if unsure whether to continue.

"Yes? Well? Don't keep me in suspense!"

"There were skeletal remains," he said, finally.

"Skeletons? You mean, human skeletons?"

He nodded. "We know the Romans employed slaves, thousands of them, to grow the food and produce the goods to supply the vast market within the Empire and to be traded with neighboring peoples. They must have coerced hundreds of the native population to work here mining clay and metal ores, quarrying stone, producing olive oil, wine, and manufacturing pottery, jewelry, furniture, carpets, and so on. Given the harsh, desert environment, endemic diseases, and the general attitude toward slaves, the death rate must have been high."

"*Allah karim!* But how does that account for the skeletons in the pottery works? Wouldn't they have buried them?"

"They probably buried most of those who died of natural causes or overwork in mass graves. But others—and knowing how fiercely the Berbers, and especially the Tuareg, cherish their freedom, there must have been many who resisted—especially those who worked around the kilns, where the heat in the summer must've been hellish. They were probably slain and their bodies stuffed into the ovens and burned on the spot. The Roman custom, of course, was to cremate their dead. But there was more to it here. There were ritual sacrifices."

"Sacrifices?"

He hesitated again, then said, "You know those straight,

long swords the Romans were famous for in war and glad-iatorial exhibitions?"

"Spathas."

"Spathas, yes. They were made of strong Toledo steel. Well, we found several of them. The Romans had just begun to use them extensively in the early first century. But there were also a few of the original Roman short swords made of inferior Italian steel—which helps to narrow the dating of the site, by the way. That early Italian steel was notoriously brittle and couldn't hold its edge. The Romans were actually introduced to the high-quality Toledo blades by Hannibal, whose armies used them against the Roman Legions in the Punic Wars. The new spatha became so popular that the Romans, who enjoyed a spectacle, and often used horses to draw and quarter their condemned prisoners in the amphi-theaters, switched to beheading them with the sword."

"I thought they used a broadaxe?"

"No. The broadaxe didn't come into common use until the late Middle Ages in Europe. Incidently, it was Nero who put a stop to drawing and quartering when he decided that the practice was demeaning to horses, can you imagine!" He gave a sardonic grunt, adding, "Think of it: Nero's said to have had captured Christians dipped in oil and set on fire in his garden at night as a source of light—but it turns out that he had a compassionate side. He was a great fancier of horses—the Romans generally, in fact. They had defined some fifty separate breeds in their time. They'd developed vast systems of stud farms to supply horses for the Army and the circus—sorry, I guess I'm babbling!"

"But the skeletons?"

"Ah, yes. The skeletons. When you take into account the

likely caliber of the Roman soldier or auxiliary who might have been deployed to oversee the slaves working the mines and workshops in the dismal desert outpost here, as opposed to those selected to man the more glorious fighting Legions of Rome, you can imagine how the punishment and disposal of the rebellious slaves must have been a brutal affair. We found piles of skeletons, but few complete. They were mostly dismembered fragments. We haven't completed the count yet, but they must number close to a hundred souls. The bones were stacked along the walls around and behind the kilns. They'd been arranged according to body parts. There were piles of thighbones and femurs next to a heap of foot bones, then a stack of arms, then another of ribs and backbones. They'd all been decapitated, and the skulls, most of which had apparently been crushed with a stone or a bludgeon or cloven with a sword, were piled separately. The open joints clearly showed evidence of intentional cuts. In other words, they'd been hacked apart. We'll have to await an examination by forensic archeologists to determine whether the limbs had been severed after death, or before. If the latter, it must've been done as a form of torture. But there were a great deal of bone fragments mixed in with the charcoal and ash in the ovens. The proportion of bone we found, compared with the oak, olive, cedar and other woods present in the ovens, suggest it wasn't a unique occurrence."

"Merciful God! How awful!" Abul-Abbas didn't want to hear any more. And yet, he heard himself say, "You mentioned sacrifices?"

Amal pursed his lips, eying him thoughtfully, before answering. "There's good reason to suppose that most of the soldiers and auxiliaries posted here came from the hinterlands.

They would've brought with them beliefs in strange gods and ritual practices even more barbaric than those in Rome. The evidence indicates that many of the slaves here were tortured, butchered and burnt as sacrifices to these gods. The body parts were probably stacked separately because different gods required different forms of sacrifice at different times. We found fragments of what must have been clay effigies of these deities amongst the shards of pottery, many of them theriomorphs—gods having the form of a beast, or a human body with the head of a beast. And there were what must have been instruments of torture: iron manacles, chains, pokers, bits of hemp. As I said, there were also some skeletons that hadn't yet been dismembered. They lay in various contorted positions, apparently just as they'd died, twisted in pain. Their skulls were shattered or their backbones broken. There was one skull with a poker still embedded in the eye socket."

"My God!"

"It's strange, Abul-Abbas. They were only bones, you understand. Dry bones twenty centuries old. But as I stood there, looking about me, it was as if I could see them dying! I thought I could actually hear their cries for help and smell the rotting flesh!"

"Enough! Please, Amal, no more!"

"Ah! Yes, sorry! You don't wish to hear any more, then?"

"No! Really, no! That's enough!"

"Yes, of course. I understand. I'm sorry. It's what I should've expected. Perfectly reasonable."

His tone was solicitous, but Abul-Abbas couldn't help wondering whether Amal had purposely been trying to make him uncomfortable for some reason. He glanced away, and his eye came to rest on the platter Amal had brought. It sat there, on the coffee table, polished and resplendent, resting in its elaborate tissue wrapper. But the gazelles in the pattern now seemed frail and vulnerable and, together with the pattern's illusion of spinning in place, it appeared that they were running in desperate flight from some unseen predator. It provoked a feeling of vertigo and he found himself suddenly nauseated by it.

"I want to pick up where we left off just before dinner," Amal said later, "when we were talking about the periodic rise and fall of cultures."

It was evening by then. Earlier, Fâtima had called them in to dinner. In deference to her and to the wonderful repast she'd prepared, the two men had taken a break to chat about family and lighter matters. Fâtima had gone so far as to make a wonderful lamb tagine for the occasion, with couscous and a spicy harissa—a welcome exception, in honor of Amal's visit, to the usual bland diet Abul-Abbas's beloved wife had been serving him, on the doctor's orders, for months on end. But now, the two were alone again. They'd stepped out into the courtyard—it was a lovely evening, with the late desert sun gleaming through an iridescent panoply of diaphanous clouds—and they'd gravitated toward the stone benches around the fountain where they used to sit in the old days to play chess and discuss the history of ideas and the fate of the world. On this occasion, they took up their earlier conversation about the cultural influences that had swept back and forth across North Africa and the ancient Mediterranean generally, and soon they were trading facts, disputing theories and arguing away in earnest again, like old times. Amal seemed quite relaxed, by then—possibly an effect of the good dinner—and they were comfortable together, with that first awkward feeling Abul-Abbas had had when Amal had entered completely dispersed—or at least the judge let himself think so. In Amal's last comment, he was referring to an observation Abul-Abbas had made just before dinner regarding civilization's debt to the Ancients. The judge had been trying to illustrate his own proposition that human civilization had been rising to more and more impressive heights by virtue of each of the world's major cultures profiting from the contributions of those preceding. But Amal, taking exception, had started to recite a long, bloody list of disastrous wars and political reversals that had seemed continually to set back any advances civilization had made through history. He'd so much as accused Abul-Abbas of being guilty of Toynbeean optimism, whereupon the judge had countered by accusing him of Spenglerian cynicism. They were simply enjoying the moment, if at the expense of a little exaggeration, because they both knew that the German historian Oswald Spengler as well as his English counterpart Arnold Joseph Toynbee had been influenced in their cyclical views of the development of world civilizations by a 14th century Arabic philosopher and historian they both admired, Ibn Khaldun.

By the time they'd started accusing one another of being under the influence of Spengler or Toynbee, Amal had raised a hand and said, "Peace! I think we're both being carried away by an excess of rhetorical glee!"—at which point they'd both laughed, and Fâtima, with her unerring sense of timing, had stepped in to announce dinner.

Now, Amal went on to speak of what he perceived as the

compound effect of historical factors that seemed periodically to coalesce and well up every three or four generations like a tidal force, impelling one people or another toward war, political uprising, or cultural revolution.

"Are you speaking of *'asabiyyah?*"

"I start from that, yes—but Ibn Khaldun applied it only to North Africa. To my mind, it's a global phenomenon—and there is something else."

(*'Asabiyyah* was an ancient and complex Arabic concept formalized by Ibn Khaldun in the first volume of his world history, to refer to an intangible but pervasive natural impetus that drove historical change, contributing to the cultural cohesion that carried certain groups to power—while, at the same time, containing within itself the sociological, economic, and political seeds of that group's eventual downfall. The term had no close English equivalent. Western scholars had loosely translated *'asabiyyah* as "social cohesion," "group solidarity," or "tribalism," but these terms were misleading simplifications, interpreting the concept of an irresistible propulsive cultural force as if it were a passive local effect. Or, at least, that was Amal's interpretation. *'Asabiyyah* bespoke destiny, he said, maintaining that while fate was passive, destiny was not. In his own reading, however, Abul-Abbas had not found Ibn Khaldun to be so explicit. It seemed to him that the ancient scholar had used the term as a conceptual fiction in his analysis of the perceived patterns of history, rather than as a determining force. Whatever the case—and notwithstanding Amal's strong arguments—the judge was uncomfortable with the idea of a deterministic view of history because it seemed to leave too little room for individual responsibility.)

In the event, Amal went on to elaborate his idea, saying the most significant early example of *'asabiyyah* for which we had a historical record was the nexus of cultural revolutions that took place throughout the world in the years around 500 BCE, a remarkable moment in history, which the German philosopher Karl Jaspers had called the "Axial Age." It was a time when the paths of human cultural development were suddenly and forever altered by new ways of thinking in religion, politics, and philosophy. These ideas appeared independently but almost simultaneously in Persia, India, China, and the Greco-Roman world. Among the Ancient Greeks, for instance, Solon and Cleisthenes introduced the first radical ideas of democratic government in Athens, and Thales of Miletus expounded the first precepts of metaphysics, mathematics, and scientific thought, while in Rome the ancient line of kings was replaced by its first republican government.

"But most important of all," Amal said, "was the fact that this was the first time in history that humanity all across the globe was struck with the notion that it might be possible for the common man to rise above the exigencies of the material world—the endless cycles of work, war, plague, famine, and the oppression of tyrants. All at once and everywhere there arrived a new idea: something far more important to the plebeian mind than democracy or philosophy, it was the concept of transcendence, a chance at an afterlife! As if in answer to an age-old cry of the soul for some meaning to the drudgery of existence, there came Hinduism and Buddhism in India; Zoroastrianism in Ancient Persia; and in China, Confucianism and Daoism! But just think of it, my friend! Can you imagine what it must've been like to be alive at such a time? Can you imagine the soul-wrenching thrill that must have shivered through the world then? Suddenly, there was more to life than struggle, sorrow, and oblivion! All men everywhere could now cling to the illusion that there was a Great Reason for all this, that they had a chance at eternal redemption! All at once, each one seemed to be an integral part of the grand scheme of the cosmos!"

"Well…except, didn't the Mesopotamians and the Ancient Egyptians imagine an afterlife a thousand years earlier? The *Book of the Dead*—"

"Books," Amal said, correcting him. "Books of the dead. Egypt had many, and they came in many forms: originally in pyramid and coffin texts, where the sundry spells and prescriptions for the soul's behavior after death were painted on the inside walls of the tomb, or on the sarcophagus or coffin. Later, of course, similar funerary texts were inscribed on long scrolls of papyrus. But when you acquaint yourself with their content, you realize that the complexity and number of hurdles the dead soul had to overcome—the prayers it had to recite, the weighing of its moral conscience against an ostrich feather, the hazardous passage through some twenty-odd gates of challenge—and the horrible consequences it would experience if it failed to pass any of these tests—in order to reach eternal rebirth in paradise, or what they called *Sekhet-Aaru,* the Field of Reeds, you realize that almost all the tribulations of life on earth were a mere cakewalk by comparison! Which of course was the point, and which was why there were as many variations of these books of the dead as there were men rich enough to commission them—the more you paid the scribe, the easier he made the passage— again, rather like the way privilege still works here on earth.

It was essentially the same in Mesopotamia, where only the elect, the great mythical heroes, could earn an afterlife—by being apotheosized into demigods. The rest simply moldered to dust. So, still not much to look forward to for the great unwashed, eh? The religious revolutions I'm speaking of, however, dramatically changed all that—the afterlife was suddenly democratized, it was now equally available to all, depending only upon each one's moral character!

"Ah," he added, "but then it all falls apart, doesn't it? With the next wave, Athenian democracy is suppressed by the Macedonians, the Zhou dynasty collapses, and China enters its violent period of Warring States. And Hannibal! Hannibal's magnificent failure to conquer Italy sets Rome on the path to empire in the Mediterranean—and the destruction of his own Carthage. Soon, the tyrants are back—but this time, they've learned to co-opt those earlier great movements of the promise of transcendence and wield them like a sword: Constantine builds his Roman empire on the back of Christianity, the Gupta Dynasty controls India with Hinduism, and the new imperial states rising in China are promoting different factions of Daoism and Buddhism in their efforts to gain ascendency over one another!"

The point Amal seemed to be at pains to make clear was that the force of *'asabiyyah,* which was as impartial and blind as the evolutionary force, might work for good or ill—but was especially terrible when it worked for ill. Whenever the unconscious rising tide of *'asabiyyah* merged with a people's conscious sense of imminent cultural ascendancy, the resulting confluence of forces tended to result in wars beyond any hope of political or diplomatic resolution, wars of attrition that were of such extreme violence as to approach genocidal proportions and even threaten to destroy whole cultures. He cited the obvious examples from our own times, the two World Wars, and the partitions of India, Pakistan, and Bangladesh. Then he said:

"You see, Carlyle was wrong! History is much more than the biographies of Great Men. Those so-called 'Great Men' are only the talented opportunists who are thrown up to give the juggernaut focus. Those who conceive of history as the comings and goings of kings and conquerors miss the real action, which surges beneath the surface, and like a riptide can gut a kingdom or an empire without warning. But such movements are often difficult to recognize at first. They may begin as trifling tribal, ethnic, or religious schisms, or a local peasant revolt. And by the time the elite, having previously dismissed them out of complacency, recognize what has befallen them, it's too late! So it was with the arrival of Christianity in Rome and Communism in Tzarist Russia. Even now, while the scholars are watching the confrontation between Communism and capitalism, expecting that the outcome of that great contest will determine the next turning of the historical tide, it's my opinion they'll be taken by surprise once again—this time, by the rise of something else entirely that they will least expect! In fact, I say it's already begun! It began twenty years ago in Egypt, in the July Revolution of 1952, when Nasser overthrew King Farouk, drove out the British, and established an independent republic. In the West, the analysts tried to dismiss it as an anomaly, a unique local event with little significance on the global stage. But then, of course, there was Algeria. And if I were to tell them that these two events were only the beginning of the coming wave of history, they would say I was deluded, how could two isolated incidents occurring on opposite sides of the continent possibly represent the seeds of a storm that will rage through the Arab World a generation later? But then, I wouldn't expect a Western historian to understand that our sense of time and space is very different from his, and our memories are longer. For us, a generation is but a sigh in passing. However, Trotsky understood. Trotsky said the events of war and those of the revolutionary mass movement are measured by different yardsticks, because while the action of armies may be measured by days and weeks, the movement of the masses of people is reckoned in years, or even decades." He paused, and then added, darkly, "And now, we've come full circle!"

Then he suddenly broke off. What he was saying sounded to Abul-Abbas as though he were leading up to something apocalyptic, but when the judge asked him to explain what he meant, he fell silent and grew pale. His features lapsed into a kind of rictus, and that same strange chill from his first appearance that evening crept over Abul-Abbas again.

Amal turned to look out over the garden wall toward the horizon, and after a moment, he said, "Have you noticed how the desert has been advancing?"

"The desert?"

"Our vineyards and olive orchards have been drying up for years. You haven't noticed?"

"Well, yes, of course. Everyone's noticed. The farmers have been abandoning the land and crowding into the cities looking for work, but there's nothing for them to do. And the government seems unable to find a solution. But excuse me, why do you mention that now?"

But he didn't answer that question, either. He just

pursed his lips, then nodded as at some inner thought and looked away as if he had nothing to add—or rather, as if it was all too obvious to require elaboration.

Abul-Abbas had realized, by then, that something was very wrong. Amal's arguments had always been cogent. But that evening, he seemed to stray further and further afield, and his assessment of the progress of civilization seemed excessively dark. He was clearly agitated, but when Abul-Abbas asked him about it, he dismissed it as the vestige of a passing fever, and simply reverted to his gloomy theme.

"Well," the judge said, finally, "all that seems unduly bleak to me! Cultures, like people, experience periods of growth and stasis, and conflicts, I suppose, will always be with us. But really, the history of civilizations in both the East and the West has been much richer than how you make it seem. For instance—"

"Even so!" he said, cutting him off. "Irrespective of outside influences, the core aspirations of each culture are unique to that culture—and while that's not news, the point I want to make is that it's a critically important idea, now especially, because these differences tend to be lost in the big picture, whenever a hegemonic culture decides to dictate the future course of development to a subject people. The technocrats of the regime always offer the same specious argument, that everyone is—or should be—evolving in the same direction, and for the good of mankind we should all be willing to conform to…well, you fill in the blank: the authoritarian idyll of the moment. But this, of course, is— you'll pardon the expression—*de la merde!* It's a teleological argument. It's an argument that says, 'This is the Ultimate Good, and resistance is immoral or deranged!'"

"Of course," Abul-Abbas said, thinking to anticipate where he was going, "and this oppression leads to resentment, and ultimately, to rebellion. You're thinking again of the rise of Arabic resistance."

"Right now, the Arabs are being squeezed between Soviet socialism and Western capitalism," he said, nodding. "But neither will satisfy the Arab soul, because ultimately both share the same deep flaw: they both foster materialism at the expense of the spirit. 'The aim is not to win a contest between rival models of economic development,' someone wrote, 'but above all to fill a spiritual void.' Can you guess who wrote that?"

Abul-Abbas shook his head, no.

"Henry Kissinger!" He laughed, "Kissinger was talking about how Communism had made more converts through the theological appeal of Marxism than through the materialistic aspect it took so much pride in. Imagine, even an American Secretary of State could understand that! But of course, once the socialist system is put in place, reality grinds the theological aspirations to dust! Do you remember when we watched as anti-Western regimes came to power in Syria, in Iraq, and in Libya—do you remember how excited we were? We thought we were seeing a new wave of hope for an Arab resurgence and independence from Western influence throughout the Mideast. The Soviet Union, of course, was hoping to ride this wave and extend its influence too—they were suddenly dumping money and guns on us at every turn—so all at once, we had Arab 'socialist' regimes winning popular support with promises to destroy Israel, defeat the U.S. and imperialism, and finally bring ascendancy to the Arab ethos!" He threw up his hands in a gesture of resignation. "But now, we see what's come of that. The igno-minious defeat in the Six-Day War left the Arab world disil-lusioned, and the people gradually came to realize the failure of socialism as a way to their redemption.

"But where does that leave us now?" he continued. "The West is no longer an option. By this time, the Arab states that had tried to come to an accommodation with the West have seen how Western ideas threaten to erode our spiritual values and turn everything into a zero-sum game, disparag-ing our tradition of communal cooperation and introducing the dazzling notion of competitiveness, which leaves our youth bewildered and detached, disillusioned with the past and anxious about the future. To us, the West and the Sovi-ets pose the same threat. It's strange, you know. Throughout history, for most of the world's peoples the changing hands of empire have been of little account. All empires occupy the country, exploit its resources, and abuse its people. So, to the people of the country, it didn't really matter who ruled them, because whoever ruled them, from whatever faraway capital, they suffered physical oppression and their taxes were onerous in any case. But you see, the Western mode of conquest—and I include the Soviets here, because whether it's Adam Smith or Karl Marx, capitalism or Communism, essentially, they're both forms of Western materialism—this Western mode is something new. Whether or not it actually occupies the land, it infects the *mind*, Abul-Abbas. This is more insidious than any physical army the world has ever faced before!

"You smile!" he said, suddenly, eyeing my expression. "You think I'm exaggerating! But tell me if you think it might not be true!"

Abul-Abbas wasn't conscious of smiling, but he was certainly bewildered by his friend's tone. Compared with the Amal he thought he knew, this Amal's whole manner that evening seemed strangely intense, even overbearing, and his argument a little wild. He couldn't tell where Amal was going, and that made him apprehensive.

"Tell me, Abul-Abbas, if you think it might not be true," he continued, "that we've arrived at a turning point. In this Cold War world, divided between Western and Soviet spheres of influence, we must finally understand that it is an existential necessity that we carve out a third way. And to be free to do that, will require a violent resistance!"

"Excuse me, but are you speaking immediately of Qarmat now, or the Arab world, generally?"

"We're about to see the rise of a new generation of rebels," he continued, not quite answering the question, "a new jihad, Abul-Abbas. But this time, I foresee a much more vengeful war than before. We may be at a disadvantage in a war of armies, so we will have to wage a war of terror. We are a proud people, but we've been pushed to the extreme, and so, the terror will come on a scale the West has never known!"

He paused, and Abul-Abbas stared at him for a moment, not knowing quite what to say. Terror? The word immediately brought back to his mind the horrors the country had experienced decades earlier, when the two men had fought together in the civil war that had brought Emir Mohamed Boualem el-Roweed to the throne. And suddenly, Amal was bringing it up again now—and in a way that almost seemed as if the thought excited him. Abul-Abbas felt somehow entrapped by his logic, but found the tenor of his remarks frightening. More than that, the judge was seeing a side of someone he'd never seen before. He felt nauseated and disoriented, as though someone he'd always looked upon as a pillar of rational equanimity had suddenly pulled him up close to peer into his eyes. Abul-Abbas felt as if he stood at the edge of a pit, staring down to where reason had fallen away into the depths of an all-consuming vengefulness! But the pit—was it in Amal, or in himself? It was strange, the ambivalence that he felt. In hearing his friend's words, there was—for a moment, he had to confess—a certain undeniable mad excitement that he could feel percolating through himself, as though his warrior spirit, so long dormant, had been rekindled at Amal's torch. At the same time, he was repelled, revolted by the implications. He thought—he didn't really know what he thought. He thought that maybe it was all just an academic exercise, that Amal was simply exploring the hypothetical case to see how the Algerian model might apply to Qarmat, imagining the rise of a popular guerrilla action against the French colonial presence there at the time. Abul-Abbas never imagined, he certainly could never have imagined, the scope, the profound depravity of what his friend was actually planning. But whatever it was, he felt he wanted to get away from it, to remove himself from the base heat Amal had brought to his door.

"Terrorism? You mean—but terrorism?" he stammered, as though he'd lost his footing. "I'm afraid I don't understand, Amal, you almost make me think you relished the thought! But terrorism is self-defeating! When you start attacking the civilian population you lose the sympathy of the very people whose support you need to accomplish anything. I thought we'd learned that lesson twenty years ago, when the other side used it only to alienate their base of support and then lose the war."

"That was then. But it worked in Algeria, didn't it?"

"It…well, I suppose—well, maybe, in that case. But I think only because at the same time, France was financially and morally depleted. They'd just been defeated at Dien Bien Phu. France was in political turmoil, and the French people were fed up with the moral cost of colonialism. They wanted out. The timing just happened to be fortunate for the Algerians."

"The timing is fortunate for us, now!"

"In fact, historically," Abul-Abbas continued, caught up in his own attempt to derail Amal's argument—and not catching the significance of his friend's last comment— "and as a student of history, Amal, you must know this—people, as a whole, tend to respond to terrorism paradoxically. It only seems to increase their resistance. Think of how the British responded to the intense aerial bombardment of London at the beginning of the last War. It only provoked their courage and fighting spirit—more so, I think, than any mere propaganda could have. Or, later, when the Allies carpet-bombed Dresden. The effect of the bombings in Dresden, Berlin and elsewhere only hardened the German resolve to fight to the bitter end!"

"You're absolutely right!" he said, surprising Abul-Abbas with a sudden concession. "Historically, there's no question about that. But the fact is, after generations of oppression and failed attempts at negotiation and accommodation, there comes a time when you must be ready to act on instinct—or be annihilated. Between Western mind-control and terroristic resistance, a desperate people has little choice—really, none, no alternative. Between these two evils they must learn to use the one against the other.

"Wait!" he continued. "I see you're about to object. But hear me out. Yes, I spoke of terrorism. But terrorism is only a tactic, not a strategy. To have any hope of success, such terrorism, which is driven by exasperation and hatred, requires intelligent planning, realistic goals—and, as you say, fortunate timing! It *can* be effective! It was effective in Algeria, not only because of the French fatigue, the Algerians also had the advantage of brilliant leadership in Ferhat Abbas and Boumedienne. Those men understood the uses of terror, and understood, too, that they had to look beyond it, for hatred and terror have their limitations, and even when they seem enabling, they can only destroy a thing. Once you've destroyed a thing, you must have something ready to replace it. If you don't do that, you're faced with a void, and the void will devour you!"

He was quiet then for a long time, and as Abul-Abbas brooded on his words and how to respond, he thought he saw Amal actually shaking. He continued to stare into that dark corner of the courtyard. It was a relatively cool evening, but certainly not chilly enough to cause him to shiver. But he continued to stare into the bushes as if he saw there, in his mind's eye, some dreadful beast shambling toward them. Abul-Abbas was completely taken aback by his vehemence and this new, bitter tone from one he'd known for so long as an apostle of reason and an indefatigable idealist.

Finally, on impulse, Abul-Abbas reached out to touch his hand, and said, "Amal, are you all right? I don't—is there something you want to tell me?"

Amal looked at him, his eyes suddenly large and haunted,

and put his hand over that of his friend, pressing their hands together—and even allowing for their long intimacy, it was a gesture of warmth and intensity that was rare for him.

He said, "Abul-Abbas, I need to ask you something."

The judge waited, but Amal didn't say any more. Then he glanced away again—and that, too, was unusual for him, because Amal would normally hold your gaze—but he glanced away, as if embarrassed by his own ominous tone.

Abul-Abbas prompted him, "Amal, what is it? What did you want to ask me?"

But Amal only laughed—a dry, harsh laugh—and withdrew his hands, "No, nothing. I was being melodramatic, that's all."

"No, really, go on. What did you want to ask me?"

He waved it away, and got up and walked to the far side of the fountain. He stopped a few paces beyond and stood for a moment staring into the bushes in that same dark corner. Then, he suddenly glanced back over his shoulder and, changing the subject, he said, "Khalid and I used to chase each other around this fountain when he was little, do you remember? He was such a bright, sweet boy. It's very sad! I remember, when I heard the news, I felt as if I'd lost a son of my own...." He paused for a moment, as if revisiting those days in his mind.

"Amal, excuse me, I don't mean to pry, but from the moment you arrived tonight you seemed agitated, or at least preoccupied by something. And you just said you wanted to ask me something. What is it? Is something wrong? Is there anything I can do to help?"

He looked up sharply, as though startled out of his reverie, and when he spoke, his voice had a hard, defensive edge, "Let's forget about that, Abul-Abbas, if you don't mind. Besides, talk isn't going to change anything."

"Who knows? It could. Sometimes, talking can help us to understand—"

"There's nothing to understand!" he said, cutting him off. "And in any case, understanding would be useless!"

"Useless?" the judge stared at him, not knowing what to think. For a moment, Amal seemed a stranger. "How can understanding ever be useless? We've been talking all evening, and now I've just asked you—"

But Amal cut him off again, his voice almost shrill, "Completely useless!"

Then, suddenly, he burst out in laughter—but now, it was a full-throated, congenial laugh, and this abrupt return to a tone of apparent light-hearted banter only disconcerted the judge further. Abul-Abbas thought it was unlike the person he knew and it seemed unbalanced. And then he began to feel really anxious without knowing why. It seemed that even the depth of his friend's sarcasm escaped him.

"For example," Amal continued, as if teasingly, "what exactly could we have expected our conversation this evening to accomplish, hmm? I mean, beyond whiling away a few pleasant hours? I think it would've been unrealistic for us to hope it could've changed anything—don't you agree?"

"I think that would depend on what it is you wanted to change!" Abul-Abbas said. But he was hurt that Amal had so lightly dismissed their evening together. At the same time, he couldn't escape the feeling that, whether or not it was his own fault, an important moment between them had slipped by. Amal had said that he wanted to ask him something. His friend must have come to ask him something. And later, when it had all unfolded, Abul-Abbas felt that, had he pressed Amal at the time, had he been just a little more perceptive, even aggressive, the conversation might've taken a different turn and—just possibly—it might have prevented a catastrophe. But in the moment, Amal had taken on a strange and sardonic aspect which he found repellent, and he slowly got up and said, "But if you feel that way, well, then…perhaps we shouldn't waste any more of the evening."

But Amal immediately shook his head and raised his hands, as if in mock surrender, and yet his tone was harsh when he muttered—and Abul-Abbas couldn't tell whether he was addressing him or himself— "You have to try harder!"

They both stood there a moment, as if puzzled by a voice that had come from somewhere else. Abul-Abbas found himself running his tongue over his lower lip, as if to taste the meaning of words that he couldn't quite make sense of by just hearing them.

Finally, Amal nodded his head, then turned and in a voice that seemed to be trying to be reasonable again—but by this time the judge couldn't tell from his tone whether he was speaking to him or lecturing some imaginary audience—Amal said:

"There are instances when understanding may be…if not exactly useless, not really useful, anyway. When I say understanding may not be useful, I'm really asking a question: What is at stake? What is the highest priority? How does the subject under consideration—philosophy, number theory, poetry—change anything that matters? What good was all the understanding of Athenian philosophy when confronted with the superior militarism of autocratic Sparta? Of what use is understanding in politics or war?"

"What are you saying? Countless thousands of innocent lives are lost in wars. Understanding would—"

"More specifically," he continued, as if he hadn't heard him, "suppose, now, Qarmat were to go to war with France. What then, hmm? It would be costly, of course, but there are plenty of good reasons for Qarmat to go to war with France."

The words began to rush out of him, as if he were warming, at last, to the subject he'd had in mind all along, but his voice retained a cold, analytic edge as he continued.

"'But,' you might say, 'understanding should prevent such a war!' Except you see, Abul-Abbas, you'd be wrong. Because for many—and especially for those who would avoid the truth, or twist it to suit their own nefarious purposes—'to understand' only means to simplify! And the fact is, the truth isn't simple at all—quite the contrary, it's often very complicated. But if your purpose is to manipulate the public, you don't want to make things complicated. You want to make them simple and clear. To take an interesting tidbit from history that I think might serve to illustrate my point: when the American President Harry Truman wanted to raise funds to help rebuild Europe after the wholesale destruction of the Second World War, he ran up against an obstructionist Congress, who felt that the United States had done its share to help win the war and that Europe should take responsibility for rebuilding itself, without further expenditure of American tax dollars. But then-Senator Arthur Vandenberg understood something profound about politics and foreign policy. He knew that while statesmen may approach foreign policy from the vantage point of hope—hope for world peace and international trade, say—the general public tends to be more effectively motivated by fear. So, he told Truman that if he wanted the people to back him and to put pressure on their representatives in Congress to provide the funds he needed, he was going to have to scare them into it, scare the hell out of them. He was going to have to create a bogeyman. He was going to have to go around the country and speak to the people and explain to them, in terms clear enough for them to understand, that if America didn't help Europe get back on its feet, Europe—and possibly the rest of the world—might fall under the sway of Russian Communism, and then America, the last bastion of Western Christian democracy, would be alone and vulnerable to succumbing to the worldwide threat of atheism and Communism! So, Truman and his team did just that, they followed Vandenberg's advice. It worked. It worked so well that America has been paying the price for it ever since: building arms for an endless Cold War; encouraging—indirectly through the NRA—even the civilian population to arm themselves in case the regular army should fail to protect them; fighting dubious foreign wars it couldn't win in Korea and Vietnam, and infiltrating and alienating itself from its natural allies in Cuba, El Salvador, and elsewhere—not to mention eroding national self-confidence in paranoid witch hunts for Communist sympathizers at home. Notwithstanding this outcome, Truman's secretary of state, Dean Acheson, later defended the tactic in his memoirs, claiming that it was sometimes necessary to make things, in his words, 'clearer than the truth' to advance a greater cause. But I must ask you, what could be clearer than the truth—save a lie? Because the problem, you see—as an earlier president, Woodrow Wilson, realized when he deliberated bringing America into the First World War—the problem is that once you open the floodgates of fear and hate, you can't close them again. They become a self-regenerating force. Whether you do it as a statesman with 'ethical' intentions, or as a self-serving demagogue, once you simplify the truth, you forge a weapon beyond the pale of reason to control. We both remember Jacob Burckhardt's warning against the 'Terrible Simplifiers!'

"So now, here, Abul-Abbas, is a complicated truth: this is the 16th Safar, 1392, by our Islamic calendar, which is to say, April 1st, 1972, Gregorian, yes? France has occupied Qarmat for a hundred and forty-seven years, seven months and thirteen days—ah, yes! Some of us have been counting! And during that time, we've been studying each other intently. The French 'understand' us very well, and we them. They know that we're weary of the yoke of colonialism, that we've long outgrown any benefits we might once have deluded ourselves into thinking it held for us. They know that we've grown restless, impatient of the political and economic inequities we experience, that we want to be free to develop our own resources, to trade with whomsoever we please on our own terms, to walk as equals among the other nations in the corridors of international diplomacy, that we don't want to answer to anyone anymore—in a word, that we want to be free! We, on the other hand, have come to understand that for any people to put its destiny in the hands of strangers is to be caught in a precarious situation. We understand that France is greedy and selfish, that France is arrogant, patronizing and complacent—as any world power is tempted to be. We understand that France has no intention of abandoning the economic advantages and international prestige of being a colonial power—insofar as France can hold on to what's left of that illusion. We understand, in a word, that France—and the West, generally—thinks of us as 'sand niggers' and undeserving of the wealth of the land we were born in and have cultivated for a thousand generations. France and Qarmat have come to 'understand' each other thoroughly—but this has not promoted much sympathy between us! The only understanding that's kept the peace all this time has been the simple awareness that France was too strong and we'd lose too much and gain little in such a war. And yet we've seen the resentment on both sides increasing inexorably year by year.

"But now, there's a change in the air. The French are no longer the great colonial power they used to be. They've been demoralized by their international losses in recent years. The French people are fed up with the weak Fourth Republic and its costly attempts to claw back the anachronistic self-image of being an imperial state. The French people have had enough—and so have the Qarmatians! Sooner or later—and probably, sooner, we both know it's true—that confrontation is coming! It's inevitable!" He hesitated a moment, as if unsure whether to continue.

"But Amal, with all that being true, what you're calling 'understanding' here is just the opposite! What's needed is an open dialogue to penetrate and unravel the complicated history and truths of our relationship with France."

"Ah, but that would take time and good will," he answered, with bitter sarcasm, "but there is no sign of good will on the French side—and time, my friend, is running out! Besides, we've been "talking" for over a hundred years! The thing is, in such a war, we would need the sympathy of the world, as Algeria had it, to put pressure on France. And in the eyes of the world, it's much more sympathetic to act heroically, to simply cut a knot, than to try to unravel it."

He broke off, and his expression suddenly sobered again, as he added, "Abul-Abbas, you and I have thought deeply about these matters, and we've talked about them for so long. We've honored each other for so much of our lives, but you know—I don't know if I've ever told you—you've really been a sort of mentor, to me—"

"What!" In the context, the sudden compliment—if that's what it was—came across to Abul-Abbas as facile, as if Amal was being patronizing. "What are you talking about?"

"I mean, your high moral standards, and your sense of justice. You've been like a sort of higher conscience—"

"Amal Koraoun el-Mudharrisi! Please! I don't know whether you're trying to flatter me, but please don't! It's embarrassing! And anyway, what has this got to do with anything?"

Amal just stood there, studying him for some time, without answering, and when he did, the sudden question caught the judge by surprise, "What would *you* do?"

Abul-Abbas couldn't see his eyes. He'd turned away to look toward the window, as if he'd just become aware, as the judge had, that the sun had gone down. They'd been talking all evening, and neither had noticed the gathering shadows until now, when a servant had apparently turned on a lamp in the house. But the moon was out. It was a full moon, and its light filled the courtyard with a silvery, nostalgic glimmer. And in the moonlight, Amal's face in profile, that once-youthful face, had taken on the age and the pale luster of a stone.

"What would *I* do?"

"If…"

"If, what?"

Amal hesitated again, then turned back to look at him with a penetrating gaze, he said, "We fought together on the same side once, remember? You were very brave when we were both young soldiers fighting to unite the country under the old Emir."

Abul-Abbas dismissed the remark with an irritable wave of the hand, "Soldiering is a young man's game—but what are you saying? Are we on different sides now?"

Amal bit his lip, then came forward and drew him down to sit beside him on the bench, and speaking quietly, he said, "Of course not, of course we're on the same side. What I meant was—" He paused again, then leaned forward, his expression, in the dim light, seemed even more somber than before and his voice grew hoarse with intensity as he added, "I wanted to—I'd like to tell you something, my friend, in confidence, just between the two of us: lately, Abul-Abbas, I've been having a recurrent dream, it's about that final confrontation, and it's terrible!"

That was what Amal said. But it was a lie! It wasn't a dream, Abul-Abbas thought to himself, now. It was the nightmare he'd been planning all along—he and his *Jaysh Damm*, his Blood Army! The reality was more terrible than any dream!

7.

The sound awakens him. It seemed so real that as Samiel opens his eyes he looks around to see where it's coming from. The sound he heard was the opening fugal passage from the Adagio, Opus 131. But when he sees the walls around him now, he realizes he'd only imagined it, his inner ear drawing it out of memory or some dream already forgotten. For the reality to which he wakes hardly evokes lyricism. It's late at night and he's in jail, of course. There's nothing to look at but the deceptive geometry of this prison cell, where he waits out the hours between the acts of the ongoing farce in court, nothing but the horizontal planes, vertical bars and cinerious walls that give one the feeling of peace and finality, the gray, vague darkness of the tomb. But in fact, there is no peace, for he's being beset by things he thought he'd left behind long ago.

Someone or something is shuffling across the concrete floor, and he hears the distant clang of an iron gate echoing back through the whine of mosquitoes—might it have been only that? Beethoven's serene, melancholic C-sharp minor quartet called back to his ear by the whining of mosquitoes in a cell above the killing floor? The stench of ordure and old wounds, of fear, sweat, and dried blood, all the miseries he'd imposed on others, still clings in the air, investing the cracks in the walls, along with the teaming vermin, like a mosaic of agonies. And the chains and racks and break-bars have all been put on display now, neatly catalogued and labeled for the titillation of tourists.

"…We come, now, to the question of the *Neo-qaada*," the prosecutor is saying in the courtroom seven months later, "a certain group of male youths conscripted by the QPR into a sort of junior revolutionary organization. Is the defendant familiar with this organization?"

"Yes," Samiel says.

"Yes. Well, then, would the defendant please describe the nature of the *Neo-qaada* organization for the Court?"

"The *Neo-qaada* was a small group, or cadre, of young men of promising abilities whom the QPR selected and trained in preparation for possible leadership positions when vacancies arose within the QPR hierarchy."

The prosecuting attorney nods then asks, "And how were these 'young men of promising abilities' selected?"

"Candidates were selected from youths we encountered throughout the country, ranging from twelve to sixteen years and nine months of age. Those who met certain standards of health, strength and basic intelligence went through a screening process, involving interviews and recommendations."

"Who conducted the interviews and selected the candidates for the *Neo-qaada*?"

"Myself and other officers of the QPR."

"Can you be more specific? Besides yourself, can you name some of those officers?"

Samiel considers a moment before answering, then says, "Initially, Mumi el-Hawhza, our imam and leader, would make the final selections, based upon preliminary interviews and recommendations made by myself, Musheikhi 'el-Aqrab' el-Barzan my adjutant, and other lieutenants, including

Abdillah Hammadi, Muhammad Falah, Ali Kamel, Mustafa Daoudi, Muhammad el-Beghal…later, there were others. As the QPR organization grew and our responsibilities grew, many other officers took part."

The prosecutor turns to address the bench. "Please the Court, let it be noted that the men mentioned by the defendant are all known to these proceedings. Mumi Malagawi el-Hawhza is deceased. Abdillah Hammadi is currently imprisoned for an unrelated conviction. Muhammad Falah is known to have fled to Dar el-Nar. Ali Kamel is believed to have fled the country, but we don't know where. Mustafa Daoudi is deceased and Muhammad el-Beghal is assumed to be in hiding somewhere in Qarmat.

"It has just come to light, however, that Musheikhi el-Barzan, who is listed as a witness for the prosecution in this case and who was scheduled to testify in court within the next two weeks, will not be available. We received a communication to that effect this morning—may I repeat, we received the news *only this morning!*—from the office of the Inspector of Police in el-Rawi. We ask the Court to recall that the inspector had accepted the official responsibility of monitoring the whereabouts and securing the safety of el-Barzan and other witnesses who were otherwise left at liberty in the city. And again, we ask the Court to note that it was *only this morning*, as court was being called into session, that we were told that *fourteen months ago, one year and two months ago!*—specifically, three weeks before the defendant, Samiel, was apprehended and scheduled for trial—el-Barzan, whose nom de guerre was 'el-Aqrab,' the Scorpion, and who, according to the pretrial depositions and testimony of others in this courtroom, functioned under the defendant's direct supervision and was in charge of most of the torture sessions and executions conducted at the QPR's main prison, Bustan el-Barzakh, this man was found dead—*murdered*, in fact—in his hammam, a bathhouse he owned and operated in the old Jewish quarter of the city."

The prosecutor turns to give Samiel a long, accusatory look, before continuing. "Returning to the matter of the *Neo-qaada*, would the defendant please tell the Court where this cadre of young men was housed and trained?"

"At the camp at Bustan el-Barzakh."

"At the execution camp?"

"At the prison camp."

"Were there two camps at Bustan el-Barzakh, one for executions and one for…other purposes?"

Samiel lets a sigh escape his lips before answering, "There was really only one camp. But it was a large camp, a large facility with many activities. The members of the *Neo-qaada* were kept in a dormitory apart from the prisoners. Their classes—in political history, Arabic literacy, with special emphasis on Qur'ânic studies, some rudimentary principles of mathematics, and management skills—were held in a separate building set aside for that purpose, with an attached yard for physical exercise."

The prosecutor nods, "I see. Thank you for that clarification. Please tell the Court how large a group the *Neo-qaada* was, how many youths were selected for this cadre?"

"Four hundred."

"Four hundred," the prosecutor repeats, quoting him. "Is that an approximation, or an exact number?"

"An exact number," Samiel replies, then adds, "Well, permit me to explain. Four hundred were initially selected, and as trainees 'graduated' from the program, so to speak, other youths were selected to replace them. The group was never larger than four hundred at any one time."

"An exact number, then. Four hundred at a time, no more, no fewer. Is that correct?"

"Yes."

"And these four hundred were selected from…how many potential candidates? How many youths would you say were initially brought forward for consideration to be selected during the existence of the *Neo-qaada* program?"

Samiel hesitates a moment, then says, "I cannot say, exactly. There were many."

"How many?" the prosecutor prompts. "Approximately. Would you say hundreds? Thousands? Tens of thousands?"

Samiel takes another moment to consider, and then, waving his hand in a vague gesture, answers, "I would say, a few thousand. Perhaps five or ten thousand."

"Five or ten thousand. So, the Court may understand you to say that as many as five or ten thousand young men between the ages of twelve and sixteen years and nine months were rounded up throughout the country to undergo the selection process for membership in the *Neo-qaada*? Is that right?"

"Yes."

The young prosecutor pauses, as if to let the Court absorb the impact of the statement. Then, after a moment, he says, "And what happened to these other youths, the thousands who were not selected for membership in the *Neo-qaada*?"

"They were eliminated."

"Eliminated? Meaning?"

Samiel looked at him blankly, "I beg your pardon?"

"What does 'eliminated' mean?" the prosecutor persists. "Eliminated how? In what way were they 'eliminated?'"

Samiel shrugs. "Eliminated from consideration. Excluded from the group selected."

"And what became of them? What became of the thousands of young men not deemed fit for selection into the *Neo-qaada*?"

"They were reassigned to other projects, often to other camps. There were many work projects in the camps. They included quarrying stone and manufacturing bricks for construction materials, the actual construction of buildings to house the inmates, building walls and putting up fences at the perimeters, digging ditches for irrigation, sewage, and so on."

"I see." The prosecutor pauses a moment, as if considering whether to pursue that line of questioning, then tilts his head and changes tack.

"What was your relationship to the *Neo-qaada* organization?"

"The *Neo-qaada* was organized on my suggestion, and I took initial responsibility for the group's training and discipline. After the first few months, I delegated those responsibilities to others, but I remained the nominal head of the group and retained responsibility for determining the group's direction, the maturity of the graduates—that is to say, their readiness to move on to responsible positions of their own within the QPR—and for recommending them for vacancies in the hierarchy as they became available."

The prosecuting attorney pauses to study Samiel for a moment, and a mischievous gleam creeps into his pale blue eyes. Finally, he says, addressing the judges' bench, "The defendant was the supreme commander of the QPR at the time—"

"With the Court's permission," Samiel says, interrupting him, "that is not correct. I was *second* in command to Mumi Malagawi el-Hawhza, who was the founder and Supreme Commander of the QPR Revolution, and who was responsible for initiating strategy and guiding the Party toward its objectives. I was only second-in-command."

"Only *second* in command." The prosecutor raises his hand and nods in acquiescence, "Correction noted, I'm sorry. Second in command. Very well, but even so, I believe you admitted you had extensive responsibility for military operations during and after the Revolution, oversight in all political initiatives and 'disciplinary' policies—including senior responsibility for the selection, arrest, interrogation, torture and execution of all those considered enemies or threats to the Revolution—"

"Objection!"

"Defending counsel's objection is sustained," the Chief Magistrate, Abul-Abbas, says. "Prosecuting counselor will please refrain from assumptions of guilt regarding crimes this court has been convened to determine, avoid leading questions, and keep the wording of his questions within proper constraints."

The young prosecuting attorney nods, "I apologize, Your Honor. Let me rephrase the question. In fact, let me begin by explaining my line of questioning. As the defendant has admitted to being second in command of the QPR Revolutionary movement, the prosecution would like to ascertain why, with all the responsibilities that pertained to that position, why the defendant took the time and trouble to create and to retain control over the *Neo-qaada* organization, what importance the *Neo-qaada* had for the QPR, and to what extent the defendant was responsible for the ultimate fate of those who were selected for membership, as well as of those not selected."

The Chief Magistrate confers a moment with his associate justices, then nods his approval. "Very well. Counsel may proceed."

"Thank you, Your Honor. Would the defendant please recapitulate, for the Court, his rationale for creating the *Neo-qaada* organization? In fact, would he be so kind as to begin by explaining the name. '*Neo-qaada*' is a made-up word, I believe."

Samiel looks at the youthful American with blond hair and pale, almost-transparently-blue eyes with renewed interest. He was aware of the fellow's background. The young man was another appointee made by the International Court of Justice from the international roster to act as principal prosecuting attorney. He was a Harvard Law alumnus who had clerked for Chief Justice William Rehnquist of the U. S. Supreme Court and had subsequently made a name for himself, even at that young age, defending victims of humanitarian abuses on several continents. Samiel guesses that the young attorney hasn't run up against someone quite like himself before, but the boy's smart, he grants, and he's learning. He gives an ironic smile, beginning to enjoy the exchange.

"Yes," he says, finally. "'*Neo-qaada*' is a neologism. I made up the name. 'Neo' comes, of course, from the Greek root, meaning new. But I borrowed it from the English word, 'neoteny,' a term employed in zoology and anthropology referring to the retention of juvenile characteristics and developmental potentialities in the adult. I might give an example of the process in a termite colony. In a healthy termite colony, a selected group of juvenile termites are kept in reserve in case the queen dies, in order to replace her and keep the colony intact. '*Qaa'id*' is Arabic for leader, or chief—the plural being '*qaada*.' Hence, the *Neo-qaada* were conceived as a reserve force of ready-trained new leaders to infuse a youthful vigor and new vision for the future QPR as it grew...."

He pauses and turns to address the judges. "There is an important point I would like to make here, but it would involve a small digression. With the Court's permission, may I explain?"

"Please the Court," the prosecuting attorney interjects, rising, "the prosecution feels the defendant's elaboration in this instance may provide substantive background information bearing on the matters being considered here, and we request he be allowed to continue."

The Chief Magistrate, after an inquiring glance toward the defense counsel, who nods, indicating he has no objection, waves his hand toward Samiel, "You may proceed."

Samiel clears his throat, and continues, "The concept of a provision for new leadership had been embedded in the QPR plan of action from very early on, well prior to the initiation of military action. The reason for this is that it was deemed that, historically, the responsibility for the failure of many previous revolutions throughout the world lay at the feet of the initial leaders of those revolutions. That is to say that once those leaders had achieved power, they became enamored of power for its own sake, at the cost of losing sight of the original objectives of the revolutions they had led. It is a commonplace that power corrupts, but this is usually meant to refer to the abuses of power, particularly with regard to exploitation of those governed. In the case of a revolutionary government, the more consequential effect of corruption of power is, rather, the subversion of the core vision of the revolution itself. This corruption usually takes two forms: temptation to hold on to power, once achieved, and the tendency to complacency.

"This was, in essence, the failure of the regime the QPR rose to overthrow, the regime of King Saddahi el-Roweed, which—while not a revolutionary government—nevertheless came to power with promises of a just, enlightened, and beneficent monarchy that would unite the disparate warring tribes and bring stability to the country. These promises were not kept. The Saddahi regime became grossly corrupt and more oppressive as its power grew over the twenty years of its reign, during which time inequities became increasingly apparent, as the King and his cronies created an oligarchy by appointing public officials entirely from within their own tribal circle. They oppressed, abused, and exploited the general population, and pawned our national heritage and resources to the French.

"We in the QPR were determined to avoid these mistakes. Nor did we intend to become liable to the vagaries of a cult of personality. Those misguided leaders who succumbed to the temptation to believe in their own auto-mythologies came to believe that they, themselves, in their own personage, embodied the Revolution, that the Revolution would succeed or fail in their shadow. But the truth is that it was always the Revolution that lent them any significance they might have had.

"Ideally, one would want to look for some 'Wise Man' to lead a nation through the pitfalls of political reality. But wisdom, by which I mean a certain inborn ability ripened by prolonged life experience, immune to temptation and prescient in crisis, is all too rare. We in the QPR sought to compensate for any lack of wisdom by training in the techniques of governing. In other words, we sought to develop a cadre of professionals as a democratic surrogate to the concept of the Philosopher King. We understood that our leaders were only human. Mumi el-Hawhza was the primary leader and inspiration of the QPR, but he accepted—we all accepted—that there would come a time when he—or any one of us—might become a liability to the Revolution we had created and have to step aside and be replaced. We felt that the future health of the Revolution depended upon the injection of new blood to replace older leaders before they became too comfortable with power and allowed the Revolution to become philosophically *arthritic*, if you will. These new young leaders were intended to bring fresh perspectives to bear on new political and foreign policy challenges as they would arise, keeping the Revolution vigorous and viable into the future as far as possible, *inshallah*."

Samiel pauses, then turns a hand in the air and sits back, indicating he's finished.

The prosecutor lowers his head in thought, as if digesting—or allowing the Court a moment to digest—the import of Samiel's words. "So…" he says, then, "so you—I mean, the QPR—had planned for the long term. And so could one say that your plans for the *Neo-qaada* were projected far into the future? Would that be correct?"

"Yes."

"Hmm…." The prosecutor pauses again, briefly, then continues, "The *Neo-qaada*, then, how long did this group exist?"

"Five years and four months. It was implemented in February of 1972, during the last phase of the Revolutionary War and two months before the QPR took power. It continued until June 1977, when the QPR government was overthrown by the invading Army of Dar el-Nar."

"And during those five years and four months of the existence of the *Neo-qaada*, how many 'graduates' were eventually placed in the QPR hierarchy?"

"Seven."

"Seven. Not eight, not six, just seven."

"Seven. That is correct."

"I see. How many graduates did you have during those five years?

"Two hundred."

"Two hundred. And when these two hundred were graduated, they were replaced by two hundred more—'undergraduates,' so to speak—is that right?"

"Yes."

"So, you had—the *Neo-qaada* had—two hundred graduates during the five years and four months of its existence, and out of that two hundred, seven were placed within the QPR hierarchy, is that right?"

"Yes."

"What happened to the others?"

"The others?"

"Yes, the other one hundred and ninety-three. Two hundred were graduated, and only seven were placed. What happened to the remaining one hundred and ninety-three graduates?"

Samiel pauses a moment to consider the question, then says, simply, "They were not placed."

"Not placed." The prosecutor's hand moves briefly to cover his mouth, as if to hide a smile, before he continues, "Two hundred young men were graduated, and seven placed. The prosecution would like to ask the defendant again, to be more specific: What happened to the remaining one hundred and ninety-three graduates who were not placed?"

"Standards were very high," Samiel says. "The seven who were placed met those standards. But only seven positions came open in that time. So, the others were eliminated."

The prosecutor raises his eyebrows ironically, "Eliminated? You have used that word before, today. What do you mean, now, when you say, 'eliminated?' Were the one hundred and ninety-three graduates who were not placed simply 'reassigned to other projects,' like those who were not selected in the first place?"

Samiel's lip turns down in a wry smile, as though trying to be patient with a slow student, and switching for the moment from Arabic to a clear, unaccented English, as if with the ironic intention of by-passing any possible vagueness introduced in translation, he says, "They were not included among those recommended for placement."

The prosecutor rolls his tongue behind his lips, as though taking a moment to temper his own response. "I think that much is clear to the Court," he says, "in Arabic, in English, in French, in German and the many other languages into which your responses are being translated, concurrently as you speak. But now, I would like to ask you, what happened to those who 'were not included among those recommended for placement?' I mean, once they were 'eliminated' from consideration for placement, what happened to them? Specifically, what became of them *then*?"

As Samiel pauses to consider his answer, a man shouts out from the gallery in the rear, "*Yakdhib! Buraaz al 'anta! Yatabawwal al 'anta! Assassin!*"

There follows a brief scuffle, as the bailiffs rush to intercept the man, who is running forward down the aisle with a shoe in his raised hand, apparently intending to throw it at Samiel. The court officers manage to restrain him, and after a brief struggle, eject him from the courtroom.

When order is restored, the Chief Magistrate directs Samiel to answer the prosecution's last question.

Samiel clears his throat, and reverting to Arabic, says, "Those who graduated from the *Neo-qaada* and were not placed within the hierarchy of the QPR were no longer considered members of the *Neo-qaada*. Their places within the *Neo-qaada* were taken by other youths, and they themselves became…in effect, they became nonpersons. Within the QPR, they were considered to be no longer relevant to the struggle. In fact, they were considered a liability to the struggle, because a certain degree of boldness and initiative were among the native qualities required for their selection for membership in the first place, and at that point, having been trained to be leaders—training which greatly enhanced these qualities—and there being no leadership positions open, they were thought to be susceptible to egotism. They might become fractious and a divisive element within the Party. To counter that, they were expelled…that is to say, for all intents and purposes, one might say that, officially, they ceased to exist."

"They ceased to exist! Officially? What does that mean? What about *un*officially?"

Samiel shakes his head. "I'm sorry, I don't understand your question."

The young attorney is showing signs of losing his patience, now. He screws up his mouth and says, "I mean, physically. *Physically!* What *physically* became of them, what *physically* happened to these one hundred and ninety-three graduates who were not placed?

Samiel shrugs and says simply, "They were dismissed."

"Dismissed! You let them go?"

"In a sense, yes."

"In what sense? Specifically, in what sense did you let them go? Did you let them go *free*?"

"That would be a good way to put it, I think," Samiel says, adding, "*Allah karim.*"

"You mean it would be a 'good way' of saying that they were freed *of the cares of life,* that they were *masHooq—?*"

"Objection!"

"Sustained!"

"—A 'good way,'" The prosecutor continues, raising his voice to be heard over the objections of the defense, and leaning forward, pounded his fist on his desk for emphasis as he spoke, "A 'good way' of saying one hundred and ninety-three innocent young men of teenage years were *executed—!*"

"Objection! Objection!"

"—Savagely killed, the backs of their heads smashed in with the blade of a shovel, and thrown into a *mass grave!*"

"Sustained! Prosecuting counsel will desist—"

"We found the bodies, Samiel! We found the skeletons

of one hundred and ninety-three young men where you buried them—"

"Objection!"

"—in a mass grave in an abandoned mine shaft in the Hercules Mountains!"

"Objection!"

"We found them!"

The courtroom is in an uproar. The Chief Magistrate bangs his gavel several times to no apparent effect as he attempts to admonish the prosecuting attorney and bring the court to order, until he finally orders the bailiffs to clear the room.

"Court is adjourned!" he says, loudly, over the clamor. "Court is adjourned until ten o'clock tomorrow morning! *Alhamdulillah,* Court is adjourned!"

8.

One morning three weeks earlier, during a recess in the trial, Abul-Abbas, still in his slippers and reading the newspaper on his smartphone over breakfast, had received a text from Toufiq, the foreman, informing him of a major accident at the phosphate mine owned by his family in Qâf Khamsah. He'd called Youssef immediately, but it had taken some moments to get through, as Youssef was on the phone at the same time getting details and organizing the rescue operation. When they finally spoke, it was brief, and by the time they'd rung off, at 7:23, the headline had already popped up as "Breaking News" on the website of *El-Kilma el-Rawi*: "Landslide at Phosphate Mine! Many Buried & Feared Dead!"

He'd insisted—against Youssef's resistance—that they ride down to the mine together. He felt they needed to talk. In the fifteen years since he'd retired from active oversight of the mining operations and put the family business into his son's capable hands, he'd made every effort to keep out of Youssef's way. He'd always had complete confidence in Youssef, and—at least, until now—he'd never had reason to regret it. But recently, he'd been hearing troubling rumors, and so long as he was still head of the family, he intended to make sure no slander tainted its good name.

In the car on the way to pick Youssef up, as his driver

wove the Mercedes expertly through the rush-hour traffic of the Capital and sped onto the highway heading southeast with official emergency lights blazing and siren wailing, Abul-Abbas ruminated on just how he was going to put his questions. The business itself was doing quite well. Production had increased over forty-three percent in the last seven years alone. Youssef had proven to be a talented manager with a gift for anticipating business opportunities. Personally, he could be a little gruff, with a quick and acid tongue. But his one real fault, as far as Abul-Abbas was concerned, was a certain arrogance that made him resent intrusion into matters he considered his own responsibility, and this caused him to be dismissive of opinions diverging from his own. Recently however, there had been another strike at the mine—the second in as many years. The el-Irewat Mining Company had never experienced a strike before. And according to the news reports it had been harshly put down by security forces. He'd seen some of it himself in clips they'd shown on the television. A melee! Dozens of miners had been injured. This had come after he'd already been hearing worrisome rumors about possible management corruption. He'd been reluctant at first to bring these issues up to Youssef, hoping his son would address them on his own and avoid any necessity for him to interfere. But now, given the occasion of the tragedy this morning, it seemed a good excuse for them to talk.

Thirty-five minutes later, the car pulled off the highway onto a private road where the barren *bled* had been transformed into a cultivated landscape of flowering shrubs and trees. The road wound through a manicured forest of tall cedars and then climbed steadily for another five kilometers to the crest of a plateau, where Youssef's vast fortress-like compound stood overlooking orchards of orange, olive, and almond trees. Farm workers could be seen tilling the irrigated fields along the slopes. The car pulled up before a tall wrought-iron gate, where a uniformed guard confirmed Abul-Abbas's identity before allowing them to proceed along the sweeping driveway toward the main house, where Youssef stood waiting on the steps with his son, Yaqub. Despite Youssef's dark expression of barely disguised impatience, Abul-Abbas thought them two handsome men, as they stood there dressed—as he was—in white kaffiyehs, flowing white djellabas and leather slippers. He was proud of them both. And he certainly loved his grandson, but he was disappointed, nonetheless, to see him there. It would make it more difficult for him and Youssef to speak candidly in the youth's presence. As the car drew up, Yaqub stepped forward to open the door for him.

"*Salaam aliekam, Bâbâ,*" Yaqub said, embracing him as he got out of the car.

"*Aliekam salaam,* Fanakee.*"

"*Salaam aliekam,* Papa."

"*Aliekam salaam,* Youssef.*"

Youssef embraced him in turn, rather stiffly, and then, before another word could be said, he turned abruptly, "*Ta'ehla!*" he said. ("Come!")

"Wait, Youssef! We can take *my* car."

"Your driver can follow!" Youssef answered, over his shoulder.

Abul-Abbas remained where he was, put off by his son's peremptory tone, but confident Youssef would acquiesce when he realized he wasn't being followed. Yaqub, however, after wavering uncertainly for a moment between them, saw his father resolutely striding off, and with an apologetic smile toward his grandfather, turned to go after him. Abul-Abbas felt his face reddening. He managed to control his temper, but he thought it was an inauspicious beginning. He turned to his chauffeur, and told him to go on without him. But Jibrîl, a tall, powerfully-built Berber who'd been with him for many years, hesitated and looked at him askance. Jibrîl was very protective of him and never liked to leave him on his own. Abul-Abbas made a sign to placate him and turned to follow his son.

Youssef led them down a path skirting the house that traversed a maze of arbors of white-blooming wisteria interspersed with gardens where sculpted water fountains played among overhanging fruit trees and flowering shrubs. When they finally emerged, at the edge of a large square tarmac well behind the house, Abul-Abbas was startled by the sudden roar of an engine, after the buffered silence of the gardens. He stared at the bulbous nose, tapered body and whirring rotor blades of the machine, squatting there before him like a giant insect glistening in the sun, and was suddenly seized with distaste and apprehension. He'd never ridden in one of those things. The helicopter, perched precariously on two thin skids, looked for all the world like a large, fragile glass and metal ornament that was about to shake itself to pieces at any moment. He was accustomed to flying in large planes and he'd been rather daring in his youth, he reflected. He'd raised and raced camels, fought skirmishes on horseback, won medals for valor in a civil war and faced down the powerful on more than one occasion. Now, he was old, he'd had a good life, all in all, and he had no regrets. He wasn't put off by the risk of dying, so much as by the embarrassment of voluntarily putting himself into harm's way in such an absurd contraption. But Yaqub and an attendant, apparently a maintenance man for the helicopter, stood waiting for him beside the open passenger door with their heads stooped in the draught of the rotor blades. Well, he thought, they would certainly get there a lot quicker this way, and with a sigh of resignation, he tucked his chin and stepped out onto the tarmac.

The second rude surprise was that it was even noisier inside the small cabin, which accommodated only two passengers, beside the pilot. Yaqub, who climbed in after him, guided Abul-Abbas to the front passenger seat and proceeded to buckle him into a complicated leather harness that seemed designed, Abul-Abbas thought, to restrain a madman. Yaqub then clamped headphones over his ears, which Abul-Abbas found only slightly helpful in mitigating the BAT-TER-BAT-TER-BAT-TER of the engine. Yaqub then buckled himself into the rear passenger seat, and while Abul-Abbas was still seeking a comfortable position for his feet in the cramped cabin, they were suddenly airborne.

"Wait!"

But the helicopter rose with a jerk and plunged forward. The engine roared louder and Abul-Abbas could feel its alarming noise vibrating through his body as they ascended with astonishing speed. He gaped at the ground dropping away from him at a heart-stopping rate and, feeling as though he'd left his stomach there, hastily glanced away, only to realize that they were riding in a Plexiglas bubble completely transparent to the air. He felt as if they'd been suddenly thrust into empty space with literally nothing between them and the receding ground, toward which they must inevitably plunge back down to their deaths at any moment. Reflexively, he clutched at the leather straps of his harness.

"Speak into the microphone, please, Papa."

"What microphone?" he replied, surprised by Youssef's voice in his earphones.

His grandson reached over and gently twisted the microphone attached to his headset around into position before his lips.

"What did you say, Papa?" Youssef prompted again.

"Nothing, never mind." Abul-Abbas was now made giddy by the sensation of falling away to his right, toward the apparition of Youssef's estate, a sheer couple of hundred meters below, as they banked steeply to starboard and swung south. Youssef handled the helicopter with aplomb, as he did everything else—and of course, it was typical of him to pilot the craft himself, although he could certainly have afforded to hire a pilot if he'd wanted—but that gave Abul-Abbas little comfort in the moment. He saw his limousine down there, diminished in the distance like a child's toy, pulling out of Youssef's driveway and racing toward the highway to follow them. But they quickly left it far behind, and he gave a nervous laugh as the thought escaped his lips before he could stop it: "It's like those children's stories of riding on a magic carpet!"

Youssef chuckled, "I'll race this against your magic carpet any day!"

"How long have you had it?"

"How, what?"

"How long have you had the helicopter?" Abul-Abbas repeated, more loudly. Youssef was sitting right beside him, but even with the headsets, it was hard to hear over the noise of the engine.

"A little over three years…. Gbdlwk…'second-hand' from a Russian mining executive, but in fact…never used! He…mshzgh…but by the time …ghbyd…delivered here, he'd been…trzfd…to the Black Sea!" He laughed again.

"It's a Kazan Aktai 2, *Bâbâ!*" Yaqub interjected, leaning forward with the enthusiasm of youth. "It has a 270 horse-power engine. It can…mzzg…600 kilom…ghtrz…cruise at 155…and climb…meters per minute to a ceiling of… thezzd…!"

"*Taijib!*" Youssef added, slapping the dashboard affectionately, "Very reliable!"

Abul-Abbas smiled and nodded, but much of what they'd said had been inaudible to him, and he realized that under the circumstances he was going to have to wait to have the more serious conversation he'd been hoping for.

They flew on for some moments without speaking. Abul-Abbas watched their shadow gliding over mile after mile of rock-strewn hammadas, and then over a great sandy plain riven by dry gullies where a number of settlements had been left abandoned with their orchards desiccated by drought, and then finally out onto the great, wind-swept erg where, for all its sweep and grandeur, nothing grew and, save for the majestic Hercules Mountains in the distance, nothing was visible under the bleak, blue sky but waves of sand stretching out to the horizon. The sun glare was unrelenting and despite the air-conditioning in the cabin he could feel the heat like a fourth presence among them.

After some time, they overtook a column of Tuareg mounted on camels who turned to look up at them as they passed. Draped in their traditional hooded blue djellabas and doubtless following some ancient, instinctive path along a dry gully, the little band seemed doomed to be lost in that vast eremitic wasteland. It wasn't true, of course—or at least, it wasn't true that they ran much risk of being lost. The Sahara was their ancient home and the Tuareg were born survivors, the oldest known inhabitants of one of the most inhospitable environments on Earth—the scale of whose cruel beauty he was appreciating anew, now, from his present height through the big glass bubble he rode in. At the same time, seeing the Tuareg making their way through the endless sands from this perspective brought to mind a darker thought. The desert was changing, and it seemed inevitable that, sooner than one might have imagined, the age-old lifestyle of the Tuareg *would* be doomed. It was curious, he thought, how despite the dramatic panorama with its sculptural flow of light and shadow playing over the immensity before him, there was so little hint of the more subtle colors and the interplay between shapes perceived and remembered that one observed and instinctively triangulated to find one's way at ground level, the shifting scents on the wind, the infinitely variable textures of sand and stone beneath the feet—all the hints, for those familiar enough to distinguish them, of landmarks in the desert. Survival depended on these details. Without benefit of GPS or compass, the Tuareg knew, for example, how to find direction in the wide, apparently featureless desert—even when the pole star was invisible and the sand dunes crept back and forth bewilderingly with the wind. They knew that if the moon rose before sunset, the light side faced west, and if it rose after midnight, the light side faced east. They knew to draw an imaginary line between the horns of the crescent moon and the horizon to find south. They could tell how long it was before sunset by holding their hand horizontally up to the sun, knowing that the width of each finger approximated fifteen minutes, so that if one could line up the width of four fingers between the bottom of the sun and the horizon, it meant that the sun would set in one hour. They knew to look for water where birds circled, or to dig for it where a dry *wadi* bent deeply into the shade of towering rocks. They were intimate with all the tricks of the desert. And yet lately, even the Tuareg were finding their age-old tricks unreliable. One couldn't see it from where he was, but down there on the ground it was becoming increasingly evident that the desert was changing. More and more often in recent years, one heard of travelers crossing the desert who experienced increasing difficulty in finding water. One looked for it in the usual places, but found none. The water level in known oases was falling, and some wells had dried up altogether. These were not singular events. It used to be that, if one followed animal tracks to lower ground, or managed to come upon a swath of dense vegetation or the shaded bend of a dry stream or river where water flowed during the rainy season, one usually needed only to dig down a half-meter or so to have a reasonable chance of finding water. But that wasn't true anymore. *Bahr Belá Má*, "the Waterless Sea," as the Tuareg called the Sahara, was being transformed before their eyes. The Tuareg, who knew the desert better than anyone, now had to carry their goatskin sacks into the canyons and gullies of the mountains to look where clouds, caught between the high peaks, might have dropped some moisture. If one were lucky, rainwater might be found stored in steep crevices, like cisterns, in the rocky surface, where it was protected from evaporating by the shade of the surrounding cliffs. But rain was increasingly scarce. Rainfall in the Sahara—rarely more than 25 cm (10 inches) a year, had dropped precipitously in recent years.

But there had always been periods of drought, and this alone didn't really explain the problem. From time immemorial, the Sahara had been crisscrossed by vast aquifers deep underground that fed the more superficial wells and springs. In fact, early sedentary Berbers in North Africa had developed *qanāh* networks, an ancient and ingenious system of transporting water by gravity through underground channels dug just above the water table that usually started from an aquifer or well in the higher foothills of the mountains and led to lower agricultural lands that were miles distant. The technology dated back to the mists of time, and communities of early peoples had built them in dry areas all over the world—but those here were petering out now too. Recent mining surveys by his own company and others had reported even the natural subterranean Saharan aquifers receding. The question remained, Why? The natural aquifers had been established over 10,000 years earlier, at the end of the last Ice Age, when precipitation was plentiful and melt from the receding glaciers left great lakes scattered all across North Africa. In the thousands of years that followed, as the Earth's orbit changed and the climate warmed and dried, the lakes subsided and were covered by windblown sediment, sand, and rock-fall. During all that time there'd been many periods of extreme drought, but the subterranean lakes remained, sealed against evaporation by the desert above. So, even while the surface area of the desert was known to be spreading under the ongoing drought of the last couple of decades, that didn't explain why the underground aquifers were drying up. The diminishing rainfall, alone, couldn't account for it. It was as if something else was going on, some deep geological phenomenon that no one understood.

Whatever it was, it was decimating the vineyards, olive orchards, and farmlands of the region that had flourished for generations. The whole population was growing restless. They seemed to be at the beginning of a great migration, in which the farmers and vintners from the countryside were moving to the cities to look for work. Except there wasn't any work for them there. They hunkered down in tents or hastily rigged shanties on the edges of the towns and villages and congregated in the markets offering their services as day laborers, or their women as prostitutes, or begging or stealing, and becoming a general nuisance to the resident urban population and an apparently intractable problem for the government. But for those displaced it was becoming dire. The Qarmatian economy was under stress at the moment, but still doing fairly well in relation to the rest of North Africa, and was ranked second, in fact, after Morocco. However, little of the government's revenues from tourism, petroleum, and mineral exports—not to mention the agricultural products grown by the peasants themselves—ever made its way back to the farmers. And the farmers, who subsisted on whatever they could raise, grow, and sell on their own account, were abandoning their farms because of the drought. Only the previous week, a well-meant attempt on the part of the government's internal ministry to distribute food to the hungry in a few of the hardest-hit rural districts had led to fatal consequences. The distribution effort had been poorly organized, with little appreciation for the level of desperation among the people, and in one district,

Sidi Duliyyah, where nearly a thousand had gathered, some women—it was mostly women and children in the crowd—apparently afraid that the baskets of flour, sugar, and meal would run out, rushed the lines. Twelve of them were crushed to death in the ensuing stampede and half-a-dozen more injured. Images broadcast of the aftermath showed victims being loaded into ambulances, survivors fighting over the remaining baskets, and the field strewn with torn-off *qamis*, slippers, *abayas,* and other personal effects. And neither Parliament nor the King had responded as yet to the public outcry for help.

Meanwhile, there remained the question of what was to become of the Tuareg. These perennial nomads had spurned the more sedentary life on the farms or in the towns taken up by their Berber cousins. They called themselves *Amazigh*, a word in their language that signified "freemen," and during their long habitation of the desert they'd resisted countless attempts at entrapment by all the encroaching populations that had encountered them. They'd been there before the rise of Ancient Egypt, but the Egyptians hadn't been able to conquer them, nor the Carthaginians to enslave them. Neither the Hellenic Greeks nor the Romans had been able to co-opt or colonize them, any more than had the Turks or the French of Modern Europe. But now, the Tuareg—to whom that great procession of civilizations at the verges of their beloved desert must have seemed but a passing pageant over the millennia—the Tuareg, too, were about to be undone by a profound transformation of the very environment that had once been their pride and sanctuary.

The helicopter climbed to a higher altitude as they approached the mountains, and Abul-Abbas, rousing himself from his reverie, turned to Youssef, in the pilot seat next to him. Shouting to be heard over the engine, he said, "Did you get any details about what happened this morning?"

"No, Papa—well, not much, really. Apparently, it… suddenly. These things aren't unusual, as you know. The last one…once in awhile, especially…rainy season, after the dry months. The first rains…dry layer of dust and the digging, of course…. But this was bad. A whole side…Pit Number 3… and collapsed."

"Toufiq said over eighty men might be dead or missing!"

"Could well be more."

"Terrible!"

"At least fifty or more…buried…tunnel."

"*Allah karim*! Hopefully, they got them out by now!"

"They're trapped, *Bâbâ*—under a dragline!" Yaqub put in.

"Dragline?"

"Yes, *Bâbâ*! A huge excavator capsized…blocking… escape!"

Abul-Abbas turned to stare at his grandson, trying to grasp the hideous implications of what he'd heard, "They're trapped in a tunnel *under* a dragline excavator?"

"Yes, *Bâbâ*!"

"Somehow," Youssef said, his face expressing perplexity at the logistical problem, "—I don't know…going to do it— but…to move another dragline from…into position…and raise it before…try to free them, *inshallah!*"

Abul-Abbas shut his eyes against the terrible image. The foreman who'd texted him that morning hadn't mentioned the overturned dragline. The news horrified him. Their dragline excavators were of a type commonly employed in strip-mining and open-pit mining operations. After smaller backhoes dug out the overburden that was carted away in dump trucks, the draglines advanced along the excavated "benches," or terraces, spiraling down the walls of the open pit and extracted the phosphate itself. These draglines, consisting of huge bucket-wheel shovels mounted on the ends of long, articulated, mobilized cranes, could extract as much as 12,000 cubic meters of mineral per hour. But they were among the largest construction machines in the world. They had to be shipped piecemeal from the factory and built on site. Each one could weigh 10,000 tons or more. To imagine one capsized—and with men trapped under it! "May God have mercy on them!"

"*Inshallah!*"

An extraordinary spectacle opened before him as they came over the mountains and it took Abul-Abbas's breath away, despite the fact that he knew the place very well. He'd made numerous visits to the site over the years—though not since he'd relinquished control of operations to Youssef— and never before by air. Qâf Khamsah was a little village, or *qarya*, that the company had appropriated almost a century ago to use as a base camp. The village had originally been a remote cluster of yellow clay buildings on the slopes of the foothills with one mosque and a market square surrounded by struggling sheep pastures and fruit orchards from which the local farmers were just barely able to eek out a living, dependent as they were upon the uncertain flow of a meager mountain stream that flooded only once or twice a year in the rainy seasons. In the early years, his father's father, Sheikh Abdul Rahman ibn Khalid, who'd founded the family business and had made the first mining surveys at the site, had put in roads, built workshops and installed an extensive irrigation system that provided water year-round. When Sheikh Abdul Rahman's son, Sheikh Nizar ben Khalid (Abul-Abbas's father) had taken over, he'd added a school and new housing for the laborers brought in to work in the mine, and Abul-Abbas, in his turn at the helm, had endowed a modern hospital that included advanced facilities for radiological imaging, diagnosis and trauma care, and a capacity of eighty beds. He remembered his early amusement when his father brought him to visit the place as a child and he first saw goats in the trees and people on their knees picking through the goat manure. It was explained to him then that those trees, actually spiny, evergreen shrubs, produced a leathery, olive-sized fruit, called argan, which was very valuable. The goats were encouraged to climb the trees to eat the fruit, and then the farmers would recover the pits from the goat manure and pulverize them to produce argan oil, which they used for cooking, but which they also sold, providing the district with its greatest source of income. Argan oil was used as a basis of cosmetic products sold all over the world, and producing it was a long-established tradition that went back to the Berbers' earliest history, even prior to the arrival of the Phoenicians.

Over time, of course, the growth of the mine had imposed some trade-offs. Excavation and the expansion of operations eventually spread over what had once been open pasture and orchards. But the locals had been more than compensated for this by finding steady employment at the mine and having their standard of living generally improved. Some had even risen to first-level field management positions in the firm. In any event, when Abul-Abbas had previously approached the site, by car at ground level, his first impression was of dust, noise, and the industrial processes involved in extracting phosphate from an open pit. But as they came upon it now, he was astonished to see that the mine had more than doubled in size, so much so that Qâf Khamsah, the town and base camp, visible only because he knew where to look for it, seemed to have diminished to the size of a small, congested extrusion at one corner of the lip of Pit Number 3, while the pit itself opened before them like a stunning, gargantuan and incongruously beautiful flower, a flower that in blooming had split the earth to its core. Abul-Abbas estimated that the open pit had grown to cover some five kilometers in length, about three in width and hundreds of meters in depth. Excavated terraces crisscrossed the contours of engulfed foothills like the whorls of giant metallic petals, all glittering in the sun with the variegated colors of phosphate crystals interlaced with veins of silver; copper; iron-manganese; green-flecked pink, purple, and blue quartzite; cadmium; nickel, and other trace minerals. But in the midst of this splendor, a huge dragline lay over on its side, sprawled down the collapsed western slope of the pit like an ugly canker with its great bucket-mouth agape and its wheels on one side, each half-again as large as a pick-up truck, high in the air.

There were other aircraft circling the area. Some displayed the Red Crescent emblem of the medical corps and were apparently part of the rescue effort. But others were probably carrying journalists and photographers here to cover the story as it unfolded. Youssef circled slowly and finally brought their helicopter to a standstill, hovering low over the scene of the accident. The terraces spiraling down the earth wall had been excavated at 50-meter intervals, and the dragline had apparently been tracking along that area when the wall had given way. The landslide had left a great gash through the terraces and a heap of rock and soil at the bottom. Emergency vehicles were ranged around the area above the open pit and rescue teams were climbing up and down the ragged slope carrying victims in stretchers to the ambulances waiting above. A half-dozen rescue workers, suspended by ropes anchored to the rock face by steel bolts, were hunkered down under the neck of the crane digging bare-handed through the fallen gravel and shouting to survivors apparently trapped in a tunnel beneath the overturned machine. Suddenly, as Abul-Abbas watched, there was a loud roar and in the next moment, the whole dragline shifted some twenty meters downward. Most of the rescuers had jumped back in time to avoid being caught, but one man remained pinned under the crane. All you could see of him was his lower abdomen and his legs, which were kicking in the desperate effort to free himself. The other rescue workers stood about for a moment, gesticulating wildly, apparently in a quandary. The slope was steep, the gravel loose underfoot, and there was no telling when the dragline would shift again.

At that moment, his son's voice came loudly through Abul-Abbas's earphones as he called over the radio, "Attention! Youssef el-Irewat to Red Crescent! Attention! Youssef el-Irewat to Red Crescent! Emergency! Answer at once!"

A voice responded over the radio, "Red Crescent to Youssef el-Irewat, yes, *ya beyh! Salaam aleikem, ya beyh!* How may I be of service?"

"*Aleikem salaam.* Who is this?" Youssef demanded. "Are

you the officer in charge here?"

"Yes, *ya beyh!* Colonel Hafid bin Moussa at your service! How may I be of assistance?"

"The capsized dragline just shifted and it's likely to slide further down the slope. I need—do you have a heavy-lift helicopter here, a Skycrane or something?"

"We have an air-ambulance, *ya beyh*, that's all. Actually, I'm here in it, now."

"Where? I don't see you."

"Here, *ya beyh*. We're hovering over the second crane they're trying to bring in to—"

"What the fuck are you doing over there? You're not a crane operator! The accident's *here*!"

"Yes, *ya beyh!* So sorry, *ya beyh!* But—"

"I'm in the Kazan Aktai, right over the fallen dragline. Get your ass over here immediately!"

"Yes, *ya beyh!* Of course! But I think you should know this. We've just found many skeletons, *ya beyh,* many! I think you should know."

"What?"

"Many, many human skeletons," Colonel bin Moussa repeated. "They were buried in an abandoned shaft here, just below me, where the second crane is. The shock of the collapse on your side of the pit must have weakened the earth wall that sealed off the shaft here, and when this second crane entered the ramp, the wall collapsed, and skeletons started falling out!"

But Youssef, incredulous and dismissive, yelled at him in anger, "What the fuck are you talking about! Skeletons? Fuck the skeletons! Get your ass over here! I don't want this overturned crane damaged any further if we can help it, *inshallah.* I want you to lower a cable to hold it in place until the other crane can get here to right it again, you hear me! *Now,* do you here me? *Do it now!* I'm pulling out."

"Yes, *ya beyh!* Immediately, *ya beyh!* We're coming immediately, *inshallah!*"

As Youssef shifted gears and they climbed up and out of the pit, they saw a large Sikorsky S-76 air-ambulance rising and coming toward them across the chasm.

Youssef took them back to a point above the edge of the pit and they watched as the Red Crescent helicopter moved into position over the toppled dragline and began lowering a cable toward where the rescue worker was trapped. Abul-Abbas became aware, now, of crowds of people at various points along the rim of the pit watching the operation, and a mile further on, in the direction from which the ambulance had flown, another dragline was slowly making its way toward an entry ramp. Moving such a huge machine into a mine pit was a delicate and dangerous operation at the best of times, but there seemed to be another problem, now. The men there were apparently trying to maneuver the second dragline down into position to raise the one that had capsized, but the ramp, although nearly a mile from the landslide, had suffered some damage, too. A portion of the outer edge of the ramp had broken away and there was the question of whether the surface was stable or the second huge excavator was about to be put at risk.

After a moment, Youssef banked and they moved toward where this second excavator stood. As they approached, one of the men working there looked up and waved at them. It was Toufiq, the foreman. He waved again, directing them to land nearby, on a level patch behind the entry ramp to the pit.

"La' Shughl!" ("No Work")

"Tahta Sheikh Nizar Acheron!"

"Yatabawwal al Youssef Acheron!"

"Strike! Strike!"

"Fuck the Sheikh!"

"Tahta Sheikh Nizar Acheron!" ("Down with Sheikh Nizar Acheron!")

"Yatabawwal al Youssef Acheron!" ("Piss on Youssef Acheron!")

"We're Not Slaves!"

"Fuck the Sheikh…!"

They had landed in the midst of an angry crowd of demonstrators holding signs and yelling. There must have been a hundred or more of them. Abul-Abbas, already overcome by the sight of the disaster, was astonished by this wave of hostility. The angry mob parted reluctantly to make way for the aircraft to touch down, only to surge forward again as soon as Youssef cut the engine. The men were yelling verbal abuse and pushing their homemade signs against the Plexiglas cabin of the aircraft, while the women and children began to beseech the passengers as they disembarked to rescue the miners, their fathers, sons, and husbands, who were injured or who remained trapped in the tunnel.

In addition to the protest signs Abul-Abbas heard voices crying out:

"No foreign workers!"

"We want clean water!"

"We want money for our lost land!"

"No toxic sludge!"

"We want more pay!"

"Free our prisoners!"

"Fuck el-Irewat Mining Company!"

After a moment, a contingent of company security guards rushed forward to set up barricades and forcibly press the crowd back to clear a path for Abul-Abbas and the others to pass.

But Abul-Abbas, Youssef, and Yaqub made their way through the crowd of demonstrators only to find themselves besieged by the press. Photographers were shooting video of their arrival amid the hostile reception and reporters were shouting questions over the background noise of the protestors:

"How many men are trapped in the tunnel, *ya beyh*?"

"Do you know the number who've been killed and injured?"

"*Ya beyh* Acheron el-Irewat! Please, *ya beyh*! How soon will the trapped men be freed, *inshallah*?"

"How many miners are locked up in your prison here, *ya beyh*?"

"Is it true, *ya beyh*, that the groundwater is contaminated by radiation?"

"Do you have a comment, *ya beyh*, on the fact that this is the fourth fatal accident here this year?"

Abul-Abbas, disconcerted by the implications of what he was witnessing, took it all in but left it to Youssef to respond. Youssef, however, merely strode on, plowing his way through the jostling crowd with an imperial air. Yaqub followed his father, who ignored the press and headed directly toward Toufiq, who'd come out of the pit to meet them. The foreman, a small, wiry, clever man, had been with the firm for over quarter of a century. All of his five sons worked in the mine. He greeted them, now, with warm respect and brought them up to date on the situation—including the fact that Fariq, his third son, was still trapped in the tunnel. They spoke together for a few minutes, then Toufiq led the way back to the pit, where Youssef intended to direct the operation to get the second excavator into position to raise the toppled one. Abul-Abbas, meanwhile, was approached by several older miners and their families who recognized him from his earlier visits during his stewardship of the firm and who were begging him for help now. Satisfied that Youssef was quite capable of supervising the rescue effort without him, he turned to speak with them.

"*Salaam aliekam, ya beyh!*"

"*Allahu akbar*, we're so happy to see you, *ya beyh!*"

"*Aliekam salaam*, Moufdi. *Aliekam salaam*, Raisha, I'm so sorry about your son. But please be patient. You see, there, my own son, Youssef, is going, now, to try and free him and everyone else trapped in the tunnel, *inshallah!*"

"*Allahu akbar, ya beyh!* I am praying for you and your great son, and my own Hammad!"

"Please, *ya beyh*, please tell them to clean our water! Yazid, my youngest grandson, died of the sickness, *ya beyh!*"

"Sickness?"

"Our sheep are dying, *ya beyh!* Our olive trees bear no fruit!"

"Our goats are wasting away! The land is poisoned, *ya beyh!*"

"Poisoned? What do you mean?"

"Please help us, *ya beyh!*"

"Remember me, *ya beyh?* Muhammad! I have worked for you over fifteen years. I work hard, and you know that I am honest. But they fired me last year, *ya beyh!* They fired me and hired a black boy from Chad to replace me, because he work for less! It's not fair!"

"Me, too, *ya beyh!* I was replaced by a black from Sudan!"

"Please help us, *ya beyh!*"

"The children are dying, *ya beyh!*"

"The children?"

He asked to see the sick children. They led him past a row of work sheds, the sides of which were covered with protest signs and slogans and amateurish murals, and continued down the slope to the village where, in the house of one woman whose husband was still trapped in the tunnel, three of her five children, ages four to seven, were lying in bed. They were reduced to skin and bone, pallid, jaundiced, shivering, and bent over with cramps.

"What's wrong with them?"

"They are sick, *ya beyh!* They are dying!"

He felt their foreheads and found them feverish. "Bring me some water," he said, "They must drink!"

"Begging your forbearance, *ya beyh*, we cannot give them water. The water is making them sick!"

"How do you know that?"

"See here, *ya beyh*, see for yourself!"

They brought him a jug of water, and he could smell its foulness and acidity even before he looked into it. It was greenish-yellow with a gelatinous cast, and when he put his hand into it, it felt oily and viscous. "This is the only water you have to drink? What about the stream?"

"This *is* from the stream, *ya beyh*. There is no water from the Company pipes."

"They cut the pipes off last month because the government inspector said the water was unhealthy!"

"We drink sheep's milk or camel milk or have to fetch water from high up in the mountain, *ya beyh*."

The judge, taken aback and growing angry, bit his lip, and after a moment turned back to the sick children before him, "What does the doctor say?"

"The doctor hasn't seen them. He left last week."

"Left? What do you mean? What about the other doctors?"

"Gone, *ya beyh*."

"All gone, *ya beyh*. All the doctors gone!"

"What are you talking about? The hospital's right there, in the center square. I left it fully staffed with doctors, nurses, technicians!"

"It is empty, *ya beyh*. There's no doctor, no nurse, nobody!"

"What!"

"The last doctor, he stayed a little while. A good man, he tried to stay, but he said he couldn't do it all by himself, without medicines, without nurses. There were too many of us sick."

"They stopped paying him, *ya beyh*. He had no money to live on. We had no money, either, but we gave him some of the little food we had so he could stay and help us. But it got to be too much for him, *ya beyh*."

"We took the sick children back home from the hospital, *ya beyh*. They are dying…!"

He rose and, followed by the villagers, stalked off in the direction of the hospital, determined to inspect it for himself. He found the corridors and wards filthy, the beds soiled, and beside a distraught clerk at the admittance desk, the only other living person in the building was the janitor, whom he found napping on a gurney in front of the CAT-Scan machine. The offices and laboratories and diagnostic machines were unattended. At his request, the villagers led him to the mountain stream, where he saw the once-fresh water now burbling out of the mountain green and foul. They showed him their reconstituted pastures and olive orchards, planted on reclaimed landfill over an exhausted and abandoned pit, where the waste dump had been leveled and stabilized. He knew that the waste, composed of tailings and trace metals from active pits, contained sulfides and should have been covered with a thick layer of clay to prevent moisture and oxygen in the air from oxidizing the sulfides and producing sulfuric acid, before a top layer of soil was applied and vegetation planted to consolidate the material. And yet he could see areas of discoloration of the topsoil where the heavy metals and acid were apparently leeching out. The sheep looked weak as though they were wasting away, and the olive trees were stunted, bearing few fruit, most of which had shriveled on the limb. He was aware that even when the job was done properly, sooner or later the layer of clay might be susceptible to erosion. But it was generally hoped—there were no long-term studies to prove it yet, unfortunately—but it was assumed that the rate of leaching would be sufficiently slowed by the clay cover to allow the environment to absorb the acid and associated heavy metals to a safe degree. So if acid was leaching out already, it suggested that for some reason— and what other reason could there be but to cut costs?—the clay had been layered too thinly, or possibly even eliminated entirely. The effect of course was to endanger the health of the community and leave the environment toxic for possibly a thousand years.

While he'd been pondering these things, the reporters— who'd been barred from following Youssef, who'd gone to deal with the overturned dragline—had been dogging his every step and badgering him with questions. He'd forbidden them to take photographs or videos—although he was sure they would sneak in a few—and notwithstanding his polite demurrals ("No comment. No comment. I am no longer officially associated with the firm. Please address your questions to the front office!")—the tenor of their questions disturbed him:

"Is it true the company is illegally importing cheap labor from the Sahel to replace local workers, *ya beyh?*" one asked.

"*Al Arabiya* has published a report that this is the deadliest mine in North Africa. Do you have a comment, *ya beyh?*" asked another.

"How many illegals do you have working here, *ya beyh?*"

"Today, *Al Jazeera* accused el-Irewat Mining and the Morteggan-Krafft Bank of colluding to manipulate the phosphate market. Is it true, *ya beyh?*"

"How's that?"

"In their news broadcast today, *Al Jazeera* claimed that el-Irewat Mining and Morteggan-Krafft are—"

"No!—I mean, never mind! No comment!" Turning away from the reporters, he suddenly realized there was someone he'd been expecting to see there, but hadn't. He searched the faces about him for one he'd known from previous years, the village elder, and not seeing him, asked of those around him, "*Sheikh* Abdullah? Where is *Sheikh* Abdullah el-Qâf Khamsi?"

"He is in the jail, *ya beyh*," Muhammad, one of the miners who'd been fired, said, speaking up from the crowd.

"In jail! What jail? For what?"

"Up there, *ya beyh*," Muhammad said, turning to point

toward a new fortified building Abul-Abbas hadn't noticed before, on top of a ridge overlooking the village. "*Sheikh Abdullah* complained one time too many about the conditions here, and they arrested him."

Just then, someone in the back of the crowd threw a stone. It was a small stone and it bounced harmlessly off his shoulder and fell to the ground. But it was immediately followed by a sandal and then rotten fruit and clumps of mud. A large group of younger mine workers who didn't know him—who knew only what he stood for in their eyes—had quietly come up to surround the crowd around him and they began to push their way through the reporters and the older, more friendly villagers, cursing him and throwing dirt and stones. A rock struck him just above the eye and he began to bleed from the cut on his brow. There were two security guards who'd accompanied him on his walking tour, and they, together with some of the older villagers, tried to intervene to protect him. Even so, the guards, Abul-Abbas thought, were too aggressive. They waded into the crowd swinging their batons left and right, bashing the heads of friendly and hostile villagers indiscriminately, then drew their pistols and began firing, first in the air, then point-blank into the crowd. Abul-Abbas saw one stone-thrower fall bleeding, then an innocent old woman, and then a child. But the guards' actions only seemed to provoke the young toughs to greater violence, and they surged forward and were about to overwhelm the guards, when all at once a siren wailed close by and screams went up from the back of the mob. Suddenly, people were panicking and fleeing left and right, as Abul-Abbas, frozen to the spot, saw a black Mercedes-Benz plowing through the crowd and bearing down on him with its siren wailing, its horn blaring and riot lights spinning. It swerved to a stop barely two meters in front of him, and in the next instant, he sighed with relief to see his chauffeur and bodyguard leap out and rush toward him. Jibrîl enveloped him in his strong arms and guided him into the limousine, shielding him from the angry crowd with his towering form. Sticks and stones and old shoes continued to strike the car as Jibrîl spun it around and they drove off. The judge, meanwhile, sat slumped in the back seat with his head in his hands, overwhelmed by the experience. He was distraught at the deteriorating conditions of the village and the fact that the medical staff had deserted the hospital he'd built. He was dismayed by the hostility of the young miners, and stung to his heart by the questions of the journalists implying that his company had resorted to greed, corruption and wanton disregard for the workers and their environment—the company he and his fore-fathers had been so proud of and had labored so hard to develop, to keep honest, and to serve as a model for the country and a beneficent influence in the community! Colluding with Morteggan-Krafft, for God's sake—even if it was only an unsubstantiated rumor, the very idea that the el-Irewat Phosphate Mining Company could possibly stoop to that! Morteggan-Krafft was probably the most rapacious of all the international banking houses! It was too much! Seeing blood on his hands, he pulled out his handkerchief to staunch the wound on his forehead. How could things have come to such a pass in just a few years, he wondered? How could he have misjudged Youssef so completely? He'd tried to be a good father, to set him a good example, to foster in his first-born son a sense of ethics, of social as well as organizational responsibility! But then, he had to admit, there was also the question of why he'd allowed it to go so far. He'd heard some rumors years earlier, but he'd chosen not to pursue them. He hadn't wanted to interfere—but had that been the result of simple over-confidence on his part, or worse, a selfish, self-imposed blindness? But now that he'd come here and seen with his own eyes how things were going, his conscience couldn't ignore it, he had to step in and reassert his family's good name, *inshallah!* He couldn't allow things to continue like this. Of course, having removed himself from active management of the company for so long, he had to expect resistance to any effort he might make now to reassert his authority. Youssef would certainly resent it, and would, he knew, go to great lengths to try to stop him. But so be it! He would have to accept that, he'd have to accept his son as a rival, and even—if it came to that, Allah forbid!—as an enemy!

The last thing he saw, as he glanced back through the cloud of dust toward the young toughs running and throwing stones after them, was the mural painted on the high wall of a work shed with the portrait of a man with an intense gaze pointing accusingly at the viewer while a group of miners behind him raised their fists and their tools in defiant support. The portrait was amateurish, but there was no mistaking its subject. In fact, he'd been seeing similar posters on billboards in several villages outside the Capital in recent months, and it troubled him, for he could not imagine what forces were at work, after all these years, to resuscitate the reputation of the one he now had on trial for crimes against humanity. The caption below the portrait said,

"He will return!

He has not forgotten us!
Samiel will free us again!"

The forensic report came in two weeks later, confirming that there were a hundred and ninety-three skeletons exhumed from the abandoned mine shaft, all young men between the ages of sixteen and twenty. They had been buried there for at least twenty-five years, and all had fatal wounds, their skulls crushed by a blow from a sharp instrument.

9.

t's a labyrinth, Samiel says to himself, alone in his cell later that evening, a labyrinth from which he still can't escape. It was a work of so many years, of so much deep thought. Again and again he'd thought to leave it, but it had compelled him then—as it entraps him now. Once begun, he really couldn't turn away from it. All the work, the preparation, the dreams and hopes would have collapsed. Mumi el-Hawhza had had the vision, but it had needed an architect. Malik, Hammadi, Falah, el-Beghal, they were mere engineers, and what they'd all sought merely to repair had already collapsed. Qarmat would've fallen back into Jâhiliyya, into that primordial barbarian state of lawlessness out of which it had first risen, with sectarian wars, tribe against tribe, the country going to wrack and ruin, and the French, or whatever Western power would've succeeded them, waiting in the wings until all of Qarmat's talent and strength lay bleeding on the battlefield— whence they would simply walk into the waste, pluck the spoils, enslave the population again, and despise us for being the same backward biblical aborigines they'd always imagined. He could not have allowed that to happen.

And yet, in spite of everything, it seems to be on the verge of happening again, after all—

But why should he care anymore? He has nothing at stake now, certainly not his reputation. And still, he feels his anxiety mounting. It isn't just the fever, there's something else, as though he's on the verge of an abyss beyond which nothing seems sure. He stares through the darkness of the cell at the wall opposite, and it's as if he can see wall after wall after wall behind it. It isn't the physical imprisonment he's thinking of. What they're walling up is the fount of ideas! The walls are willful ignorance, misunderstanding—worse, disinterest. The court "judging" him doesn't care. The truth is, he probably doesn't either anymore. They're all willing actors in a charade. He's dying anyway, it doesn't matter if they put him before a firing squad. But what would they learn from that? Well, of course, he knew they wouldn't have him shot, execution is banned in the International Court, and even if it wasn't, the Qarmatians wouldn't dare to do it. Dead or alive they are still afraid of him. But the media, emboldened by the rising tide of the worldwide humanitarian movement, are calling him a beast and a monster. Well, it may be, as the poet said, that from time to time monsters appear in order not to frighten but to be questioned. His trial offers them the opportunity to try and grasp the historical complexities that had led to his actions, so that—draw what conclusions they may—they might at least benefit from the deliberation, at the calming distance of a quarter-century, over those numinous events that had rushed past too quickly and seemed too disorienting to comprehend at the time.

But their questions are a mockery. They have an agenda, and they don't care that it may eventually lead them back into the same old historical quagmire. His trial is really an elaborate funereal proceeding, the whole point of which is simply to bury and forget another irritating and irreconcilable problem.

And yet he can't help considering it a personal failure. The world has moved on and he's left engulfed in a solitude of truth that pales the specter of death.

A feint sound rouses him from his reverie. Has he imagined it, the sound of footsteps approaching? He listens. There's nothing. But of course, there's nothing! He's already been told that he would not be allowed any visitors during trial. Everything is being conducted out of the public's eye. The Hague, the U.N. and the world at large are to have their satisfaction, but here, in Qarmat, nothing will be said, no one will know! What could be more absurd?

"Pssst! Samiel!" A rasping whisper thrust through the bars of his cell. "Samiel, you have visitors!"

It's well past midnight, and he's startled as the cell door swings open and they slip in all at once in a disreputable tangle, like a skulk of foxes in a mating frenzy. The guard closes the cell door behind them and then stands on post outside.

"*Salaam aleichem*, Samiel!"

"*Salaam aleichem*, Samiel!"

"*Salaam!*"

"*Aleikem salaam,*" he replies.

There are six of them, led by his old lieutenant, the huge, wily, garrulous Muhammad el-Beghal, who lost an eye in their very first battle, sporting a big gray beard now. There's sharp-shooting Ali Kamel with the wall-eye; quick, sly Abdillah Zinedine; Ali Bourada, who fought all day after swallowing a bullet fired from a French rifle in the Oued Ben Hahri and had spit it up again that night at camp; one-armed Khaled Slimani, who rode three days and nights without food or water to warn him of an Army detachment on its way to ambush him at the Sennai Railhead, and the small, wiry Fouhad ben Khemais, who broke his arm in a fall during a night raid, reset the compound fracture himself and was back in action the following day. They were all older and less agile now, but they fought by his side. He embraces them warmly—and yet, even as he does so, it's as if he can feel them change under his hands from the solid, warm-blooded, faithful warriors he'd known, into the pale shadows of a dream from which he awakened long ago. There are also two others, young men he doesn't know, apparently from the new generation of hero-worshipers, who stand back, wide-eyed and grinning self-consciously.

"How did you get in?" Samiel says.

Muhammad el-Beghal smiles mischievously, rubbing his fingers together and nodding over his shoulder toward the guard.

There is another moment of mutually embarrassed silence, then el-Beghal says, "We are here to be at your service when you're ready, Samiel."

"Ready?"

"Yes, Samiel. The rest of us are camped in the north, at Aqqabat. There are three hundred or a little more. Just give us the word, and we will free you! Just tell us what to do."

"Three hundred or more."

"Yes, but it is only a beginning. Many more have promised to join us when we start. Just tell us what it is you would have us do and it shall be done, *inshallah!*"

Samiel looks from one to the other. They are all gazing at him expectantly.

After a long moment, he says, "Nothing."

El-Beghal starts a hesitant smile, "Nothing, Samiel? What do you mean? You mean, you want us to wait, Samiel?"

"There is nothing to wait for, now."

El-Beghal gapes at him in dismay. The others exchange glances, as if questioning their own ears.

"But, Samiel?"

"What I would have you all do," he says, "all three hundred of you, is nothing. Nothing! It's over. It was over twenty-five years ago! Go home."

"But, Samiel?"

"But then, why did you come back?"

"I had my own reasons for coming back," he says. "They have nothing to do with you. Go home."

But they are reluctant to believe that, or to accept it. They continue to stand there, their eyes shifting from him to one another, and then to the dark, grimy walls and the bars all around them. And little by little, he can see the warm glow of recognition in their eyes grow tarnished with disillusionment, and in its place creeps the cold and dark glint of fear, alienation, and paranoia. He can read what they are thinking clearly on their faces. They are thinking that if he hasn't returned to take up the banner of the Revolution again, then he must have returned with some ulterior motive, and what else could that be, but the intention of clearing his own name by shifting the blame to them for whatever crimes he stands accused of?

The hand of the small, wiry one, Fouhad ben Khemai, moves slowly, as if unconsciously, to pull back his robe and slip over the hilt of his knife. Now, other hands are doing the same. Samiel sees this, and looks each one in the eye, but it's like looking into dark windows.

Suddenly, el-Beghal backhands Fouhad ben Khemai across the chest, driving him backward and then wheels to glare at the others, who drop their hands and step back, abashed. The big man then turns to Samiel and nods, solemnly acknowledging and accepting his leader's decision. At that moment, an iron gate clangs shut in the distance, and then comes the sound of boots approaching. It's the captain of the guards on night rounds.

The guard at the door taps his baton lightly on the bars three times and opens the cell door, "Must go!" he whispers urgently.

One by one, his old comrades turn, bid Samiel peace and good luck, and slip away.

10.

"*Daaryah.*"
   "*Daaryah!?*"
   "*Daaryah….*"

Moments later, after his old comrades-in-arms leave, the memory of the first *majlis*, the war council that had launched the QPR into the first decisive action of their military campaign over thirty years ago, comes back to Samiel like a fresh breeze. It was in the early days, when their spirits were buoyed up by great ideals and their hearts full of hope. They were camped in the ruins of Aqqabat, an old Arab watchtower in the northern mountains dating from the period of the Crusades. It was a damp, cold night in November. The relative mildness of the lava-strewn desert plain had dropped away gradually as they'd mounted the hammada, and then turned to raw chill as they'd wound their way up the narrow, precipitous mountain trails. The schist on the steep slopes cracked with a sound like rifle fire echoing back from the mountain walls, he remembers. The loosened stones slid away under the hooves of the camels of the lead riders above in wide, thin, razor-sharp fragments that ricocheted off the rock face to slice past those following on the path beneath them and go wheeling and whistling like a shower of axe blades down into the gorge a thousand feet below. By the time they reached the old watchtower the sun was down behind the mountain and all warmth and light fell away into a sudden frigid darkness. The mist rising from the *shallaal* rose up to envelop them in its cold, phosphorescent glitter, turning their clothes, long since damp and clammy with the sweat of the long day's ride, now icy and morbid. But the cool, sweet water of the fall that poured down in a thin, steady stream from the peak fifty feet above into a natural basin at the verge of the fort was the only potable water within forty miles, and the isolation and treacherous terrain nearly guaranteed them safety from prying eyes.

For the QPR, who'd spent years in preparation, their moment had arrived. The country was in turmoil. The police were overwhelmed trying to deal with a sudden eruption of work stoppages for lack of pay and unorganized citizens protesting the ending of the bread dole in almost every province. The King and Parliament were at loggerheads over the deteriorating state of the economy, and both were being hard-pressed by the French, who'd lost patience over the drop in production of raw goods, unpaid debts, and the cost of having their equipment and ships stand idle, while the government seemed impotent to do anything about it. King Saddahi had ordered the Army and police to use all necessary force to put down the protests and get the striking workers back on the job, but to no avail. Hundreds of demonstrators had been killed or wounded in the streets, and hundreds more, accused of being agitators fomenting disruption or instigating work stoppages, had been arrested and tortured. To the countless numbers who'd been accused of treachery or sedition and executed over the preceding twenty years since Saddahi had taken power, dozens more "disappeared" almost daily while being transferred from one prison to another. But the people remained obdurate. Finally, just the week before, there'd been an "incident" between Qarmatian soldiers and a platoon of the French occupying force at an Army post outside the Capital in which two soldiers had been wounded and a French lieutenant killed. The cause of the exchange of fire was in dispute, but the incident had been escalated into a diplomatic crisis between the government and the French.

At Aqqabat, Samiel; Marwan Fareed "General Malik" Badat and Musheikhi "el-Aqrab" el-Barzan; together with Abdillah Hammadi; Muhammad Falah; Ali Kamel; Mustafa Daoudi; the giant warrior Muhammad el-Beghal, who still had two good eyes, then, and other senior lieutenants of the QPR were gathered in council in their imam's tent to plan their first action. Mumi Malagawi el-Hawhza had opened the meeting with the evening prayers, and a lively discussion immediately began.

"…Daaryah!" General Malik was protesting, "I said we needed to begin with a bold stroke! Daaryah is at the asshole end of Oued Seenib, clear across the country from the Capital! What I had in mind was a direct strike at the center of power! We could take over the Royal Palace! Or, better yet, the House of Parliament! Security around the Capital is weak or nonexistent, and we now have the strength to pull it off easily, *inshallah!*"

"Perhaps, yes," Samiel said, presiding from his seat on an old Roman sundial, "but it could just as easily backfire. First, I think, we need to—"

Malik interrupted him, sucking his teeth in impatience. "The country's teetering on the brink and the government's useless! The people want decisiveness, a lightning bolt, clarity! We've got to think in terms of the moment. We've got to think the way Lenin did in 1917. Once we control the government—"

"At that point, we would not be controlling the government," Samiel countered, "only holding it hostage. Do you expect Saddahi would abdicate or Parliament resign en mass at the first sight of us?"

"I do think this is not the moment for half-measures! Holding the government hostage might be a good idea! As for Saddahi…" Malik shrugged his shoulders, "in the end, we'll most likely have to…let's say, *eliminate* the King from the equation, anyway. But Daaryah! Daaryah's an obscure outpost. Most of the population doesn't even know it exists. And, anyway, once we've taken over the government, the Army and its installations would be ours."

Marwan Fareed "Malik" Badat, a stout man with bushy eyebrows, for the moment hunkered down in his burdah and irritable as they all were from the cold, the dampness, and the perennial lice, was shrewder than it might seem from his blunt manner and deceptively bland features—as well as being notoriously ambitious. Samiel had made him a senior strategist and spy in the rebellion because he was, at the same time, Deputy Commander of the Qarmatian Security and Intelligence Service (QSIS) in the current government. Badat also happened to be a distant cousin of King Saddahi, and it was no secret that he harbored a fierce resentment for the man. It was because of this combination of ambition and resentment that Samiel had felt him out for membership in the QPR.

"As far as 'eliminating' the King," Samiel said to him now, "Saddahi is your cousin, so when the time comes, you can deal with him as you like. But as for taking over the House of Parliament, immediately upon us making such a move, we'd be on the defensive and a target ourselves. I'd much prefer we remain on the *offensive* for the time being."

He proceeded to remind them of the fact that, until that moment, the QPR had kept a very low profile in order to come as far as they had and avoid the brutal suppression other opposition parties had suffered. The government had only heard rumors of the QPR and didn't really know who they were, what their strength was or how much of a threat the Party posed. On the other hand, most Qarmatians didn't know who they were either, and for their struggle to have a hope of success, they had to have the support of the people behind them.

"Daaryah, on the other hand, would be very desirable," Samiel continued. "Besides being one of the Army's major supply depots, it overlooks a crucial switching station for the railway, and it's the other main port of exit, besides el-Rawi, for raw materials being shipped to the factories in Marseilles. For the government to lose control of Daaryah—at the very outset of our own campaign—would strike a deep nerve. It would be a major blow to the Army's self-esteem. And it would give the French pause, causing them to doubt the government's ability to protect its own interests."

"But starting out there," another lieutenant, Falah Sabawi, said, "we'd be setting ourselves up for a long, dreary campaign to fight our way all the way back to the Capital."

"True," Samiel said. "But during that long campaign, we'd have the opportunity to garner the sympathy and support of the population. One tribe, one village, one sector at a time, we'd win them over with food, tax relief, and security from the arbitrary searches and seizures and forced conscription into military service they've been made to suffer all these years. Overthrowing one's government isn't the work of an hour—even Lenin had to prepare."

Malik flushed at the cut.

Musheikhi "el-Aqrab" el-Barzan put up his hand. He was a slow-spoken man of few words, with the broad features, prematurely receding hairline and short, powerful build of the Houdaq. The Houdaq were not really a tribe so much as a group of outcastes of ancient and indigenous stock who supported themselves as shepherds, camel-boys and goatherds in the desert, or street-cleaners, servants and laborers in the villages. They were generally looked down upon by the Arabs, who freely insulted them for sport. El-Aqrab ("The Scorpion," the nom de guerre he'd assumed on joining the QPR) had been a ditch digger. Samiel had found him three years earlier brawling in a backstreet of el-Rawi with three Berbers who'd come upon him digging a trench to broaden a street and were wielding knives trying to rob him. El-Aqrab, armed only with his pickax, had managed to kill two of his assailants and send the third packing. He'd kept the knife of one as a prize of battle. It was a handmade, chased-steel blade with a carved jade hilt, and el-Aqrab wore it proudly in his belt. He'd subsequently found that his new position, as Samiel's enforcer in the QPR, came with a certain prestige and second-hand authority. This step-up in status had pleased him and he'd proven loyal.

"With your permission, Boss, I have a question," el-Aqrab said now. "How would we attack Daaryah? At Daaryah, it's very strong, I think. There's a full battalion there. And there's the Hercules Mountains on one side, and there's the sea on the other."

"And the army guns command the whole sweep of Oued Seenib," Malik quickly interjected. "And need I mention the French warships anchored in the port? Good question! I was about to raise it myself. This could end up being much ado about nothing. If we failed, it'd be a fiasco. Not a good start! And while you're answering that one," he added turning back to Samiel, "I have a second question: even if we were to actually capture Daaryah, how would we hold on to it? Again, we'd be locked into a static defensive position, as you were so quick to point out before. Because the Army would most certainly be quick to try and take it back!"

"We don't want to hold on to it," Samiel said, simply, speaking above the voices raised in arguments back and forth across the fire, round which they were all sitting.

"I beg your pardon?" Malik said, putting his hand to his ear in a mock-gesture of trying to hear better. "Do I understand you to be saying we should risk everything on a...a mad gamble—only to give it up again immediately? This is not a time for joking, Samiel!"

"No joke is intended," he answered calmly. "Think about it. We've been organizing the QPR quietly for six years. We've been very selective in accepting new members to an organization for which secrecy has been paramount. So, yes, we're basically unknown right now—but this yields us an advantage: between the opposed powers of the government and the French, on one side, and a hodge-podge of disgruntled and rebellious citizens on the other, we enjoy a relative anonymity. Now, just suppose—for a moment!— just suppose that I could show you how we can capture Daaryah—and I will—with hardly a casualty. The timing would be perfect. We would take them completely by surprise, would we not? By the time the government realized what happened, we could bomb both the port and the railhead, putting them out of condition for the better part of a year—yes, a year, because the rains will start soon, and spare parts will be slow to come from France. The French have almost suspended shipment of finished goods to us, anyhow, while our own economy is in upheaval, and it's unlikely any work would begin in earnest on repairs until late next spring, at best. Meanwhile, we would have the opportunity to make off with all the tanks, howitzers and armored vehicles we can manage, while the Army regroups. By the time they return to take back their precious Daaryah…we'll be gone! Vanished back into the desert—only then, we'll be well-equipped to strike blows elsewhere and everywhere behind the Army's back, *inshallah!*"

He knew his own revolutionary force was already well-supplied with assault rifles, mobile rocket-launchers and other light arms. Qarmat was a notorious way station in the international black-market arms trade, siphoning surplus weapons from Ukraine and Eastern Europe, China, France, Israel and the United States to renegade militants in the Middle East, Southern Africa and East Asia. A few daring raids on the arms caches at their lightly guarded transfer points had sufficed to prepare the QPR for opportunistic light skirmishes with unprepared Army outposts. But the heavier artillery and armored motor units stored at Daaryah would give the revolutionary force the firepower and maneuverability to strike effectively whenever and wherever it chose.

"*Allahu akbar! Lah! Ay! Allahu akbar…!*" Murmurs of

approval and dissenting arguments now flowed back and forth among the men.

Malik shook his head, dissatisfied, "Except Daaryah's nearly impregnable, and again I say, failure would be disastrous. How in hell do you propose we begin this grand attack on the garrison anyway?"

"We don't."

"What?"

"The French warships will attack them for us. We'll simply slip over the mountains to finish off the garrison from the rear."

"The French!" several of the men said, astonished.

"The French ships will attack them?" Malik said. "And just why would the French do that for us?"

"Because," Samiel said, "we will begin—under cover of the night before—by swimming out and mining the French ships!"

11.

"In his testimony," the young American prosecutor is saying now, "the witness, the same, Mamoun Mzadi, who is no longer able to speak, wrote that he had been arrested one morning on his way to work as a domestic servant in the home of the mayor of Mudharris and taken to Bustan el-Barzakh—the death camp over which you, Samiel, admit you had jurisdiction. He testified that he was kept there for fifteen days, locked in a cell with a dozen other prisoners, and interrogated day and night by guards who accused him of being a traitor and informer in the service of the French and who demanded that he write a confession implicating his employer, the mayor, and listing the names of everyone he knew, family, friends, neighbors, men, women, and children, as coconspirators. He testified that he was innocent and resisted confessing to these crimes, but that he was then tortured in various ways. At one point he was shackled to an iron bar from which he hung for five straight days, with his toes barely touching a stool. He wrote that the handcuffs cut so deeply into his wrists that the guards once needed almost a half-hour to remove them so that he could be taken out to the interrogation room again. The witness testified that he tried to kill himself by beating his head against the concrete wall, but that he only succeeded in falling unconscious with a concussion and that when the guards found him, they held his head down in the bucket that served as the common latrine for the prisoners until he woke up choking. And when the guards caught him trying to kill himself a second time by biting off his own tongue, they notified you...."

Samiel lets his attention drift from the prosecutor's litany, and he glances toward the back of the courtroom—looking again, he realizes, to catch a glimpse of Ibrahim. He knows the boy cannot be there, but he finds himself wishing that he was. He hasn't seen Ibrahim in a couple of years, now, not since he'd given him the gandoura and el-Aqrab's knife, and that had been only a couple of weeks before he'd turned himself in to the authorities. The boy should be thirteen now. A little taller, he imagines, with the first downy wisps of early teenage shadowing his mouth and chin, and there would also probably be, Samiel acknowledged to himself, a deepening curve of cynicism about his lips. He tries to imagine how he might look to Ibrahim now. Ibrahim would probably see him sitting there in the dock as some legendary monster on display in a zoo! He smiles inwardly, an ironic smile at his own expense, realizing he must be suffering an uncharacteristic spasm of sentimentality after all this time. He really wouldn't want Ibrahim exposed to all of this, he certainly wouldn't want the boy to hear the sordid details of all that he was being accused of being responsible for. Still, it would have been nice to see Ibrahim there, just a familiar face—however hostile—from which he might draw solace. It might have made him feel a little less embattled, less alone perhaps, even in the company of those dark, brooding eyes.

At the same time, Samiel is struck with how time has flown since the trial began. He seems to have lost track of the days without even noticing it. With the apparently endless legal formalities, pretrial hearings, discussions with the attorneys, and so on, the days have run together so that they seem one long, interminable excursion into absurdity. The whole arrangement seemed so simple in the beginning. But at the rate they are going, it's anyone's guess how much longer it might take them to bring it to conclusion—a conclusion everybody had anticipated at the beginning.

It must be getting late, Samiel thinks, unconsciously pressing his fingers against his temple. Perhaps Abul-Abbas will soon adjourn court for the day. It's Ramadan again. He knows it's still too early, but he realizes that for the last hour or two, he's been listening unconsciously for the sound of the cannon. And with that realization comes, for a brief moment, a recollection of his mother's harira. It was the traditional evening meal that followed the day's fast during Ramadan, a peasant soup of red lentils, chickpeas and cubed, boneless, lean lamb. His mother used to spice it with onions, ground cinnamon, and coriander....

All this must be taking its toll, he thinks now. From the time he first left home as a young student, he never felt homesick....

"...And then," the prosecutor is saying, "you gave orders that Mzadi should be '*masHooq*' the next morning—we understand that that was the term you used, '*masHooq.*' Other witnesses—including you, yourself—have testified in this courtroom that the term, '*masHooq,*' literally, 'crushed or pulverized,' was the euphemism—if, indeed, one can call it such—that was commonly used in the death camp at Bustan el-Barzakh for having a prisoner executed. Mamoun Mzadi testified that he believed he only escaped execution because in the hours before dawn the following morning, the prison was liberated by the invading Army of Dar el-Nar, who set him free.

"We would like the Court to note that the prosecution feels this is a credible assumption on the part of the witness, for it is known that every prisoner brought to the QPR prison camps at that time was intended to be executed. Originally, the victims were supposed to be real or 'suspected' political enemies, but they soon included members of the QPR itself who were deemed traitors or spies or unreliable or, for some other reason, of no further use. Further, of the two-point-one million people imprisoned for whom there are documented records, only eight hundred and sixty-eight—fewer than a thousand—are known to have survived. Three escaped, and the invading Dar el-Nar Army liberated the rest.

"Do you, Samiel," the prosecutor continues, "do you admit, or do you deny the truth of Mamoun Mzadi's testimony?"

But at that moment, they all hear the muffled boom of the cannon from the square announcing that it's time for the evening prayer and the end of the day's fast. Abul-Abbas and the other judges immediately rise, and the clerk announces that court is adjourned.

As the court is being cleared, Samiel glances back to see the prosecutor standing there staring at him with a curious expression as the guards lead him out.

12.

The American prosecutor had made himself familiar with Bustan el-Barzakh, the death camp mentioned by the witness Mamoun Mzadi. As part of his preparatory investigations on arrival in Qarmat, he'd joined a sightseeing tour travelling across the desert south of the Capital to see it with his own eyes. It was a trip he would never forget:

"…Ladies and gentlemen, may I have your attention for a moment? Someone has asked about the strange bright-red splotches hanging in the air behind us. If you glance back over your left shoulder through the windows, you'll see them. Yes, they look like great pools of burning fire, or as somebody said, red, bloody eyes staring at us out of the haze. They're actually the reflection of the setting sun on shallow pools of rainwater on the erg, the flat desert plain we're crossing. You can't see the water now, the sand looks dry out to the horizon. It's the mirage. Those pools are actually miles beyond our line of sight. But if you think back, you might have noticed them as we drove past. The effect, the mirage you're seeing there, is called 'Ibrahim's Eyes.'

"Sorry? We don't know. Probably nobody knows why they are called that anymore. It must go back to some old folktale....

"Here we are, at Bustan el-Barzakh, the main attraction. This is Falah Sabawi. Mr. Sabawi will be your guide for this next part of the tour. Feel free to ask him any questions you might have, he knows all about it. Don't forget to stop at the gift shop on your way out if you want any souvenirs. I'll be waiting for you here with the buses, when you're ready to move on. We'll be making one more stop—at the souk in el-Rawi again for last-minute shopping—before we take you back to your boat. Enjoy!"

"*Salaam aleikem*!" Falah Sabawi had said, greeting them. He was a tall, elderly man in a coarse cotton burnoose, thin as a post but erect in posture with features as solemn and eloquent in repose as the Sphinx. "Come, please," he'd continued in English. "We will walk the rest of the way. The gorge is too narrow for the buses and it is desired to preserve the pristine nature of the Oued Bustan from the effects of diesel pollution. Those of you who may be thirsty will find a refreshment bar over there to the left under the palm trees. Ladies and gentlemen will find comfort stations to your right. You are welcome to return here to the bar or to sit on the benches under the trees by the oasis if at any time you feel oppressed by the heat or by the... exhibits. The entrance to the prison is directly ahead through the iron gate.

"I'm sorry? No, sir, the cyclone fencing is a new addition. That and the razor wire on top have been added to protect the site from vandals. At the time the prison was in use, such a fence was not necessary. The camp is surrounded by the sheer rock face of the Hercules Mountains on one side—you can see that before you—and barren desert extending over eighty miles in every other direction. If a prisoner had escaped, there would have been no place for him to go.

"The cells you see here are where the prisoners were kept. They have been left exactly as they were then. There are no beds. Prisoners slept on the dirt floor. The cells are mostly all about the same, twenty feet wide and eight feet deep. Twenty to forty prisoners were kept in each one. They were chained together to the iron rings hanging on the back wall, sometimes for days at a time, between interrogations. The bucket in the corner you see there was used as the common latrine. The floodlights above you, they were powered by a gasoline generator then, as they are now. The floodlights were kept on twenty-four hours a day. This was to make it easier for the guards on watch. But they also served another purpose: they were used, together with loud noises, to keep the prisoners from sleeping.

"Beg pardon? No, ma'am, I'm sorry, there is no air conditioning. There was no air conditioning then, and no heat. The temperature out here in the desert, which has been known to reach 46 degrees Celsius in the afternoon in summer— about 115 Fahrenheit—often falls below minus 7 degrees Celsius—that would be about 20 degrees

Fahrenheit—in winter, and the winds can be severe. Step this way, please.

"Here is the interrogation area. In front is the induction center. Here, newly arrived prisoners would have their identities checked and their photographs taken, and a file would be opened on each one. The interconnected interrogation cells, as you see, are only separated by iron bars to allow for viewing. The one here is typical. There are chains and break-bars, racks, gouges, pincers, forceps, pokers, knives, rusted saws, and razors. You see them exactly as they were found, except that you will notice they have been labeled with tags indicating how they were used.

"I'm sorry, I must ask you not to touch them. It is a rule here, to preserve them as they are. They are part of our history.

"As I was saying, prisoners would sometimes be allowed to choose their method of interrogation. The iron bar hanging from chains on your left was used to hang prisoners for long periods of time with their wrists manacled behind their backs so that their shoulders would be dislocated. While the prisoner was hanging there, the interrogator would use these instruments to apply torture. Also, autopsies were sometimes performed on living prisoners on the surgical table on the right. The surgical table was also used for—

"Beg pardon? Yes, there were women prisoners here as well as men prisoners. Yes, ma'am, there were also children. There were many children, although children were…not kept for very long.

"Sorry? No, sir, I'm sorry. As I said, there is no air conditioning anywhere on the site. Yes, there is electricity. As I said, there is a generator. But no, no air conditioning. No, I'm sorry, they will not put in air conditioning. "Perhaps we should move out to the prison yard. The sun is also very hot, but there are a number of parasols available. If you feel over-come by the heat, you may follow the signs back to the refreshment bar….

"…In the open pits you see here, the prisoners would be chained and left to bake in the sun, or left at night to the mercy of the cold, the leeches, and the vipers. Some of the pits form part of the camp's sewage system, and so prisoners might occasionally be drowned there in the run-off.

"If you will step this way, please, you will see the killing field.

"Beg pardon? Over there? It is a drainage ditch. For sewage. You mean, *in* the drainage ditch? Ah, it is…that is *el-Nafs el-Nafaq*, how you would say, The Tunnel to the Soul. It was a special torture here….

"Sorry? Yes, ma'am, they are tears. Well, I sup-pose I am weeping, ma'am—but never mind, it will pass…. How can I bear to do this job? Well, I guess I am…I am doing a sort of penance, ma'am. I was a QPR. It was a long time ago, and I was very young, you see. And for a while, I was a guard in this place."

13.

ate continues to baffle expectations, Samiel is thinking, late that night in his cell. He thought he was through with politics a generation ago. But the outcome of his political adventures is only now to be determined—and by parties whose interest in his country was belated and exploitative, at best, and who'll be judging him on the basis of factors which are patently hypocritical and secondary to the issues he had to deal with at the time. When he'd agreed to undergo this ordeal, it was supposed to have been a perfunctory exercise in diplomatic finessing, so one would think it should've been over and done with in short order. But instead, the indignities went on: interrogations, depositions, endless quibbling, casuistry, and backroom haggling between the prosecution and the defense—and then, the medical examinations and psychological evaluations. As if he were the subject of a teratological inquiry. As if, a quarter-century after the fact, a handful of naïve foreign academics could actually determine the right or wrong of such events! What was the point?

Nor, apparently, was there any purpose served by the confrontation, earlier that afternoon, during a court recess, with the victims' families. A disappointment, in fact. Through his attorney, he had offered the Court the opportunity for the families who had been admitted into the gallery during the trial to visit with him in jail to hear his side of things and to share their own feelings and complaints with him—for his was the face of the revolution they knew best. His attorney had willingly presented the notion to the Court, arguing that it might offer the victims some closure and hoping, perhaps, that if it went well, it might even serve to lessen Samiel's sentence in the end.

"There were many things we had to do," he'd told those poor unfortunates, "that were absolutely necessary for us to do! They were necessary to save our country from the abuses and oppression you, I, all of us had experienced under King Saddahi in his ruthless partnership with France—France, who had been exploiting our country for over a century and to whom Saddahi had bartered away what little we had left of the fruits of our labor, our land, our resources, and our birthright! There were many who had profited under this system, who had colluded in it, and they had resisted our efforts to free ourselves. They were selfish, cunning, and duplicitous, and we had to eliminate them, we had to root them out in order to achieve our greater purpose, so that you, I, and the rest of Qarmat could be free! Some of them were our friends, our family, and as we saw them taken away by the Revolution, we thought it harsh at the time. But now, look around you: the French are gone—after almost a hundred and fifty years, the French are gone!—and you have a Constitution protecting you and your right to live as you please, to speak your mind without fear of reprisal, and to work as you choose and keep the fruits of your own labor! There is a price for freedom, and that price sometimes falls heavily upon us. And so we in the QPR took upon our own shoulders the greater part of that burden, shedding our blood and our lives on the battlefield at that awful time. And now, I am here as the surviving symbol of the Revolution, I stand here willingly accepting the blame for whatever may have gone wrong along the way—whether or not

we could have prevented it. For in the heat of the moment many mistakes may be made. But it was a just war, and all of you here can testify to the improvement in your lives. But for those innocents among you who might have suffered along the way, I am truly sorry! Truly sorry! Aywá, Allah karim!"

But afterward, they simply stood there staring at him, not saying a word for nearly the whole ten minutes they were allotted. A dozen at most—peasants, workers, a school principal, widows, grandparents, bereft siblings—Samiel pitied them all, he really did. The necessities of war and revolution fell hard on everyone, but they fell with particular harshness on the passive, those who merely stood by and did nothing while others were caught up in the riptide of events. Whether out of fear or the inability to choose a side, these were the ones who, when destiny called, failed to act decisively, either to aid one side or to hinder the other. These were the ones who lived under the illusion that they were innocent, or could remain neutral, or who thought they could find sanctuary in withdrawal, in ambivalence, and equivocation, that the world around them would clash and crash and drain away its heat and horrors and leave them safe and free to live on, untouched and unquestioning. But instead, they later find themselves choked with the vague, haunting guilt of their own inaction, their souls discomfited in a way they can never make sense of in their islands of delusion.

And yet that was why he'd invited them, to give them the opportunity to step beyond their inveterate silence. That was why he'd made the offer to do so, and had publicly admitted his responsibility and apologized for the suffering of the victims who'd been killed and buried in mass graves across the country. That was why he'd invited them to say whatever they felt in their hearts that they needed to say, or to ask him any last questions about his reasons, why he'd felt under obligation to do as he did, or about their own feelings of guilt as survivors, or about the victims who were sacrificed, so that they all, he and they too, could come to terms with the abiding fears and passions and the history of exploitation and divisive violence that was their country's heritage.

But few had come. The impulsive ones, the loudmouths who'd screamed out senseless insults during the course of testimony and had had to be ejected from the courtroom, they hadn't come. And those few who had come had had nothing to say. They'd just stood there staring at him but not meeting his eyes, as if he were some alien being with whom they shared no common language. They were outnumbered by the reporters—it was the one event during the trial to which the press had been permitted attendance—without cameras. And the press crowded over to one side swinging their tape recorders uselessly about as one survivor or another stuttered forth as if to say something, only to subside again into a silence punctuated by sighs and sharp intakes of breath, as the minutes ticked pointlessly by.

Finally, one raised his hand, like a child at school, and the others parted to let him step forward, an elderly peasant.

"Allahu karim," the man began hesitantly. "Ammalet Jarrah? Do you remember Ammalet Jarrah? He was seven, only seven. My son. Seven years old. They said he was—they said they took the children up to the roof and they—"

He paused, startled by the muffled boom of the cannon firing from the city square in the distance that signaled it was time for salât el-maghrib, the evening prayer, for it was still Ramadan. Visiting time was up. The guards immediately began hustling the visitors and the press out of the room.

"Ammalet Jarrah!" the man called out over his shoulder, as the guards dragged him away. "Do you remember Ammalet Jarrah?"

As the steel door closed behind them, Samiel knew that the guards, along with everybody else, were rushing home to their evening bowls of harira, for the faithful had been fasting since sunrise. He hasn't touched food himself for the last three days, but for different reasons. He isn't religious. His father, a Sufi, who'd done well as an exporter of coffees, teas and spices, was a spiritual man but had never imposed his beliefs on the family. In fact, he was more often to be seen with a book of poetry, Rūmī's Mathnawī *or a Hafez divan, under his arm, than the* Qur'an. *What he might claim to have inherited from his father, Samiel thinks, is an abiding affection for Hafez, Blake, and the metaphysical poets—and perhaps a fondness for wine. It was his mother who, although only self-educated, had first stimulated his interests in mathematics, business, and politics. She'd had visions of her son growing up to be a prosperous and important person one day, someone who would never have to experience the effects of hunger and want that farming families like hers had experienced during periods of drought when she was a child. Well, as far as he's concerned, it has turned out well enough. He never had much interest in accumulating wealth or property, but he did liberate his country from the grip of a colonial power and the abuses of a tyrant—no small thing, he thinks, although he's gotten little credit for it and is now being prosecuted for it. And he can fairly say that he's made some small contributions to the world of mathematics. Mathematics was—and still is—his first love, after all. He never felt so comfortable with people as with numbers. He doesn't regret his time with the Revolution, but if things had been different and he'd had the option, he would gladly have devoted his life to the quiet study of mathematics. And yet it was strange in a way how that too had seemed to come full circle.*

14.

I t was two years earlier, Samiel recalls, the morning of the same day that he turned himself in to the authorities. He was in a hotel room overlooking the bay of el-Rawi and lying naked on the floor, thinking. After a moment, he crunched up and lay down again. Then again he crunched up, winced, and lay down. He felt the floor tiles cool and soothing beneath him. Crunch up, lay down—with each sit-up, an involuntary grunt of pain escaped his lips, but the movement comforted him, all the same. As he crunched up the final time, completing his set of fifty, his lips curled at the taste of bile that rose in his mouth—and at the irony of this morning ritual, a futile gesture now toward health. Climbing to his feet, he threw on a gandoura and went to the window, leaning into the shadows to look out. The morning was crisp and clear and the light spring breeze sharp with the scent of brine. Beyond the seawall he could see the beach, where the wind had driven down the dunes that had mounted so high there only yesterday. Down at the water's edge two small boys were playing in the surf and throwing stones at the sea. The tide was running out and the waves, churned by the undertow, glittered and clashed around them like steel wheels in the morning sun. He remembered being there when he was a boy and doing the same thing and feeling the exhilaration as the waves crashed around him, tugging him this way and that. He remembered it all so well! But farther out there were signs of a change. A half-dozen ocean freighters carrying the flags of places as far away as Panama, Saudi Arabia, Indonesia, and Singapore, rode at anchor, tossing in the treacherous crosscurrents that swirled in around the outer reef. It had been many years since the harbor of el-Rawi, once one of the busiest on the Mediterranean, had seen that much traffic.

Further along the beach, seagulls and terns were circling in a tumultuous clamor over the jetty. The bodies of the drowned weltered there in plain view among the breakers. He could see only two today. On some days there'd been as many as a half-dozen at a time. They were generally ignored. The scattering of families with young children picnicking on the sand paid them no mind. It was only the scavengers who seemed to notice them—and the gulls. Bold young boys, and an occasional older beggar, would rifle through the tattered clothes of the drowned in search of money, cutting the rings from their fingers and the gold from their teeth. These unfortunate dead were refugees from Dar el-Nar, the oppressive kingdom on the southern border. They could not find sanctuary in Qarmat because the Qarmatian government had a reciprocity agreement with Dar el-Nar and was obliged to return them if they were caught alive. So the desperate souls persisted in crowding into flimsy boats to seek asylum across the sea in Spain or Italy. But more often than not, their boats were wrecked by heavy seas or drawn onto the reef outside the harbor here, and for days afterward, their bodies would wash up on shore or lay rolling in the shallows. The Qarmatian government had erected a memorial over the pilings at the end of the jetty for those who'd drowned over the years. It was a stone pyramid some twenty feet high, carved out of a particularly beautiful specimen of local dolomite and inscribed with the names of some of the victims. There'd been hundreds by now, and additional names were added periodically as new victims were identified. Samiel found the monument very touching—but ironic. Qarmat was famous for its monuments and memorials to the dead, but not known for any serious attempts to ease the suffering of the victims while they lived, or to stem the tides of violence that periodically spread death like a plague over the land.

Moments later, as he walked along the seawall, a police van was driving down the beach toward the jetty. Once or twice a week, one would come by, making its way slowly over the firm mud of the berm at low tide, to scoop up the fresh bodies of the drowned and cart them away for identification, if possible, and incineration.

He turned just in time to sidestep a large camel laden with wares for market that was being driven past him along the narrow seawall. Other people were crowding by as well, most of them heading toward the medina, as he was.

The salt air was softened now by the scent of orange blossoms.

The delicate aroma grew stronger as he approached the central square, where a hundred young orange trees were all in bloom. The trees had been planted all around the square only twenty years before, to mark the reestablishment of the monarchy. It seemed to Samiel that their buds had been barely showing the evening before. But today, they were in full flower and their fragrance reached out to him with an insistence that seemed almost personal, pursuing him round every corner and down every street, ameliorating, if only by a little, the stench of rancid smoke that issued from every shop stall and alleyway he passed along the way and that came from the long, yellow Turkish cigarettes to which the denizens of the city seemed devoted.

As he walked on, faces turned toward him, as if recognizing him, then turned away avoiding his eyes. He proceeded through the crowded streets apparently oblivious to the glances that followed after him, as though aware only that it was April, that spring had come with its sudden, stunning mildness and that all along the verges of the city trees and shrubs bloomed in effusion from every corner of the once-barren sand.

He was late, but he didn't hurry. He presented his credentials to the guard at the door and entered the hall of the Royal Palace for the opening ceremony of the World Conference of Theoretical Mathematics just as the Prime Minister was approaching the microphone on stage.

Waving a hand amicably to hush the smattering of polite applause that greeted him, the Prime Minister cleared his throat and addressed the conference, acknowledging the presence of honored guests, welcoming the international audience to the city, and giving some indication of the attractions to come. Now and then, he seemed to be casting furtive glances toward the dais behind him, as if looking for someone who'd not yet appeared. There was an empty chair there, where several distinguished scientists and mathematicians from all over the world were already seated. The morning light, filtering in through the window *jalis* in the back wall seemed to cast an aura about them.

The empty chair was reserved for the principal speaker, a scholar known for his published papers on set theory, spectral theory, topological vector spaces, and commutative and homological algebras, which had led to revolutionary advances in pure mathematics. This honored guest had been awarded the Fields Medal for his breakthrough publication on refraction coefficients, a mathematical schema he'd proposed initially only as an analytical tool in extending Einstein's work on gravitational effects, but the phenomenon had subsequently been confirmed by astrophysicists in experiment. It was an effect, somewhat analogous to mirage, in which it was possible to see behind and beyond a cosmic object—a star, planet or galaxy, for example—around which light had been bent. The result was that the intervening "distance"—actually, spacetime itself—suddenly became "invisible" by virtue of a tessellated interference.

As he worked his way up the side aisle, a few seated in the audience turned their heads to watch him pass.

The dais was cordoned off and surrounded by uniformed guards. On presenting his credentials a second time, Samiel was permitted entry. When he climbed the three steps, there was some shuffling and nods of greeting among the other scheduled speakers, who made way for him as he passed to take the empty chair.

The Prime Minister, a stout man of medium height with bushy eyebrows, a high, wide forehead, and a stiff goatee, all of which gave him a vague resemblance to old photos of Lenin, paused mid-phrase to glance around at the disturbance. Seeing Samiel, he seemed relieved, then nodded in greeting and turned to continue with his opening remarks. He'd just reached the point of introducing the King. In the next moment, the audience stood and turned toward the balcony applauding, as the youthful King Essid el-Roweed entered with a small entourage. When His Royal Highness was finally seated, the Prime Minister continued, recounting to the audience the nature of the special occasion that marked this gathering. It was the opening day of the bi-annual World Conference of Theoretical Mathematics. The present Conference, co-sponsored by the King and *The Fibonacci Quarterly,* an international scientific journal on mathematical topics, was being held in el-Rawi this year on purpose to celebrate the eight hundredth anniversary of the appearance of Fibonacci's *Liber Abaci,* or *Book of Calculation.* Fibonacci's book had been first published on April 1st, 1202, by an Arabic press in el-Rawi. In the book, Leonardo of Pisa, the Italian mathematician later to be known as Fibonacci, had drawn upon his years of study with Arabic mathematicians in North Africa to introduce Europe to many mathematical novelties, including the use of so-called "Arabic" numerals, not least of which was the zero. (Both had actually been transmitted to Arabic mathematicians from India, where they had been in use, together with the decimal system, since the Ninth Century.) The Italian mathematician had also introduced the concept of irrational numbers, and the Fibonacci series, a curious sequence of numbers which seemed to occur almost everywhere in nature and which was eventually named after him.

As the Prime Minister's voice droned on, echoing back from the high, chambered ceiling overhead, Samiel squirmed restlessly in his chair and looked about him. It was many years since he'd been in the Palace, and he experienced mixed emotions as he glanced around the hall and let his eyes play again amid the splendor of its details. Rows of twenty-foot-high, paired marble pillars, bronzed with age, framed the gallery and rose to anchor higher arches that supported the ceiling. The ceiling was honeycombed and the cells, or *muqarnas*, were purported to number five thousand—one each, as the legend had it, for each of the five thousand tribes of Islam. The carving was more than merely intricate. The lines of these *muqarnas* angled, curved and re-curved, interweaving upon themselves and giving the surface the appearance of an interlaced, non-periodic tiling that formed different patterns depending upon whether one viewed them narrowly or across a wider perspective. Also, depending on the time of day, the lines revealed different quotations from the *Qur'an* as light and shadow were transposed. At such times, interior and exterior spaces appeared to converge so that the whole vaulted structure seemed to flex and breathe like a living organism. The ceiling was famous for its beauty and for being one of the most intricate of its kind in all the Maghreb. Its visual impact was enhanced by its reflection in the pool below. A fountain, spilling into a rosette at the foot of the dais, opened into this long, central pool that stretched to the rear of the gallery and divided the audience, who filled the seats arranged on either side. The faces of the audience sitting nearest the pool were also reflected in its waters, and for Samiel, the muddled resemblance of these reflections to other faces out of the past brought memories rushing back to him, the young, eager faces of his students in the village of Meena Yûsuf-as-Siddîq thirty-six years earlier....

"...So you doubt the truth of the statement," the young Samiel—then known by his birth name, Amal Koraoun el-Mudharrisi, was saying, acknowledging an objection that had been raised by one of the students in the back of the room. "Very well, but Euclid has given us a very clever proof.

Do you remember that we spoke, last week, of an elenctic argument? And we gave some everyday examples of it. It is a form of negative proof," he paused and smiled, as a few students called out the answer. "Ah, yes," he continued. "Now we remember! It's an argument of refutation in logic, one that proves a point by refuting its opposite, usually by *reductio ad absurdum*. Well, the principle has been commonly applied in mathematics as well, and that is essentially the approach Euclid used here. A prime number, you will recall, is a number greater than *1* that can only be divided by *1* and itself, such as *2, 3, 5, 7,* and so on, okay? Euclid's theorem states that all numbers are either prime or can be written as prime numbers multiplied together. But instead of attempting to calculate out to infinity to demonstrate the truth of his insight, he simply and concisely exposed the logical absurdity of supposing his theorem to be false.

"All right, so let's see how Euclid does this. How does he prove his theorem? He asks us to imagine that the theorem is wrong, that there *are* numbers that are neither prime nor can be written as prime numbers multiplied together. If there are such numbers…."

They were bright, eager students, readily grasping the rudiments of arithmetic and geometry that he was seeking to teach them and quick as hawks to pounce on apparent inconsistencies or dubious assumptions. They ranged in age from fifteen to eighteen, and most of them had only the rudiments of an education beyond a few Qur'ânic passages learned by heart. Initially shy of schooling and afraid of math in particular, several had come along much further than he'd ever hoped they would in so short a time, and already a half-dozen were hoping to prepare themselves for entrance examinations to the university in the Capital. It had been less than a year since he, a young university student at the time and a stranger in the area, had come to Meena Yûsuf-as-Siddîq. He'd come on purpose to protest the government's ongoing attacks on the village over the preceding months. There was a populist uprising going on there against the country's declining economy, government corruption, and the exploitation by the French colonial power of the country's natural resources. In the effort to suppress this uprising, the government had thrown up a military cordon to prevent shipments of food, medicine, and basic supplies from reaching the village. But it hadn't seemed to dampen the spirit of resistance, so the government had finally resorted to shelling the village with tank guns. Much to its own surprise, Meena Yûsuf-as-Siddîq, which until then had been only an obscure little fishing village in the southwest, had become a rallying cry, considered a wellspring of the new national awakening and the growing political activism among the youth in Qarmat at the time. It had all begun with the death of a local teenaged protestor in police custody earlier in the year. Despite the new-found political energy in the village, however, Amal Koraoun had had to ask Mumi Malagawi el-Hawhza, a sympathetic and revered local spiritual leader, to intercede on his behalf in order to convince the sharîf and other tribal elders of the village, who were all conservative Shi'a, to allow him to hold his classes in the mosque, which would extend the traditional syllabus of their madrassa to include modern history and mathematics.

On this day, as he proceeded with his lecture, he heard the muffled sound of a plane approaching, but caught up in the dialogue regarding Euclid's proof, he assumed it was a commercial flight or perhaps another government surveillance plane passing overhead.

We're doing very well, he was thinking, pleased at his students' progress, as he continued aloud to the class, "… Since this hypothetical number N isn't a prime number, we must be able to write it as two smaller numbers, A and B, multiplied together—"

But a sudden blast outside shook the ground beneath his feet. All at once, the air was thick with dust and flying debris and the children started screaming. A second blast, immediately after the first, knocked out the plaster wall on the other side of his classroom and the ceiling showed signs of collapsing. He saw two of the younger boys cowering under their desks in the corner there. He started toward them, but before he'd taken two steps a third bomb fell, throwing him backward. He scrambled up almost immediately and—although dazed by the concussion when his head struck the floor—started forward again, only to see that the two young boys were gone, that that whole portion of the building right down to the foundation was gone! And the bombs were still falling. The mosque's walls were caving in about him. He ran out into the street yelling—he doesn't remember what he was yelling, just screaming in anguish, anger, and fear, as was everyone else in the street. Men, women, and children, fleeing in every direction, were blown to bits before his eyes. And the bombs kept falling. Finally, when he thought it was over, he stood there stunned and gaping in disbelief at the ruins and the dead and mutilated lying in the market. And then he saw the planes. There must have been a dozen of them. But they weren't from the Qarmatian Air Force, as he would have expected. They bore the roundel of France.

He watched them bank and turn back and begin to rake the survivors with machinegun fire.

Seventy-five unarmed villagers, men, women and children, had been slaughtered and over a hundred and fifty wounded. The day had been commemorated in Qarmat every year since then. It was known as *il Yawm 'Aar*, the Day of Shame.

15.

s Samiel's symptoms gradually worsen during his overnights in jail, a guard eventually takes notice and brings his seizures to the attention of the Court. As a result, Samiel is ordered to undergo an MRI. He doesn't mind the respite from the tedium of the trial. The medical technician tells him that a certain amount of claustrophobia was normal and to be expected. But he feels no anxiety. Why should he? There will be no surprises. The findings can be only relative, an indication a little to one side or the other of the probable limits of a known outcome.

But as he enters the tube, his right elbow jams against the opening. The gurney gives a loud screech and shudders to a halt. The technician apologizes and makes the necessary adjustments. "No," Samiel says, "I'm not hurt, I'm fine. Proceed." But in fact, the impact jarred an old wound that had grown tender with arthritis where a bullet had broken his clavicle. And as the gurney inches forward again, he eyes the advancing opening speculatively: a narrow crescent above the gurney that he estimates as no more than 40 cm high and 60 wide, barely large enough to encompass a person on the small side of average. He's always had a slim, athletic physique, and he's lost a considerable amount of weight in the last few years, especially since his time in prison, for he's lost his appetite and what little he eats of the prison food disagrees with him. But his shoulders, although of uneven height since the injury, are still broad enough to extend beyond the margins of the gurney, and he wonders, wouldn't it be ironic if, after all their posturing, psychometric testing, and evaluations, he didn't fit into their mold?

But then, something else happens. As the leading edge of the MRI machine slides over him, he thinks he detects the trace of a rancid, alcoholic odor in the air, like the smell of stale beer. It might be the fumes from some antiseptic or other chemical present in the laboratory, but it suddenly evokes in him the odor that had pervaded the prison camps of the QPR thirty years before. It had emanated from the prisoners themselves and persisted even after their superficial filth had been hosed off. It was the smell of starvation, of the tissues of emaciated bodies consuming themselves. And then he is suddenly transported back to Bustan el-Barzakh and the moment when Abdullah Kamal emerged from the "Tunnel:"

Abdullah Kamal was an Amazigh. The Amazigh, more widely known as Tuareg, were a stalwart subgroup of Berbers known for being fierce warriors inured to hardship and the extreme conditions of nomadic life in the desert. They were generally of high intelligence, famous as breeders of great racing camels, and for generations—when their fealty could be won—employed as scribes, clerks, military officers, and administrative aids to emirs and government officials. Abdullah Kamal was a prisoner of particular interest because, as a government worker in a relatively privileged position, he knew many government officials, had intimate knowledge of their intrigues, and was thought to be privy to many government secrets. He was also well known to Samiel, for he was the trusted secretary to Abul-Abbas, who was at that time serving as the Minister of Culture.

Samiel had ordered the arrest of Abdullah Kamal and told the guards to notify him immediately when he was brought to the camp. In his previous role as a friend and confidant in the house of Abul-Abbas, Samiel had known Abdullah Kamal and his family and liked them. Because of this, he'd hoped to make the interrogation process go more easily with the man. He'd had Abdullah brought to his office that first evening and they'd spent some time talking privately together in a friendly manner. At least, Samiel had tried to be friendly. But Abdullah Kamal was a proud man. He'd given an oath of loyalty to the King and he knew that many of his relatives and tribal brothers had already been arrested by the QPR or "disappeared" at their hands. After the man's initial shock at recognizing Samiel in that setting—the identities of the senior officers in the QPR were strictly secret—Samiel found him resistant and uncooperative and his responses brusque almost to rudeness.

He understood Abdullah's motivations and wished to be able to take the time to convince him by mere verbal persuasion, so he had him shackled to other prisoners in a cell who were taken out and tortured one by one—while Abdullah Kamal was not tortured, but only put on a minimal diet of one slice of stale, moldy bread and two sips of water a day. Samiel hoped that, as Abdullah grew hungrier and saw his cellmates taken out and returned each day—those that were returned—with their bones broken, their nails torn off and so on, Samiel hoped that as Abdullah observed these things, he would weaken. But he didn't. Days would pass, and he would return to Abdullah's cell in the evenings and ask him, plead with him really, to cooperate. But he wouldn't.

Abdullah's body grew weaker for lack of food, but his spirit stayed firm. Samiel found this admirable, but pitiful too, for irrespective of Abdullah's staunchness, in the end his fate would be the same.

Time ran out for Abdullah, however, at the end of twelve days, when Mumi el-Hawhza, Samiel's mentor and the official head of the QPR, and "General Malik" (the nom de guerre of Marwan Badat, also Deputy Commander of QSIS, the Qarmatian Intelligence Service then) arrived together at the camp to call a meeting to discuss urgent news.

The military phase of the Revolution was then in its final stages. The QPR had succeeded in grinding down the government forces in the north and in the south, confounding the Qarmatian Army and bringing the King's line of defense to its knees. They'd managed to do this not only by a series of daring raids on military installations, blowing up trains, and sabotaging communications systems across the country, but by going undercover to light fires among the civilian population everywhere, instigating protests, uprisings, and sabotage in every sector, overwhelming the local constabulary. Their rate of success, almost astonishing even to them, had been facilitated by the general collapse of the economy, the indecisiveness and impotence of the government, the widespread resentment among the populace over onerous taxes and government corruption, and the low morale of the Army. This chaotic state of affairs had been aggravated by an imbroglio of Parliamentary intrigues among government ministers who distrusted one another and the outspoken contempt in which senior Army commanders held King Saddahi. Several Army officers had already deserted and brought their companies over to the QPR by that time. Now, General

Malik had arrived with news—good and not so good—that seemed to dandle triumph tantalizingly before their eyes. He reported that General Karim el-Akhmeinie, Head of the Army, in a secret meeting arranged by Malik, had agreed to cast his lot with the QPR. El-Akhmeinie had agreed to hand over el-Habbar, the Army's famous and reputedly impregnable fortress in the southwest, and had promised that there would be no resistance from the Army when they marched on the Capital.

The second piece of news was a mixed blessing. Malik had also arranged for the abduction of his own boss, Yassim Nasser, Commander of QSIS. Nasser would've been a great prize for interrogation, but he was wily, tightlipped, and prudent in the extreme. He kept few written notes or records of any consequence, his schedule was unpredictable, he was never without his heavily armed bodyguards, and he never traveled in the same car two days in a row. Malik had managed to anticipate him this one time, however, and he'd arranged an ambush in which Nasser was to have been abducted. The Commander's car was blocked by what was supposed to appear to be an auto accident on the road just outside of the Capital. But the plot went awry. Nasser must have suspected something, because when a QPR soldier, masquerading as an elderly woman in a burqa who was a passenger in distress from the disabled car, approached the Commander's limousine, Nasser and his bodyguards opened fire. In the return fire from the QPR soldiers hidden behind the disabled car, Nasser was killed. Malik, as Deputy Commander of QSIS in his alternate "legitimate" government role as Marwan Fareed Badat, would now take over as Commander, according to the plan—unfortunately, whatever information of value Nasser possessed had been lost with him.

Nevertheless, the QPR was now very close to victory. The occupation of el-Rawi would seem to be the next logical step. And yet Samiel reminded himself of the old saw, that one can know victory and yet not achieve it. It was better, he thought, to secure victory before the battle was fought. And in this case, the French were still an open question. The French forces had been giving fitful support to the Army until then, and intercepted communiqués gave conflicting indications as to whether the French would finally withdraw and abandon the government to its fate, or change tack and attempt a last-minute rally to support the King for the sake of their own investments. Meanwhile, they had destroyers fully manned with fighting men at anchor in several of Qarmat's harbors and bombers and jet fighters based at the airport.

With Nasser gone, the best source of information, now, would be, odd as it seemed, through the office of the Minister of Culture. The French had become fed up with the dysfunctional Qarmatian Parliament and the ambiguities of the Foreign Office. The Qarmatian Ambassador had been recalled and Fajhadi Douma, the Foreign Minister, was in open contention for power with the Prime Minister at the time, both of whom were notoriously self-serving, quixotic, and driven by greed. The French had also lost patience with the equivocations of King Saddahi. It was no secret that the state of Qarmat's relations with France rested on the shoulders of the only government minister whose integrity was proverbial and whom all parties trusted.

But the fate of that minister, Abul-Abbas, now hung

in a delicate balance, even aside from the question of the intentions of France. Abul-Abbas was a staunch loyalist, but more than that, his poise, breeding, and known wealth—his family owned the largest mineral mines in the country and, next to the King, he was one of the richest men in Qarmat—made him a public symbol of the elitism for which the monarchy was despised. So that while their plan called for most of the other government officials and MPs to be arrested immediately upon the QPR's taking over the government, Mumi el-Hawhza, Malik and others had been pressing for Abul-Abbas's immediate arrest for several weeks. Samiel, on the other hand, having been a lifelong friend of Abul-Abbas and knowing the inevitable outcome of such an arrest, had been holding them off, ordering that no one so much as approach the Minister without his express permission. And he delayed ordering that arrest—at least until he'd made up his own mind about the man. But now, el-Hawhza, Malik, and other senior officers were at his doorstep urging him to meet with them in council to weigh the impact of these new developments and to plan their next moves.

And so one morning just after dawn, he'd directed el-Aqrab to take Abdullah Kamal to the "Tunnel." It was the guards at the camp who'd come up with the name for the procedure, *"el-Nafs el-Nafaq,"* the Tunnel to the Soul.

Abdullah Kamal was let out of his cell and relieved of his shackles. This was done purposely to give the prisoner the illusion of possible leniency or even of imminent freedom. El-Aqrab, Samiel's lieutenant, led Abdullah Kamal toward the outer perimeter of the prison compound, which was located beside Oued Bustan, an oasis hidden within a tortuous gorge in the Hercules Mountains. The mountains formed part of the border dividing Qarmat from Dar el-Nar to the south. This was the northern edge of the Sahara, a vast, dull-gray plain of scalding sun and eroded marl carved up in long, twisted erratic chevrons like wind-tossed waves frozen at crest and extending to the far horizon. Out of this forbidding oceanic maze, the steep rock face of the mountains rose abruptly and almost vertically to form a continuous wall of blue-gray granite reaching heights of over fifteen thousand feet and extending five hundred miles to the sea. El-Aqrab led Abdullah Kamal along a narrow path between overhanging shoulders of dark stone inflected with pleochroistic crystals, which glittered like jewels and changed colors with the angle at which they were viewed.

There was a declivity at the end of the path, from which Abdullah Kamal could glimpse the flamingos in the pool and the cluster of fig trees, date palms, and tamarisk that ringed the oasis close by, as well as the desolate vastness beyond. At the foot of this declivity was a sewage ditch, and in it a large drainpipe. El-Aqrab and his men led Abdullah Kamal down to the bottom of the slope, stripped him of his clothes and forced him into the pipe, an isolated, twelve-foot section of rusty iron. The pipe was 55cm in diameter, barely wide enough to accommodate Abdullah's shoulders, but his arms and legs were not bound, and they told him that if he managed to wriggle out of the pipe they would let him go free. Then they left him there to roast slowly in the sun.

But of course he couldn't escape. The narrow space hampered movement, the pipe had been partially blocked at both ends and an armed guard was posted.

Samiel returned every half-hour to inquire whether Abdullah Kamal was prepared to divulge the information he needed. For the first hour, as the sun grew hotter, he could hear Abdullah struggling inside the pipe, but el-Aqrab said he never cried out or uttered a word. When Samiel stooped down to call into one end of the pipe to ask whether Abdullah was ready to talk, Abdullah Kamal merely cursed him and shouted his refusal. After two hours, when the outside temperature had already reached 95 degrees, and probably well over 110 degrees inside the pipe, he had el-Aqrab set two live rats loose in either end of the pipe. As he walked away to return to the council meeting, he could hear Abdullah Kamal begin to yell. Ninety minutes later, the guards began shoveling gravel over the top of the pipe. Abdullah Kamal would hear this, magnified by ringing echoes inside the pipe, and get the impression he was being buried alive. By this time, the sounds of Abdullah's screams and his struggles to avoid the rats were as loud as they were pitiful. But at the end of another hour, while his gasping attempts to breathe in the suffocating heat, his screams, and his physical struggles reached hysterical levels, he was still not willing to talk. The pipe, meanwhile, had grown dangerously hot in the sun. It was then over 110 degrees outside, and Samiel feared Abdullah would die before giving them any information. He ordered that sewage water be pumped into the pipe at a controlled rate. This would slow the heating of the pipe enough to keep Abdullah from literally baking inside, while allowing enough air to prevent him suffocating for at least another hour or so—while frightening him with the fear of drowning. Few prisoners had endured so long. Many had died of fright, heart attack or heat stroke before they could be pulled out and questioned. Finally, an hour later, Abdullah Kamal had gone silent, and Samiel told el-Aqrab to extract him. When they pulled him out, Abdullah Kamal was not dead, but he would no longer give useful information about anything. He'd suffered numerous broken bones, the heat had blistered his skin, the rats had got at him, and he'd gone stark mad.

———

Samiel is shivering in his cell. They forgot to give him back his opium after the MRI. Stomach cramps have him doubled up and he has little control over his bowels. The remains of his dinner sit congealing in the tin plate on the floor: chicken broth with rice and a soft-boiled egg, all he can eat, now—or might have eaten before he'd vomited in it.

...It was war, he's thinking, a revolution, and the killing was necessary, at least in the beginning. Whether it needed to be carried to that extreme he still couldn't say. It had taken on a dynamic of its own. But it had been necessary in the beginning. He'd had to root out those who'd resisted, those who'd been invested in the status quo, as well as those divisive natures pursuing other agendas for their own advantage. The government was a shambles by then, the country on the verge of anarchy. He'd had to reimpose order. For Qarmatians were no different from people anywhere, they craved order above all, above food, above family, above justice, liberty or anything. Besides, who can deny that for many who fight and die in such wars it might be a boon? When a man has little to live for, it can only exalt him to have something to die for.

But the torture, the reign of terror, was another matter. He'd struggled over that option for years beforehand. He'd had to overturn a hundred-and-fifty years of complacency under foreign exploitation and endemic corruption. That could only have been done by building up an awful and inexorable momentum. He'd had to startle the population out of their long sleep of fatalism. And yet, he'd come to realize that in the end torture was a double-edged sword. While it provoked fear, as a method of obtaining intelligence it was next to worthless. The weak would say anything but seldom knew anything, and those who did know would often only mislead or go to their graves without divulging what they knew. Even when used to induce fear, terror generally, and torture in particular, were of dubious value. Besides the paradoxical effect of stiffening resistance, the terrorist is usually seen only as a bloodthirsty barbarian.

So, after some study, he'd come to the conclusion that what he'd needed in order to control his people was to provoke not fear, but shame. Torture, he'd realized, introduced a terrible intimacy between the one who used it and his victim, an intimacy far more binding than any tie of kinship. So that when applied properly and selectively, with pity and cool detachment, the effect on the victim was similar to that of the gaze of the serpent on a bird: the initial fear and hatred were soon overwhelmed by confusion, fascination and ultimately submission. It was as if the victim were suddenly made complicit in his own degradation. And the torturer was then seen not as savage and depraved, so much as a judge of character and a spiritual guide. And afterwards, of course, those victims who survived would be filled with shame.

The point, he'd told himself, was that fear was individual, and certain persons, whether by temperament or lack of imagination, might overcome it. But shame was social, and the shame of any individual resonated through his community. This explained why, historically, so few survivors showed the courage to bear witness against their tormentors afterward—a reluctance compounded by the anticipation that their testimony would fall on deaf ears.

And this was the second point. The reason such testimony fell on deaf ears was because others were ashamed of being reminded of the terrible extremes that abide in our baser natures. Most people with any degree of self-awareness would admit—to themselves, if not to others—a natural weakness for the occasional sadistic impulse, even if only in its more passive form of schadenfreude. And this self-awareness compromised the moral authority of anyone attempting to judge the matter, because what was universal was not thought to be a crime so much as a human failing. This rationalization left the victims somehow responsible for what they had suffered, as if they had brought their troubles upon themselves—by being poor, or weak, or misguided, or merely unlucky—otherwise, goes the thinking, the victims would never have found themselves in such a situation in the first place! ("Luck" in this context being understood, by those who smugly enjoyed the privilege, to be an inherent moral quality or social class into which one was born.)

As a consequence, those later vested with the task of adjudicating guilt in cases of torture would, perforce, tend to balk, and instead try to pass that responsibility on to the accused, hoping that the accused would publicly acknowledge his own culpability and thus let everyone else off the hook. Because in their heart of hearts, the judges, like most other people, would be asking: Why had the victims not put a stop to their torture? If they were not strong enough or clever enough to escape, why, at the very least, had they not killed themselves? Sympathy would be reserved for the dead. But as regards those victims who had survived, their reluctance to kill themselves would become an excuse for others to resent them for a sort of indecency, for not having the consideration to remove themselves from the sight of the community, rather than remain as constant living reminders of the general insensitivity of their fellow human beings. The implication was that if the victim wasn't perverted or masochistic in the first place, then he or she must be a coward, and so deserving of the abuse in any case —for the brave (i.e., the rest of us) would never have put up with such treatment. In fact—the rationalization goes—these victims must somehow have actually invited the abuse upon themselves, indeed, had possibly seduced their tormentors into punishing them. And so, ironically, it would seem to be the torturer who then became the object of sympathy, because he was only guilty of a common "weakness," of being susceptible to seduction, or being drawn into expressing a base, but natural tendency (to abuse others) that we all share. Thus, all the guilt and shame would redound upon the victim.

But shame was a house easily tenanted and jealously possessed. Because, at the end of the day, no one really believed this. For the victims it was an outrageous lie, for the torturer and his judges it was merely a convenient fiction. For the revolutionary leader who had orchestrated all of this, however, it meant that everyone, victim, torturer, and judge, was morally compromised, all were bound up in the conspiracy of shame.

16.

"Tell me something, Amal, did you ever marry?"

He rolls over on his side and wipes the perspiration from his forehead with a bandaged hand. He bruised his hand in that brief attack of claustrophobia in the lab, an embarrassing overreaction to his confinement in the MRI machine. His lip curls in a wry grimace. His mind is beginning to wander, to slip fluidly, imperceptibly between the coulisses of sleep and wakefulness, dream and memory. Fever, he tells himself, just fever.

It was toward the end of the war, he remembers, now, but it comes back to him as vividly as a dream. The soldiers of the QPR were about to take the Capital. And he, in his role as military leader and senior strategist of the Revolution, had come to visit his oldest and dearest friend—a friend who never suspected his connection to the insurgency—but he'd come on a grim errand:

The house was a magnificent mess. Tiled walls and wrought iron railings verging on collapse were temporarily propped up by crude scaffolding and cables hastily strung crisscross all along the dim, unlighted halls. Costly, handmade chandeliers had been shattered, lunettes of tinted glass hung broached in the archways and elaborately carved and painted wall panels leaned, bulging and cracked, precariously out of their framework. The electricity was knocked out, but shafts of sunlight shone down incongruously through gaping holes where unexploded bombs had fallen through the roof and the floors below. Whole suites of rooms, originally intended to be glimpsed as concatenated honeycombed archways, lay a-shambles, blackened and soiled by fire and wrenched out of alignment. It was as if the house had gone mad. Yet amid all this wrecked splendor, one exquisite spiral staircase of imported marble and rare woods and both inner courtyards remained remarkably intact.

"You know something, Amal? You'd have made a very handsome carpenter," Abul-Abbas said wryly, standing back with his arms akimbo and eyeing him speculatively on the ladder. "Personally, I think all that abstract thinking has spoiled your complexion."

Samiel, his mouth full of ten-penny nails with which he was hammering the last stretch of scaffolding together, gave him a mock-cutting glance.

"No, seriously," Abul-Abbas continued, pressing his advantage. "With that baby-face of yours, you must've given those little Parisian girls a fit when you were at the *École Normale Supérieure.* What was your thesis about, anyway?"

Samiel muttered something incomprehensible through his clenched teeth.

"Really! Fascinating. More nails?"

"That'll do for now, I think," Samiel said, giving a final blow with the hammer. He climbed back down the ladder to stand beside Abul-Abbas and cast his eye along the cat's cradle of hemp rope they'd strung up to support the damaged framing in an upstairs chamber. He twitched his nose, pleased to detect, through the musty odors of smoke and plaster dust that permeated the house, a chaste hint of attar, the fragrant essential oil of the damask rose.

"Not bad for a couple of amateurs," he said.

"*Allah karim!*" Abul-Abbas said, ironically, setting his own tools aside. Shaking his head with a grim smile, he added, "Our *allies*, the French. Crazy, isn't it. They're supposed to be bombing the QPR, but they can't seem to find those brutes out there in the desert. Instead, they keep having these 'accidents,' bombing our government installations or strafing our outlying Army posts. Their enthusiasm knows no bounds."

"What do they say when you complain?"

"Oh, they apologize profusely! They blame the lowly, inept pilots for not reading their maps properly and guarantee it won't happen again." He waved a hand in a gesture of dismissal. "They like to rattle the saber and talk of De Gaulle and Napoleon, but frankly, I think they're better at wine and cheese. They just missed killing Fajhadi Douma last week, when they 'accidentally' blew up his Foreign Ministry. He'd left his office only moments before for an early morning meeting with the King, when a French sortie knocked out the whole south wing of the building. No one was hurt that time, fortunately. They don't usually show up for work in that department until midday. But I did find the timing curious. It happened only three days after Douma walked out on a meeting with the French ambassador. Then again, they also did this," he added, dryly, gesturing at the damage to his own house, "so, who knows what they're thinking? It was only my good luck to have been in a meeting at QSIS, at the time. Thanks for the help, by the way," he added, as they started back down stairs. "I'm glad you stopped by. The Lord only knows when these labor strikes will be over and I can get some workmen in here to put the place back together again."

"You were saying, about the French?"

"Only that I thought Lacet—that's the French ambassador—I thought he and I were getting along pretty well. Saddahi refuses to meet with them at all anymore, and Fajhadi Douma's been resorting to foul-mouthed tantrums lately. I've always tried to stay out of the more sordid aspect of our differences."

"Do you know where he is?"

"Who, Douma?"

"Saddahi."

"The King? Why?"

Samiel shrugged. "Just curious. I know you have cousins in Dar el-Nar, and when I heard he'd fled into exile I thought he might've gone there."

Abul-Abbas looked at him curiously. "You have long ears!" he murmured, and then flushed when he realized his thought had escaped his lips, and added, "But your comment is impertinent, Amal!"

Samiel gave a wry smile, "I'm only stating the obvious—"

"King Saddahi has not—I repeat, *has not*—'fled' the country! He's simply gone on a diplomatic trip that had been planned *long* in advance."

Samiel nodded solemnly. "I understand perfectly," he said. "But it's not exactly a state secret—and no reflection on you, of course—that your cousin lacks spine."

"Amal Koraoun el-Mudharrisi! Excuse me! You are talking about the King—and my cousin!"

Samiel stopped and turned to face him. "I apologize, Abul-Abbas," he said with a placating gesture, "I meant no disrespect. But it's true, all the same."

Abul-Abbas stared at him coldly a moment, then his voice grew husky as he said, "Of course it's true. It's horribly true. But it does me no good to hear you, of all people, say it to my face, Amal."

Samiel saw the man he once knew as a handsome young attorney, a rising star in the Qarmatian government and already Minister of Culture, as he was now, aging before his eyes. The forced levity was gone from his voice and the signature lapidary gaze had suddenly turned oblique and clouded over with misgivings.

"Frankly, Amal, I'm worried," he said. "I haven't heard from my secretary, Abdullah Kamal, and he's never been absent without prior notice. I'm probably worrying needlessly—at least, I hope so, but the times are so uncertain. He received word that his father and two brothers have disappeared, and his mother is ill. He left last week to return south to see about her and possibly help her to move in with relatives. They have no phone. He was supposed to be back yesterday morning. I know travel is difficult, now, especially south of the Capital because of all the violence. Abdullah is smart and I'm sure he's taking precautions. Still, I don't know what I'd do without him, I was never fond of keeping organized files, and I've come to rely on Abdullah's memory for everything."

They were standing, now, in a first-floor sitting room, a cozy space, sparely furnished with a banquette along three walls. It had suffered only minor damage. The late afternoon sun flooded the room with light. Samiel went to the window, and looking out into the courtyard, spied the lion fountain, round which he and Abul-Abbas had sat so often in better times enjoying leisurely philosophical conversations over glasses of sweetened mint tea.

"Have you heard from your family?" he said.

Preoccupied, Abul-Abbas sighed before answering. "My father had a stroke a couple of weeks ago which left him partially paralyzed—hopefully, it's only temporary, *inshallah*. The QPR had blown up one of our phosphate mines in the south, and I guess that and the general chaos have put him under great stress. He's in recovery, but the incident helped me to convince him to accompany my wife and children when I decided to send them east to Rabat until things quieted down here. But Fâtima wants to come home. She's been there all of ten days, but she's decided she doesn't like the Moroccans, she thinks they're crude. Well, you know Fâtima. Really, I think she just misses ordering everybody around in her own house."

He paused, then looked at Samiel ironically. "Tell me something, Amal, did you ever marry?"

"It's probably for the best."

"What?"

"That you sent them away."

Neither spoke for a long moment, during which Samiel could feel the other's eyes probing at his back as he continued to gaze out the window at the fountain in the courtyard. On so many evenings, over the years, he and Abul-Abbas had sat on the concrete benches around that fountain and enjoyed their open-ended and serpentine discussions of man and metaphysical uncertainties. He remembered once, when they had been talking about the flagrant cupidity of the local politicians and the capriciousness and gullibility of the electorate, Abul-Abbas had laughed and said, "We Qarmatians dance across the web of our own contradictions like acrobats in the palm of Allah!" Part of their pleasure, Samiel recalled, had been due to their mutual appreciation for the fact that their penchant for such deliberations had seemed special, one might even say antiquarian, in a modern world where everyday political, economic, and social aggravations seemed to leave little time or patience for abstract argument. And all at once, Samiel felt on the verge of tears. Having long ago mastered control over his emotions—or so he'd thought— he couldn't account for this sudden uprush of feeling. He realized he'd been under tremendous pressure in managing the trajectory of the Revolution, but he'd been working on it for so long by this time that he'd thought he was immune to the fatigue of war and its intrigues—and inured to the human tragedies that inevitably accompanied them. But something Abul-Abbas had just said—or, perhaps, the juxtaposition of events: the incipient culmination of his revolutionary efforts, and how that hung upon the decision he was called upon to make here, now, in this room, together with the fountain in the courtyard—how it seemed, in this moment, to represent the cost of all his efforts—all this at once appeared, suddenly, to throw open an inner gate he didn't know he'd been guarding.

"Did I tell you what Hussein Touchent said to me when he left?"

Samiel, stirred from his reverie, turned as though puzzled toward a voice that seemed to be coming to him over a great distance or from some elusive moment out of the past.

"Hussein Touchent, my houseboy..." Abul-Abbas

explained, seeing the vagueness in Samiel's eyes.

His houseboy had suddenly decided to abandon his post to join the Berber rebellion, Abul-Abbas had mentioned earlier. The Berbers in Qarmat had been suppressed for twenty years, ever since Saddahi took the throne. They were now taking advantage of this moment, when the government was besieged by the collapse of the economy and the breakout of violent protests all over the country, and the Army was overwhelmed by the rebellion, to gather their various clans and organize their own political force in the effort to reestablish their rights to speak and educate themselves in their own language.

"…His brother had disappeared the week before," Abul-Abbas was saying now, "and Hussein came to me all gussied up like a Tuareg—complete with indigo *Tagelmust* and *lithâm*, can you imagine?—and his eyes cold and distant, as though we were strangers. I couldn't actually see the foolish smirk that must've been lurking, hidden there, beneath the veil, but it shone in his eyes. He told me he could no longer work for me because he could no longer believe in what I stood for—whatever he thought that was. '*Allahu akbar!*' he said, raising his voice—raising his voice to *me!*—'I must now bend to Allah's will! I am called to join my brothers in the resurrection of the great Almoravid Dynasty,' he said. 'We will bind up again what the infidels have sundered! I must follow the truth!' My *houseboy!* Can you imagine? He was a nine-year-old illiterate orphan when I took him in. I taught him to read and write. Now, he's eighteen and talking to me about truth! I asked him, 'What makes you think you know the truth?' He said, 'We do not know the truth. We do not seek the truth. We *are* the truth. As the wind brings heat in its time, the time has brought *us!*' Very poetic, eh? But he said it without irony, and I found his tone a bit chilling."

Samiel looked preoccupied and while his gaze rested on Abul-Abbas, it was as if he were looking beyond him toward something in his mind's eye.

Abul-Abbas shifted his position, and Samiel saw a curious expression pass briefly over his face, as though his friend were experiencing the momentary absurdity of feeling uneasy in his own house.

Then, apparently recovering his composure, Abul-Abbas said, "But maybe Hussein Touchent was only caught up in the spirit of the times, after all. It seems to be a time when all sorts of fanatics have suddenly found truth. The country is overrun with what I remember you, quoting Jacob Burckhardt, once called 'Terrible Simplifiers.' It's everywhere you look. I imagine it must be the same even in that quiet little village where you are, in Mudharris? The Salafis are cursing the Shi'a in the streets, throwing Molotov cocktails into their funeral processions—it's rumored that they were the ones who burned down the *Qubbah*, here, last week, did you know about that? I'm sorry, of course you knew. Everybody knows. And these ad hoc mobs, calling themselves the *Umma Mujahedine* or the *Qarmatian Jamâ'ah el-Jihâd*, or whatnot, are vandalizing government buildings and power stations all over the country and chanting slogans out of context from the *Qur'an* that they don't begin to understand. But it's likely they're being instigated by the QPR, too. Well, the citizen protests, at least, I can see. The economy is in dire straights and we've had to cut off the wheat dole, so, yes, many are starving. I know they're starving. But what can we do about it? The drought has killed off the grain, the treasury's empty, and our credit is nil!

"But the QPR!" he continued. "Have you heard the latest? They've actually taken to taunting us! They've been posting notices in town halls and railway stations warning in advance of their impending attacks. At the meeting in the Intelligence Serivice Marwan Badat actually cursed out General Karim el-Akhmeinie in my presence, infuriated that the Army seems incapable of stopping the QPR even when they're told ahead of time what they're going to do. And, of course, the General was railing back at him, claiming that he had his hands full trying to deploy army units to take over responsibility for local disturbances all over the country on short notice because the commandant of the national con-stabulary had just been assassinated by the QPR, and what was worse, he was getting no help from the 'dimwitted ass-holes'—you'll pardon my expression—at QSIS, who apparently couldn't tell a camel from a canard and couldn't seem to give him better intelligence! This is what a high-level strategy meeting between the General of the Army and the Deputy Commander of Intelligence has come to! It wasn't a meeting, it was a brawl! Meanwhile, Dar el-Nar, apparently having heard of the possible development of our oil reserves, has been massing troops along the border, but nobody seemed to want to deal with that issue. I said to myself, *Allah karim,* thank God for the French, at least! For all their ineptitude, I don't know how we'd survive without them."

He paused, and after a moment, shook his head and murmured, "My God, my God, what are they doing to my country! I keep asking myself, what could we have done to prevent this? If we'd known…but known what? How could anybody know it would come to this!"

"How could you *not* know."

Abul-Abbas looked at him askance.

"I wasn't being flippant," Samiel said. "The signs were all there."

"What signs? What are you talking about?"

Samiel turned away a moment, then turned back, and said, "Abul-Abbas, what is this country you hold so dear? No, seriously, think!" he added gently, seeing a new wariness appear in the other's eyes. "Qarmat," he continued, "a country we both love—but what has it become? A kingdom without a king: our King has fled. A nation on the sea without access to its own ports because the French, under the guise of protecting our mutual interests, have set up a de facto blockade. Our treasury has no funds because our ministers are corrupt. We have a government impotent to govern. We have an army that can't defend its own garrisons. We're supposed to be an independent state, but we're dependent upon, exploited by, and subservient to a foreign power—one that keeps us divided and weak by manipulating our tribal and religious differences to keep us at each other's throats! So what is Qarmat now, but a broken state? And with all due respect, it's obvious King Saddahi doesn't have whatever it takes to put it back together!"

Abul-Abbas gaped at him. "My God, Amal, you sound like those revolutionaries, now!"

"Never mind that. Just think. It's been over twenty years since you and I fought to unite the country—under the great Emir Mohamed Boualem el-Roweed. It was for *him* we fought, remember? Not for his son, not for Saddahi! We just didn't anticipate that when the old Emir passed on he'd deputize his feckless eldest son to succeed him—it was the only serious mistake I'd known the old man to make. But Saddahi is old now too—in mind, if not in fact—and his spirit is shrinking and beginning to show its true colors. This upheaval was inevitable, you must know that. The population's anger and resentment were there all the time, just simmering under the lid held down by the likes of Yassim Nasser; Sheikh Nizar ben Khalid Acheron, your father; Fajhadi Douma; el-Akhmeinie, and the others. But look what's become of them: Douma's turned into a flabby, complacent, corrupt voluptuary. El-Akhmeinie has grown dull and timid. Your father's old and ill. Nasser is dead and the others are fading into irrelevance!

"So, I ask you again: What is this country of Qarmat you say you love? And who should rule it? *Think! Whom would you have rule it?*"

Abul-Abbas, astonished, took a step forward, challenging him. "Are you suggesting the QPR is the answer? Are you mad? Amal Koraoun, I begin to wonder if I know you at all, after all these years! The QPR are like madmen! The horror stories we hear! A woman clutched at me in the street only yesterday to tell me how they'd barged into her house in the middle of the night to beat and tie up her husband and son, and then forced them to watch as they raped her and her daughters and slashed their throats, before dragging the men off in a truck. She showed me the gash on her own throat, it was still bleeding under the stiches. It was only a miracle she survived."

He paused with a look of horror on his face, and Samiel imagined him thinking of the stories he'd been hearing that he'd found almost too brutal to believe. But the country was full of such stories now. Samiel had heard them too. Renegade bands of rebels had been hacking their way through the populations of several villages with swords and machetes, then forcing the survivors into their own houses and setting fire to them. Samiel had punished several such renegades when he'd been able to apprehend them, but the times had caught fire and such behavior was difficult to control.

After a moment Abul-Abbas, following his own thought, said, "No wonder they call them *el-Jaysh Damm.* They are, indeed, a bloody army! We're hearing about torture and killing on a scale such as we've never known here. So many disappeared, so many families torn apart! It's much, much worse than the last time, those years of chaos and civil wars that preceded the unification under King Boualem. Yes, there was bloodshed then, of course, but not like this. And not torture! I tell you, they're madmen! I don't know what drives them. I lie in bed tossing and turning all night, trying to understand! I try to think of reasons—even bizarre, wrong-headed reasons—but I can't imagine any *excuse!* And this one they call 'Samiel,' from what they say, he must think he's the next Grand Mahdi!"

"You've been under a strain, I understand."

"Those poor souls!" Abul-Abbas continued. "I can't help thinking about the victims, it brings tears to my eyes. And I keep telling myself, there but for the grace of God go I!"

"God gave Moses twelve commandments," Samiel said, "do you remember the story, Abul-Abbas? But the Devil gave him only one: 'Never say *I!*'"

"What's that supposed to mean!" Abul-Abbas demanded, looking up sharply.

"As for those poor souls you spoke of," Samiel continued, as though ignoring the question, "'so much the less should they be wept for, the more they are wept over!'"

"What?" Abul-Abbas said, taken aback.

And again Samiel, who knew this gentle man so well, could imagine the turmoil in his mind. Abul-Abbas was trying to understand him, wondering whether he was being facetious. Samiel saw Abul-Abbas studying him, looking into eyes that he no doubt suddenly found opaque, disconcertingly calm in an impassive face. The quotation from Augustine of Hippo would probably seem to him rude under the circumstances. And then he saw Abul-Abbas seized with an involuntary shiver, and Samiel guessed that his friend had recalled something else Augustine had written at the time of the Roman massacre of 7,000 innocents at Thessalonica:

"…Many perished in different terrible ways. If one has to lament this, then one should remember that it is the destiny of all who were born to this life. As far as I know, not one man died who wouldn't have had to die sometime anyway…. What the weak and frightened sense of the flesh shrinks away from is one thing, and what the carefully considered reasoning of the mind finds convincing is another!"

Samiel saw Abul-Abbas looking back at him bitterly now, as though thinking that his oldest friend had suddenly become an unwelcome stranger in his house.

Just then, the telephone rang.

Abul-Abbas ignored it. He continued to stare at Samiel with growing alarm. But as it kept ringing, he turned and realized it was the red phone, the secure government line. He looked back at Samiel, who nodded and stepped discretely out into the hall.

And as Abul-Abbas answered the call, Samiel quietly picked up the extension.

"Hello?"

"Abul-Abbas?"

"*Oui, M. l'Ambassadeur, c'est moi,*" Abul-Abbas replied, responding in French, on hearing the accent at the other end.

"*C'est Lacet…. Ah, je suis désolé, mon ami, mais il fait mauvaise!*"

The French were pulling out. That was what Samiel needed to know. The QPR could easily overrun the remaining Qarmatian Army forces and proceed to take the Capital. Qarmat would be freed at last of its colonial yoke! And there was no need to put Abul-Abbas through an interrogation. No need. Samiel put the receiver down carefully beside the telephone, purposely leaving it to be found off the hook. His friend would understand and flee before some rogue band of QPR rebels, drunk with the exhilaration of victory and bloodshed, came after him. With a sigh of relief, he left the house.

17.

One Sunday morning, as Samiel's trial was entering its third year, Abul-Abbas sat with his head in his hands staring, unseeing, at the food Fâtima had placed before him, a platter of figs, black olives, and dates pitted and stuffed with almonds, a dish of walnuts and pistachios, a small bowl of cooked semolina, and a wedge of khobz, the traditional flatbread which he normally loved. They were all favorites of his, in fact—except for the semolina, of course, which Fâtima insisted on boiling bland, without salt, pepper or other spice, following his doctor's orders. He wasn't really supposed to have the nuts, either, which were said to aggravate his diverticulitis, nor much fruit, because he was diabetic. But he'd talked the doctor into allowing him the figs, at least, because of their high fiber content—and because he grew the sweetest Lob Injir figs outside of Smyrna in his own orchard. But Fâtima was being particularly indulgent with him this morning. He seldom complained, but when he realized, on waking, that Samiel's trial was approaching its inevitable conclusion, the weight of it suddenly oppressed him terribly, and he couldn't hide it from her. Despite her kindnesses, however, and her gentle prodding as they sat down to breakfast, he hadn't really wanted to talk about it, and he hadn't been able to bring himself to eat anything. Finally, with a warm hug and parting words of encouragement, she'd left him alone to poke absently among the figs and brood over how he'd allowed himself to get into such a fix.

We're finally coming to the end of it, he was thinking. The evidence has all been entered and documented, the witnesses deposed, and tomorrow the final arguments will begin. And yet so many questions were still unanswered! Had he not been fettered by the restrictions imposed by the World Court, he would have had the prosecution delve much deeper—and broader. There would have been many more witnesses, not only the survivors, but also officials of the government at the time, many of whom are still alive and certain of whom, he was convinced, were hardly as innocent as they liked to pretend—not least Marwan Badat himself! The Revolution couldn't have happened—even allowing for the ingenious and devious manipulations of one such as Samiel—it couldn't have happened without some complicity on the part of those in power at the time.

But after the final arguments, it will be his turn to pronounce judgment. But how can he possibly do that— knowing Samiel as he has, resenting him as he does—and convinced there is so much more to be discovered that he was not at liberty to pursue?

And what if he'd kept to his resolve and recused himself? There would've been no trial at all! But there had to be some accounting! Such heinous crimes cannot be simply ignored anymore, not in the world we live in now, with a World Court and international agreements on the criminality of atrocities.

He'd been over this again and again in his mind, and he still didn't know! He was still asking himself the same question: Is a sham-trial better than none at all? Was he wrong to let himself be snookered into it that evening, three-and-a-half years ago, when Badat invited them to supper…?

"*Salaam aleikem, Abul-Abbas!*" the Prime Minister had bellowed, with exaggerated heartiness, as he greeted them at the door, "*Salaam aleikem, Fâtima!*"

"*Aleikem salaam!*" they'd replied.

"It's so good, as always, to see you!" Badat had added, stepping back to admit them. "I'd be so honored, if you would be kind enough to enter my poor, little house!"

Poor, indeed! Abul-Abbas had thought to himself, ironically, as he and Fâtima were ushered inside. In the twenty-five years that had passed since the fall of the Revolution and the return of the monarchy, Marwan Fareed Badat had done very well for himself.

In the event, Badat and the beautiful Lilah, the most beautiful of his three wives, had had their servants stand back and had come out to welcome them personally. Lilah and Fâtima were old friends, and Badat embraced Abul-Abbas with a great show of affection. As they entered the house, the judge couldn't help noticing that it was redolent of the same fragrance of the damask rose with which Fâtima scented their own house—although Fâtima's application, he noted mentally, was more subtle. He and Badat were about the same age, but Badat had put on a great deal of weight over the years. He'd always had a tendency to be stout and a bit ostentatious, but he'd grown, both in girth and attire, positively opulent. His bushy eyebrows and goatee, once prominent features in an otherwise undistinguished visage, now seemed comically diminished, stuck like smudges on the great orb of his face. He was largely bald, but his remaining fringe of hair, brushed back in keeping with the elegant Western suits he wore when out and about on his daily rounds as Prime Minister, was pomaded and teased out, now, making it seem as if he was being closely shadowed by a quizzical gray cloud. His kaftan, an exquisitely wrought teal-green silk robe in the old fashion, flowing in bountiful folds to the floor, was embroidered with gold and azure threads and beaded with pearls, which glinted wickedly from under the gold chain and badge of office he wore draped across his chest. The badge and chain, normally reserved for ceremonial occasions, seemed a bit of overkill, Abul-Abbas thought. Badat had clearly donned them that evening to impress somebody. Abul-Abbas, however, wearing a plain, white cotton gandoura, was merely forewarned, wondering what the ostentation might imply on this occasion. Badat had extended the invitation to dinner in such a manner as to lead him to think it was to be a cozy reunion among a small group of old friends, but as it turned out he and Fâtima were to be the only guests.

"After too many years absence, I'm honored by your presence, Abul-Abbas! Welcome to my humble home." Badat said, bowing with all the humility of a hothouse gardenia.

"God is great," Abul-Abbas replied, dryly, "and great is His mercy to each of us, in His way."

Lilah led Fâtima back into the *harîm* to catch up, while the judge followed the Prime Minister, who led him to a private sitting room for a preliminary tête-a-tête. Badat took a circuitous route on purpose, apparently, to give Abul-Abbas an opportunity to admire some of the elaborate renovations that had been made to the house since he'd seen it last. Several spacious rooms had been added, including a formal reception room with elaborate mosaics and a high ceiling bracketed by arches festooned with a *mocárabe* motif. The complex array of vertical prisms, like stalactites, that formed the motif would have been more appropriate in a grand mosque. There was also a new staircase leading up to two new floors rising above the original three. Then, there were the servants. They seemed to be in every corner, hovering conspicuously like flowers sconced in the shadows.

"And how are your sons and grandson?" Badat said, frowning as he reached absently into a nonexistent inner breast pocket for his cigarettes, only to remember that he wasn't wearing a suit. When they reached the sitting room, a ceramic teapot was already steaming on a trivet. As they settled on the cushioned banquette, there was a low rattling sound. "*Allahu akbar!*—excuse me," Badat murmured, without explanation, and quickly adjusted his kaftan, which rustled softly with a sound like parchment, as if the silk was still new and a little stiff. Immediately he was seated, a servant rushed up to place a beautifully wrought silver-filigreed cigarette case on the cushion beside him. The PM opened the case and offered him a cigarette, before taking one for himself. Abul-Abbas declined, having finally given up the habit on doctor's orders. As they exchanged a few pleasantries, Badat rose and poured them tea.

"You look wonderful, my dear boy, half your age!" he said. "*Alhamdu l'illah*, I don't know how you manage it— just look at what the years have done to me, eh?"

"*Allah karim!*" Abul-Abbas dutifully replied ("God is merciful!") But he knew the PM's comments were sheer flattery, because Badat must have noticed how pale and thin he was and must have been aware that he had only recently come out of hospital again. Badat, meanwhile, obviously took pleasure in executing the tea-pouring ceremony with panache, pivoting from one glass to the other and pouring from waist-height, so that the hot, green liquid, suffused with mint, streamed from the long, graceful neck of the teapot in a coherent arc, leaving it bubbling expertly in the tall, narrow-necked glasses resting on the floor tiles. He also noticed that Badat, unlike him, stricken as he was with Parkinson's, was still light on his feet.

"How's the family?" Badat asked again, apparently having forgotten the question had already been asked and answered.

"Very well, thank you, *Allah karim*," Abul-Abbas said, "And yours, equally well, I hope?"

"Magnificent, *Allahu akbar!*" Badat said, adding, "but hardly so distinguished as yours, I dare say! *Mashà allah*, your sons have grown up to be formidable citizens of the community. You must be very proud of them."

Abul-Abbas smiled politely, "Allah's bounty is beyond the questioning of one so humble as myself."

"And so it is for us all!" Badat replied solemnly, but then, with a mischievous wink, he added, "But, as I'm sure you know, Allah has unfortunately only blessed me with five useless girls!" He gave a disarming laugh, and after a brief pause said, "But I'm looking forward to offering your grandson, Yaqub, a place on my staff the very moment he graduates." Badat had spoken lightly, but Abul-Abbas, knowing him as well as he did, perceived it was only the hint of a subject that would likely be brought up again later in the evening. Yaqub had just started his last year at King Boualem University, and in addition to setting out on a career, Abul-Abbas assumed that Badat was implying that the boy would also be looking to start a family.

As the conversation moved on to the current drought and the news of the day, Badat suddenly said, "Have you heard about this fellow, Cloze?"

"Who?"

"Cloze, Cloze," Badat said, repeating the name.

Abul-Abbas shook his head, "The name doesn't—"

"Cloze. I think his name is Paul Cloze. A very curious man," Badat said, absently offering the cigarette case again. Abul-Abbas patiently waved it away, and as Badat lit up, he went on to describe a tall, gray-haired, austere stranger who'd recently appeared in Parliament as a special envoy with plenipotentiary powers commissioned by the United Nations to assist the government in its preparations to enter the U.N.'s hallowed circle of trading partners. "I don't know where he's from," Badat said, petulantly. "He looks like just another one of these self-important Western bureaucratic assholes—standing there smoking like a chimney and talking down to you, you know, in sunglasses that he never seems to take off—total lack of courtesy—and looking like somebody's notion of a flimflam man! Except he seems intelligent. He speaks Arabic fluently too—which is also unusual for them—but he has some kind of accent I can't place."

He'd risen to refill their tea glasses, and he paused to lean over and add, with a salacious grin and a familiar tap on Abul-Abbas's knee, "He does, however, have at least *one* readily identifiable *taste!* Within a fortnight of his appearance, Ruhani…hee-hee!" (He was referring to Ahmed Ruhani, current Minister of the Interior and a mutual acquaintance with scandalous habits known for frequenting the whorehouses of the casbah.) "Ruhani said he nearly tripped over him in an orgy at A Thousand-And-One Nights—Cloze was flat on his back, with that fat cow, Fâtima, sitting with her bare arse on his face and jerking him off! Hee-hee-hee!" (Badat, shaking with laughter, emitted a sound from behind him like a loud bark. He immediately flung one hand back irritably, as if to dismiss the intrusion, and consequently spilled the tea, which splashed over the floor and on the hem of Abul-Abbas's gandoura.) "—Oh my God, I'm so sorry, my dear Abul-Abbas, so terribly, inexcusably careless!"

A servant rushed forward to mop up the spill with a silk cloth, as Abul-Abbas became aware of a sudden, rancid tinge to the air. He glanced away, in stony silence, toward a decorative arrangement in the corner, where tall, delicate spikes of crimson amaranths were displayed in a sea-green vase. Fâtima was a common name of course, but his wife had unfortunately also put on weight in recent years. Badat, meanwhile, quickly changed the subject, launching into a litany of the difficulties of governing such a country at such a time, but Abul-Abbas, now listening for a hint of the Prime Minister's real purpose in inviting him, was rescued from his dull preoccupation by the arrival of a servant to announce dinner. As they rose to be ushered into the dining room, they were joined by the women, who emerged from behind the jali screen followed by servants bringing a delicious array of spicy *maz-za.*

Lilah, striking in a diaphanous, rose-colored kaftan, smiled and came up to give the judge another warm embrace of welcome. "Fâtima has just been telling me you've been a bad boy, Abul-Abbas! You don't take your medicine!"

He grinned, embarrassed, and tried to wave it away. He

actually did take the Levodopa, at least—although erratically, because it made him nauseous, and the dopamine inhibiter that was supposed to alleviate that side-effect gave him headaches.

"No, really!" she insisted, as they took their places in the dining room, "You must take your medicine! We're very fond of you, and we don't want anything to happen to you, you hear? Promise you'll take it?"

He smiled and nodded. It was hard to refuse Lilah anything. Her name was Dalilah, but her old friends called her by her pet name, Lilah, and she was just as lovely as he remembered. He let his eye linger on Lilah as she and Fâtima returned to the kitchen. Age hadn't affected her straight, graceful posture nor spoiled her lithe figure. Lilah's luxuriant hair was swept up in a bun beneath her veil and he'd noticed, when she'd embraced him, that it was scented with almond oil. His own beloved Fâtima, sweet and demur in a tasteful blue kaftan, had the more beautiful eyes, but advancing age had etched its lines across her features. He loved Fâtima, but it gave him a special pleasure to see that Badat's rise to power hadn't spoiled Lilah's youthful, unaffected charm. He himself was a bent old man now, but he had once been tall and slender, and as a young man some had even considered him handsome. He'd always been shy, however, and rather conservative in his habits—despite an inherited weakness for gourmet cooking. He pondered, for an instant, the vicissitudes of fate: how it was that Marwan Badat, notorious in youth for being a feckless lothario, had risen so high, while he, the eldest son of a wealthy mining entrepreneur, had turned away from the ostentatious life and a possibly large role in international trade for which his father had been grooming him. But I have no regrets, he mused, I've done well enough as a jurist and I've loved every moment in the Court—*and* I've kept my good name.

But then he caught himself and shifted to lighter thoughts and the gustatory gratifications to come. Lilah was still known as one of the best cooks in the Capital.

And, indeed, it proved a cozy, but sumptuous repast. No doubt at Badat's prompting, Lilah had prepared some of his favorite dishes, beginning with the traditional *harira*, for which she was justly famous; khobz, and then a seafood pastilla. This was followed by a *kefta,* in which the meat balls, made of minced ground beef, chicken, and lamb, were mixed with an unusual and delicious assortment of spices of her own devising; *chakchuka,* a grilled tomato and green pepper salad, and a fragrant, steaming couscous with spiced sardines. Abul-Abbas hadn't had the opportunity to relish such a rich feast for years, as his beloved Fâtima watched his diet like a hawk and prepared his food with her own hands. Loyal and devoted as she was, Fâtima, he reflected glumly, would keep him alive forever if she could—if dietary boredom didn't kill him first!

The ladies remained discreet, gossiping quietly between themselves, while he and Badat chatted of "more worldly" matters. The Prime Minister, of course, being naturally talkative, dominated the conversation. At one point, while discussing the fragility of the Qarmatian economy, Badat, scooping up a handful of walnuts and pistachios to sprinkle over his couscous, said, "I really feel sorry for the ambitious young men coming out of university now. There're so few opportunities for them to look forward to. Growth is at a standstill—*Allahu akbar!*—excuse me!" (He'd emitted that low rattling sound again, but continued without pause), "—and the old folks are not retiring. The pension funds are bankrupt and nobody wants to give up his paycheck. By the way, did I mention that I might have a position for Yaqub when he graduates?"

"As a matter of fact, you did, yes," Abul-Abbas said. "That would be very generous of you, Marwan." But he spoke absently, his attention drawn to the *harissa,* which a servant had just brought out and at which his nose was wrinkling instinctively with pleasure as he caught the first searing whiff of it. One normally added the fiery chili, onion, and garlic sauce in moderation to the bowl with which one was presented, and this was especially true with Lilah's *harissa,* because she made it hot enough to singe the palate. However, Abul-Abbas loved it very spicy, and he made a point of avoiding Fâtima's eyes—and ignoring her throat-clearing— as he reached out to heap the hot spices on. Meanwhile, they'd long since graduated from mint tea to wine, a fine Syrah *blanc* to wash down the spiced fish, and a merlot from Meknes to accompany the *kefta.* As practicing Muslims, they shouldn't have been drinking wine, of course. But Badat had begged his guests' indulgence upon this special occasion, and they were now at work on a third bottle of superb *les Coteaux de l'Hercules Premier Cru rouge* from Badat's own vineyard.

"He's studying economics, isn't he?"

"Who, Yaqub?"

"Yaqub, yes! Your grandson, Youssef's son. That's his name, isn't it, Yaqub?" he added, glancing inquiringly toward Fâtima.

"Ah, yes," Abul-Abbas said. "Yes, economics. And law. But he's just toying with them. He's a brilliant student—if

Allah will forgive me saying so—but he's still undecided about what he wants to do with his life. I'm confident he'll settle down soon enough," he said, adding, with his eyes raised to heaven ironically, "*inshallah!*"

"*Inshallah!*" Badat nodded, in earnest agreement, adding, "The youth of today lack the seriousness of our generation." Then he laughed, "Yes, but you know," he added, speaking around the roll of stuffed pancake he was munching on, "there's one thing that your Yaqub does seem to be quite serious about already!"

"Oh?"

"You seem surprised. He hasn't told you?"

Abul-Abbas shook his head, no.

Badat paused to wink at the women, then looked at him shrewdly, "Yaqub hasn't mentioned Aisha to you, eh?"

"Aisha?"

"Aisha, my baby, my youngest daughter. He hasn't mentioned her to you?"

Abul-Abbas shook his head again, and exchanging a look with Fâtima, who seemed equally in the dark, said, "No."

Badat laughed and rocked his head from side to side, "I tell you, these children, nowadays! You know—*wehish, wehish!*—" ("beastly, beastly," he added, using a common term to dispel the evil eye when one is about to express a compliment.) "Aisha's very pretty, a very pretty girl, if I may be permitted to say so myself. And a good little housekeeper. Her mother's brought her up quite well. But I admit, she's not so young anymore, fourteen—but *only* fourteen! But I mean she's already a little saucy. But absolutely honest, you know—which is good, eh?—but she just has trouble keeping her frank opinions to herself, sometimes." He shrugged, and added, "A lot of young fellows still aren't used to that from girls. But the girls, they're growing up faster than the boys these days, eh? But fourteen, I mean, she's still really a child—and your Yaqub doesn't seem to mind that at all! When he comes to visit, I have to admonish Aisha sometimes for the things she says. But Yaqub just laughs! A fine boy, your Yaqub!"

Abul-Abbas pursed his lips thoughtfully. "Has he…has Yaqub approached you?"

But Badat didn't answer, he merely smiled mischievously all around and shook his jowls at him, and then changed the subject.

After a little while, with the pungent odor of *merguez* lingering in the air, just as Abul-Abbas, savoring the aftertaste of the grilled, ground lamb sausage, spiced with sumac, fennel, and garlic, sat back happily patting his stomach and thinking he'd finally discovered what Badat was up to—suggesting a betrothal between Yaqub, and Aisha—Badat went off on a different tack altogether, speculating about Qarmat's future role in the world. Abul-Abbas, perhaps more affected by the wine and rich food than he cared to admit, had some trouble trying to follow him. Besides, Lilah, who'd run back to the kitchen briefly on some errand while a servant whisked away the empty dishes, had just returned in a fresh, alluring, low-cut *qamis* with silver trim, and ushering in a servant bearing a pot of excellent coffee and a round of desserts. Unobtrusively, Lilah had changed clothes with every course. Abul-Abbas, exchanging a discreet glance with Fâtima, had wondered briefly why Lilah had found it necessary to go and return again to direct each serving of the meal, but he was so pleased at each appearance that he gave it no further thought—and then determined to pay no further attention, as he realized Fâtima was beginning to notice his glances. Spread before him then were dates; apricots and oranges seasoned with cinnamon; nougats; baklava, and *kaab el ghzal* (gazelle's horns), a pastry stuffed with almond paste and topped with sugar. But he'd turned his attention to what, for him, was the crown of the evening, his favorite dessert, *b'stilla*. Over Fâtima's objections, he'd wrapped his long, thin fingers around the warm *ourqa* dough pastries and sunk his teeth rapturously into the filling of diced and blended quail, chicken and over-cooked eggs poached in a mild lemon sauce until his tongue swam in the viscous mix and his head reeled in sensuous delectation.

The dinner throughout had been utterly delicious and exquisitely presented. He couldn't help being flattered by the attention. All the same, despite the food, the wine, and Lilah's seductive appearances, as the evening progressed he'd gathered that Badat had been setting him up for something. He'd known Badat all their lives and thought he could read him like a book. But one of the things he also knew about Badat was that he was wily—not subtle, but devious. The feint toward a possible betrothal between Yaqub and Aisha was clever, but it seemed there was something else on the Prime Minister's mind. He had all the power and prestige he wanted. And he was probably almost as well off as Abul-Abbas was, now—although Abul-Abbas's fortune was inherited, while Badat had had to earn his own—exactly how he'd done that was another question. But the one thing they both knew Badat did not have, and did desperately crave, was respectability. Having his daughter marry Yaqub would provide a claim to an elite, old nobility—and also bring a member of the Supreme Court into his family circle, and that was well worth scheming for. But, as he discovered later that evening, it was more complicated than that. Badat, in his egotism, seemed to be trying to turn the tables, offering his daughter to Yaqub as a way of granting the family of Abul-Abbas future favor with the government—something Abul-Abbas was confident his family and descendants could do well enough without. Badat had nevertheless assumed, apparently, that such an offer of favor could tempt Abul-Abbas to undertake something much more significant—but what that was had yet to be revealed.

After dinner, the women retired to the *harîm* and he and Badat strolled arm-in-arm along the cloister surrounding the inner courtyard. Abul-Abbas remembered it being previously a small, bare concrete square. It had been enlarged, he noticed, and tiled and set off by a great enameled fountain in the center. It was now more like a proper *sahn* and separated the main house from the *harîm*, which had been removed to a recently added wing. The grand effect was somewhat spoiled, however, by a caustic stench that drifted over the walls from time to time, as the wind shifted, an unfortunate effect of the tanning pits in the leather factory located to the south of the city. That, Abul-Abbas thought, was probably another reason for Lilah's heavy-handed use of perfume in the house. Meanwhile, the Prime Minister, a fine host, however crude he might seem otherwise on occasion, had waited until they'd finished the last course and were taking their private stroll along the cloister, before raising the real subject of the meeting.

"I think its time, now, don't you?" Badat was saying. "I think it's necessary that we bring him to account." Acting in his official capacity as head of government, but unofficially, Abul-Abbas realized, as the minion of France and the U.N., Badat had finally come to the point. He was proposing to put Amal el-Mudharrisi, alias Samiel, once head of the Qarmatian People's Republic, on trial for genocide and crimes against humanity perpetrated over a quarter-century earlier. "The country needs to have the whole business finally put to rest, eh?"

"Why now?"

Badat shrugged, "They need a *dhabîhah*," he said, speaking with casual irony. "France, Germany, America, the United Nations, they need somebody to sacrifice as a sign of the purity of our intentions! Times have changed, you see. I suppose to a certain extent France still hasn't forgiven us, they still think of us as a rebellious colony. But we've proven our ability to endure independently, and…" he hesitated and gave him a shrewd look, before continuing. "I'm going to trust you and tell you something, Abul-Abbas—but you must promise me not to breathe a word of it to anyone, not to Fâtima, not to your sons, absolutely no one! It's top state secret! Do I have your word?"

Abul-Abbas allowed him a small smile and said, "I'm flattered, Marwan, of course. But really, there's no need for me to be privy to state secrets."

"Not generally, of course," Badat said, with a ministerial clearing of his throat. "However, I make an exception in this case, as it bears on the matter at hand. It will be public knowledge within a few weeks anyway, but we have an interest in keeping it quiet for now."

Abul-Abbas nodded sagely and gestured for him to continue.

"You're probably aware that for the last several months there've been offshore platforms digging exploratory wells in the deep waters off the Qarmatian coast." He paused for an affirmative nod from Abul-Abbas before going on. "Well, it's ExxonMobil and Nexen Petroleum, and they've just sent us word that of seven holes bored, *only one* came up dry! They estimate one of the fields alone at 1.4 billion barrels!"

Abul-Abbas gave him an incredulous look. "That's extraordinary," he said, "but do we know if it's real? Remember what happened the last time, when they discovered the oil sands in the south."

(That discovery had proven a great disappointment, Abul-Abbas recalled. Oil prices were skyrocketing at the time, but the Anglo-Persian Oil Company and Royal Dutch Shell, who'd made the find, decided soon after, when prices had dropped, that the field wouldn't be worth developing. The technology at the time was inadequate to make refining such poor grade oil economical.)

"Forget the oil sands!" Badat said, waving the notion away like an irritating gnat. "This is absolutely real! They have six fields under exploration now, and combining them, they say the reserve may possibly range to more than five billion barrels! At current prices, that's more than fifty billion dollars, American—and this doesn't even take into account the natural gas! My dear Abul-Abbas, do you realize what this means? Tiny little Qarmat has suddenly become a very big dot on the world map!"

Abul-Abbas pursed his lips and shook his head, as if unable to take it all in.

"I'm telling you!" Badat insisted, as if he needed the other's enthusiasm to make the news real to himself. "They said, and I quote, 'This seems to confirm that the seafloor beneath Qarmat's coastal waters contains one of the richest oil and natural gas discoveries in decades. It would be comparable to Angola!' And Angola, as you must know, is second, after Nigeria, in sub-Saharan oil production!"

Abul-Abbas shook his head again, but laughed, this time. "I'm afraid I don't know what to say."

"Say nothing!—but inside, I give you permission to dance for joy!" Badat laughed, then continued, "As I said, in a few weeks it will be public knowledge. The government will announce our intention to build a two-hundred-million-dollar petroleum processing and service center, plus plans for pipelines and other infrastructure. It's a huge investment for Qarmat, of course, but now that we're rich…."

"But what has all this to do with me?"

"Not to worry, my friend," Badat continued, mishearing his question, "ExxonMobil told me they intend to invest over three hundred and fifty million themselves in the venture. These six fields, you understand, are only part of a block of over seven million acres the companies are exploring—can you imagine? Seven holes and only one came up dry!"

"Yes, yes, amazing! But, tell me, Marwan, what has this to do with me?"

"Eh?"

"You said you were telling me all this because it bore on the matter at hand—I assume you mean something you and I are to discuss?"

"Ah. Yes. Of course." Badat paused and rummaged through his pockets for another cigarette. He finally came up with a rumpled pack, offered it to Abul-Abbas, who politely refused again, and lit his own. He drew deeply, then blew the smoke out, as though suddenly lost in thought. He was clearly taking his time, as though considering how best to phrase what he wanted to say. But instead, as he opened his mouth, there was that sound again from behind him, and he said, "*Allahu akbar*—excuse me! It's these damn pills I'm taking!" He sounded exasperated by his own flatulence. "The doctor says my cholesterol is too high. I smoke too much. I'm developing gout, and Merciful-God-only-knows what else. He has me taking Lipitor, Cozaar, Chantix and a positively disgusting concoction called 'cat's whiskers tea!' But the medicine's worse than the disease. I can't sleep, I've practically no appetite, and—you'll pardon me for speaking so plainly—I'm full of gas! I haven't had a good movement for three days! It's absolutely disgusting!" He took a step, then turned back, "*And* now I have high blood pressure!" he added as he walked on.

"How high?"

"What?" He looked around, as though irritated that someone should follow up on what he'd last said—and forgotten—because his mind had moved on.

"Your blood pressure," Abul-Abbas said, in an effort to be solicitous. "How high is it?"

"It's gone up to a *hundred!*" Badat replied, apparently seriously appalled.

"A hundred?"

"Terrifying, isn't it? I tell you, it's horrible getting old!"

"A hundred!" Abul-Abbas repeated, as astonished at the value as he was at Badat's apparent concern about it. "My God, man, you'll live forever, *inshallah!*"

"*Inshallah!* If I don't asphyxiate myself farting first!"

Abul-Abbas, falling in step beside him, was still

wondering about the real reason Badat had wanted to speak with him that evening, and the distinct feeling he had that the Prime Minister was relishing keeping him in suspense only compounded his apprehension.

"So now everybody wants to do business with Qarmat," Badat said, after a moment. "They all want to trade, but they're trying to gain some leverage, you see? ExxonMobil already has a contract on my desk—but they won't execute it until or unless the U.N. gives its blessing! It's an outrage!"

"I don't understand. What's the problem?"

"The problem—damn them all!—is the Revolution!—*our* Revolution, the QPR Revolution! They're using our Revolution as an excuse to wipe the slate!"

"I'm sorry, but I still don't—"

Badat exploded with a string of expletives, then said, "Forgive me, Abul-Abbas, I mean no disrespect. But it's a most aggravating situation! They think our Revolution was too *bloody!*" he added, with exaggerated irony. "I dare say, the colonial period under France was equally bloody—if not more so—but that I suppose they consider *blue* blood, whereas our own revolution spilt *red* blood!—I know, it's ridiculous! Completely hypocritical! They don't say that literally, of course, I'm just giving you an example of their twisted logic. The Revolution happened twenty-five years ago! Ancient history! But they're trying to use it as leverage, you see. The point is, they're fully aware that France bares some guilt for that bloodbath—the way they fucked us over for a hundred and fifty years—we're not slaves, we couldn't be expected to take that colonial shit forever, eh?—but, now, they want *us* to take full responsibility for it—exonerating them in the process! So, in effect, they're telling us, if we come up with a guilty party—specifically, if we crucify Samiel—we'll be free of our sins!" Badat chuckled, pleased with his trope, "A Western solution to a Western conundrum, eh?"

"Except, the sacrifice seems one-sided," Abul-Abbas interjected.

"Of course!" Badat replied, "Or so it would *seem!* But appearances to the contrary, it's not completely unreasonable after all, is it. Samiel is a bad man, he did some terrible things, it's not unreasonable he should have to pay for them."

"As you say, but he should, perhaps, have been called to account for them years ago. If you recall, Marwan, I approached you—the first time—less than two years, I think, after the monarchy had been reconstituted, but you told me the government wasn't yet ready to prosecute the case. You told me that again only two years later, when—"

But the Prime Minister waved it away, "Tsk! Things were still in upheaval, you know that. We were still dealing with Dar el-Nar's hostile incursions in the south. Witnesses would have been too scared to testify, anyway, with the country still in the grip of paranoia. And the treasury was empty! We couldn't have afforded such a trial, even if we'd wanted to."

"Forgive me, Marwan, for pressing the point, but only last fall, when we were discussing the prospect of my retirement and the future of the Court, I brought up the question again, remember? And you said it was too late. 'It's ancient history,' I believe was how you put it then too. 'People have short memories,' you said."

"Did I? I don't recall—but in any case, that's ancient history now too. The oil discovery and the arrival of this

Paul Cloze fellow have changed all that. We're going to have to bring Samiel to trial now. That's going to drag up a lot of unpleasantness, but it can't be helped. Unfortunately," he added, ominously, "there are certain difficulties...."

The way he described it, the trial would be choreographed by a legal team, set up as a special subunit of the International Court of Justice, which would appoint the prosecutors, defending attorneys. and ancillary judges from its roster of international jurists. They required Qarmat to provide a native jurist to serve as Chief Magistrate, while the subunit of The International Court would dictate— Badat didn't use that word, he said "prescribe"—the case for the prosecution and provide "guidelines" for the sitting magistrates.

"Why, then," Abul-Abbas asked, with a frown of distaste, "why doesn't the U.N. try Samiel with their own Chief Magistrate at the new International Criminal Court they've just established in the Hague?"

"Political considerations," Badat replied. "While doing that might suggest impartiality, it would also impugn Qarmat's ability to take responsibility for its own crimes. In the eyes of the world, it would suggest that civilization in our country hasn't evolved sufficiently to allow us to judge the behavior of our own citizens with respect to crimes against humanity, you see," he continued ironically, adding, "Frankly, I simply don't think they know what the fuck they're doing. The Hague Tribunal that's trying Slobodan Milosevic now is a joke! They're so tied up in trying to establish their legal precedents that by the time they get around to putting Milosevic on the stand, they won't remember what it was they wanted to accuse him of. Personally, I think they're hoping to use Samiel's trial, here in Qarmat, as an example for the new Court to follow." Then, with a dry laugh, he added, "Never mind the bullshit—the real point is, if we don't try Samiel they'll use that as an excuse to deny us membership as a trading partner—and there goes ExxonMobil. The only way around that—the only way they've *allowed* us to go around that—is for Samiel to be tried here, in the High Court of Qarmat, with the Chief Magistrate being a native Qarmatian."

So, Abul-Abbas thought to himself, the trial was to be a sham. Except perhaps it could serve as an opportunity for something more. And so, as Badat talked about the pre-scripted show-trial, Abul-Abbas took the opportunity to press for changes. Contrary to the U.N.'s restrictive guidelines, he wanted the prosecutors to have access to unredacted, seques-tered government documents, to be free to question wit-nesses irrespective of their possible self-incrimination, and to have the freedom to pursue any lines of inquiry the Court might deem necessary. He saw the trial as an opportunity not only to explore the warped reasoning of the one who'd conceived and perpetrated those crimes, but to reveal the conditions that had allowed such a demon to gain so much power in the first place. He argued for the mandate to allow for bringing further indictments at the Court's discretion. He passionately wanted to see real justice done, but Badat seemed to stonewall his arguments, cleaving to the Interna-tional Court's restrictions and the government's conservative position of wanting to minimize belated recriminations. They didn't want to open old wounds and stir up unneces-sary trouble in the country. The judge persisted, offering to exploit his reputation for fairness to try and help maintain calm and order while he lent whatever assistance he could to the investigation. He said such a sham-trial would be almost worse than none at all—although, secretly, he wasn't convinced whether that was true, under the circumstances.

Badat referred again to the economic fragility of the country and the need for the trade agreement. "Times have changed," he said, again.

Indeed they have, Abul-Abbas thought, ironically. For as they talked, it became clear to him that colonialism, while continuing in fact, was now to be euphemized under more politically acceptable terms. What had once been a "colony" was now to be a "protectorate," or "favored nation." Essentially, the effect was the same: an arrangement for the exploitation of weaker nations by those more powerful, who were now to be called "trading partners." Except, there *was* a difference, but it was subtle. Responsibility for crime, corruption, violence, and the abuse of law in the colony used to lay at the feet of the colonial power, which, in return for the fruits of its dominant relationship, took on, however arbitrarily, the role of moral guardian for that colony. When colonial powers in the old days felt obliged to defend their reputations for guardianship in the eyes of world opinion they referred to it euphemistically as "the white man's burden." Under the new "free trade" agreements, however, the old colonial powers were now freed of that burden—for the burden of morality had been transferred to the shoulders of their erstwhile colonies, who were suddenly obliged to prove their own moral worth in order to be admitted into the "purified" circle of international commerce....

"...Ah, but they underestimate us, as usual!" Badat was saying. "They think that once we've bowed to their demands, they'll have another go at exploiting us again. But, *Allahu akbar*, I have a surprise for them! Yes, we have orders for goods and services pending from France, and a huge order of construction materials on a freighter on its way to us right now from America—but our ace in the hole is *China!* I mentioned Nexen Petroleum before, that's the other oil company besides ExxonMobil that's been involved with the discoveries—but do you know who Nexen is? Ah, no!" he said, answering his own question, and continued, "Their full name is CNOOC Nexen Petroleum. CNOOC stands for China National Offshore Oil Corporation—Nexen Petroleum, my friend, is a wholly-owned company of the Chinese government! And Nexen has made it clear they have no qualms about our Revolution! I could sign with them tomorrow! But of course," he added, somewhat sheepishly, "one has to be careful dealing with the Chinese, there are side-issues. And it's the same with Russia, too, of course."

"Russia? But—"

"Yes, Russia! Russia's back in the fray! Russia went broke with the collapse of the Soviet Union, of course. But since Yeltsin handed over the reigns to Putin—you might not have been paying attention—they've been on the upswing! Putin put down the Chechen insurgency, and now, high oil prices, together with increasing demand and investments, have driven the Russian economy up for two straight years! And now they want to get into the act. They've put out a feeler to us too! Do you understand what I'm telling you, Abul-Abbas? The good old days of the Cold War are *back*, you see—only it's even better, this time: now, we can cut our pie three ways! And I have every intention of playing one against the other to keep our independence and our trading arrangements advantageous to ourselves, *inshallah!*"

Abul-Abbas listened, but he had reservations. On the one hand, while Badat might be hoping to parlay the recently assessed oil reserves into a bargaining chip to hedge his bets between Asia and the West, he didn't seem to be taking seriously enough the risks involved in playing such a dangerous game with much more powerful partners. As clever as Badat might think he was, Abul-Abbas didn't think he was quite up to that level. Still, he asked himself, why was he beginning to feel a certain personal apprehension with the scenario Badat was sketching? Why was the Prime Minister telling him all this? If it was necessary, at this late date, to bring Samiel to trial, he could understand that Badat might want his advice, as a retiring member of the Court. But why was he beginning to feel uneasy about it? Why did he feel that Badat was encircling him, somehow, drawing him into a situation he would find uncomfortable? As he and the PM continued talking, the anticipated details of Samiel's trial remained a bone of contention between them. They argued late into the night.

Finally, Badat said, "Well, I don't know…maybe they would allow some accommodation." Then, turning to him with a look of feigned surprise, he added, "But if you feel that strongly about it, Abul-Abbas, I suppose you'll want to preside over the case yourself. I'm sure I could probably arrange that for you."

Abul-Abbas laughed inwardly, realizing the Prime Minister had almost snookered him. "Very gracious of you, Marwan," he said, "but that's not possible. I'm afraid I would have to recuse myself from taking any official role in the proceedings whatsoever. My objectivity would obviously be impugned. Don't forget my nearly lifelong previous intimacy with Amal, we were very close friends from our schooldays—or, at least, I'd thought so, until I realized that I'd been one of his imminent targets. Someone else would have to officiate. I can suggest other names, certainly."

But Badat waved it away, "Tsk! Come, come, Abul-Abbas, I thought I'd made it clear that objectivity has nothing to do with this business. We all know Samiel is guilty, we just have to go through the formalities—and the International Court has even made that easy for us, we just have to follow their guidelines."

"The Supreme Court is not a joke, Marwan. As I'm sure you well know, objectivity lies at the heart of justice. I'll give you a list of names you can call upon."

"Bah, don't bother! I suspected you might have some qualms, so I already went through my own list. I submitted the names of all those who might have the necessary credentials, but Cloze and the legal team from the International Court rejected all but four outright as having inadequate standing."

"So?"

"They all declined—the other three, I mean."

"Why?"

"They're afraid."

"Afraid of what?"

"Afraid of their own shadows!" Badat said with a derisive laugh, adding, "Afraid, I suppose, that Samiel or his loyal followers could still retaliate in one way or another. *You're* the only one I thought who might have the courage to do it—at least," he added, in a sly, patronizing tone, "I'd *hoped* so, anyway."

Abul-Abbas brushed the innuendo aside. He wouldn't be so crudely manipulated. He had nothing to prove. They were both aware of his reputation, that he'd been threatened in the past and had simply ignored the threats and conducted all his trials according to law and his conscience. He didn't care to be a martyr and had no pretenses to heroism, but he was a serious jurist and they both knew he would seek justice irrespective of the consequences. "That's not acceptable!" he said, aloud, referring to the refusal of the other judges to serve. "If they are who I think they are—"

"They are."

"Well, then, that's not acceptable! As official members of the Court they are under the obligation to serve!"

"They're not—"

"And even should they refuse," Abul-Abbas continued, "unless they have a valid legal or medical excuse, you, as head of government, have the authority to serve them with a warrant requiring them to—"

"*Merde!*" Badat growled, irritably, interrupting him, "I tried, but somebody must've tipped them off! By the time my warrant reached their doorstep, all three had already left the country on medical emergencies!"

"What!"

"Well, I mean, fuck it," Badat said, "it doesn't matter now! They were only fallbacks, anyway."

"Meaning?"

"Meaning the International Court had already made up its mind who it really wanted to preside at the trial. This Paul Cloze fellow made it very clear who their first choice was! The others were just-in-case."

Abul-Abbas gave him a shrewd look, and waited for

him to continue.

Badat took two steps, then turned to him and said, "They specifically named *you,* Abul-Abbas Acheron el-Ire-wat! The International Court named *you* as the Chief Magistrate to conduct the trial against our old friend, Samiel!"

Abul-Abbas gaped at him, uncomprehending, "But that's not possible! I must recuse myself! It's not possible!" He was just told the trial would essentially be a charade, he wanted no part of it—not to mention the obvious conflict of interest. But as Badat, in his Machiavellian logic, had just made clear, objectivity was not a concern. The future development of Qarmat, he said, was being held hostage by the arbitrary demands of France and the U.N. They wanted the country to purge itself of the onus of crimes against humanity perpetrated by a bloody revolutionary force. So without the trial it seemed the country's current economic crisis and future political stability would be at stake. And while Abul-Abbas realized that under the circumstances the government could serve him with a warrant, he could stand on principle and refuse to comply. That of course would risk threat of arrest and imprisonment which, at his age and medical condition, he knew he might not survive. But he was willing to face that risk. For him the real problem was, as Badat articulated it, if he didn't accept the responsibility of presiding, there would be no trial at all. A quarter-century had already passed. Any remaining first-hand witnesses would not survive much longer. Samiel's crimes were too great to go unpunished and unexamined. This appeared to be the only opportunity for a trial. But under the circumstances—

"Marwan Badat, it's not possible!" he repeated.

But the Prime Minister simply stood there, smug and

silent, gazing back at him with eyes bulging at the irony.

"Marwan, please! You can't possibly mean what you say! But, this is ridiculous! They can't force me to…."

For answer, Badat merely reached under his kaftan, pulled out a large piece of parchment and, stepping close, placed it into the judge's hand. When he tried to pull away, Badat clasped his hand firmly between his own two hands, "I'm sorry, Abul-Abbas. It's out of my hands now."

"You can't be serious! A warrant like this could never stand up in court, I have a long association with the accused!"

Badat nodded his head understandingly from side to side, as if to say, I agree it's a messy business and not strictly *hallal* but we're stuck with it…. However, what he actually said was, "It's not a warrant. Be so kind as to read it. It's a Royal Decree, signed by King Essid himself. It overrides any juridical exception. I'm afraid you're *it!*"

As Abul-Abbas continued to stare at him with narrowing eyes, the Prime Minister threw up his hands and sighed, "*Allah karim!* Please understand, cousin, these are very trying times for all of us."

That had been over three years ago, in August, Abul-Abbas recalled now. The trial was to begin that October, the month of Sha'ban in the Islamic calendar. "Sha'ban," which literally meant "separation," referred to the dry season when the Arab tribes in the olden days would disperse and go their separate ways to wander across the desert wilderness in search of water. He should've known better….

18.

How have things come to such a pass? Samiel is thinking, sleepless in his cell one night between court sessions. Where was the place for sentiment in the life of cool calculation he'd tried to maintain? Tossing and turning through the restless night, Samiel finds himself floundering. Impressions from the past and the present sweep over him in contrary tides, leaving him plunging about in a maddening simultaneity of sensations as he tries to find his way forward again to some clarity. But it's like trying to distinguish reality from mirage, and clarity, once his strength, is eluding him now! Like a drowning man clinging to a straw, his mind veers back to mathematics, to a class of certainties he can define and demonstrate, as for example in that Math Conference he'd taken part in, just before his arrest.…

"…This brings us to the main attraction of our World Conference of Theoretical Mathematics," Marwan Badat, the Prime Minister, was saying. "It gives me great pleasure to have the honor of introducing our featured speaker this afternoon. This great man, scientist, mathematician, and educator, a scholar known for his work on set theory, spectral theory, and commutative algebra, has been the recipient of countless honors conferred by the most prestigious academic institutions of Europe, Asia, and America—including the illustrious Fields Medal, considered comparable to a

Nobel Prize in mathematics, which he was awarded for his breakthrough research on refraction coefficients—but which he refused to accept...."

Samiel, drawn out of some reverie, turned his attention, almost unwillingly, back to the Prime Minister, who was dragging out his preliminary comments. Over the years, he'd managed to become the most powerful politician in Qarmat, but to hear that short, stout man with bushy eyebrows and shifty eyes deliver a public speech was to wonder how he'd done it. His bland, almost soporific demeanor was proverbial. Political cartoons in the local newspapers made fun of his flaccid expression and desultory manner on public occasions. He spoke in a dull monotone and his remarks, which generally amounted to little more than an uninspired rambling among platitudes, gave no hint of the irreverent wit Samiel knew he was capable of in private conversation— or of the wily politician he'd become since Samiel had first known him.

"...But the topic he will speak on today," the Prime Minister continued, "is the subject of groundbreaking research he led over the past several years in the Department of Bio-Information and Cognitive Technologies at the Moscow Institute of Physics and Technology, commonly referred to as 'the MIT of Russia,' and for which he was granted, earlier this year, the coveted Crafoord Prize by the Royal Swedish Academy of Sciences—a prize, I must tell you, that he also—and incomprehensibly—refused to accept! Incomprehensible to the likes of me anyway!

"Anyway," he said again, "our featured speaker's topic, I've been told, is to be 'swarm intelligence!'" Badat paused to smile ironically, but irony didn't suit him and the effort devolved into a vapid smirk before he continued, "Swarm intelligence, I'm told, has something to do with birds and bees—and who knows, maybe people, too! But I will leave it there, and let our honored guest explain it all to you, for he is the expert, and I only his longstanding admirer!"

Samiel, growing impatient, as he was sure everyone else was, with the endless patter, had begun to squirm about in his chair and have second thoughts about his participation in the event. He was on the verge of walking out, when the Prime Minister appeared to be winding up his introduction at last.

"…And now, ladies and gentlemen," the Prime Minister said finally, "without further a-do, let me present to you the famous and universally esteemed Dr. Amal Koraoun el-Mudharrisi!"

The audience applauded at length, as Samiel rose and came forward.

But as he approached the microphone, the Prime Minister suddenly reached down to take a tall package, wrapped in a white silk cloth, from the hands of an assistant in the front row of the audience.

What, Samiel was wondering, was the tricky Marwan Badat up to now?

Badat gave him a mischievous wink, and leaving Samiel standing there awkwardly, turned back to the audience and said, "For my last word, ladies and gentlemen, before putting you in the hands of our esteemed guest, I am going to be a little naughty. I'm going to take a liberty here—something our guest's deep and unaffected humility would probably disapprove—but I purposely didn't give him any warning about it!"

He showed a toothy smile, apparently pleased with the chuckles he'd elicited, then continued, "It's an open secret within the profession that our featured speaker, despite having made so many contributions of incontestable and permanent value to mathematics and science has—because of his own uncompromising moral code—refused to accept any of the honors he has been awarded previously over the years on 'ethical grounds!' He did not approve, he said, of the capitalistic and exploitative policies of the corporate entities that sponsored them. Imagine! It is our hope, however, that he will accept the surprise award we are bestowing on him today. It is a nationally sponsored award, supported solely by funds out of the Royal Treasury of Qarmat, and this is the first time it is to be presented. I am privileged to say that it redounds to the pride and pleasure of Qarmat that we have the opportunity to designate a native son, and one so deserving on the world stage, as its first recipient!"

Turning back to Samiel, whose surprise and embarrassment were evident in his face, Badat said, "Dr. Amal Koraoun el-Mudharrisi, the nation of Qarmat takes pleasure in awarding you the King Essid el-Roweed Award for Lifetime Contributions to Science and Education in the Mathematical Field!"

And with a flourish, the Prime Minister drew away the cloth and presented Samiel with an exquisitely wrought solid gold statuette of the venerable Leonardo "Fibonacci" of Pisa inscribed with his name.

Samiel, recovering his customary sober expression, but experiencing an involuntary tremor—the result of a flood of conflicting emotions he couldn't analyze in the moment—took the statuette, admired it briefly and mumbled a "Thank you," almost too softly for the microphone to catch. And then, finding no other resting place, he abruptly handed it back to the Prime Minister. "If you don't mind," he said.

Badat, clearly delighted at having flustered the stoical Samiel at last, accepted the statuette with a graceful bow and withdrew.

Samiel, still trembling, moved to the microphone and addressed the audience in a dry, uninflected voice, "Your Highness, Honorable Ministers, honored guests, ladies and gentlemen…."

And then, without reference to the award he'd just received or other preamble, he launched into his talk.

"The tendency of the intelligent mind to expand its domain," he began, "that is to say, to extend those startling but untraceable arcs of sentience that exceed any predictable capability or achievement measurable simply by calculating the number and position of synapses in the brain, has been extensively studied, but remains a little-understood everyday feat of man—but also, to a curious extent, of many other animal species. It is not possible to anticipate, from any set of observations or measurements of an individual, the capacity of a vigorous community of the species for building a tunnel, a tower, or a dam—as is accomplished, for example, by colonies of termites and beavers; or for herding another species for food, as ants do with aphids; or for communicating direction, distance, and goal, as bees do for a food source.

"After exhaustive study of the brains of birds, it remains a mystery as to how hundreds, even thousands of birds in a migrating flock, establish and maintain in concert direction, positional rotation, and pattern of flight. One only has to behold a murmuration of starlings against the sky at dusk to be left almost breathless at the faultless display of intriguing, swirling patterns they form, or to contemplate the unerring navigational skills even the smallest birds exhibit flying through storms or the dark of night over thousands of miles during migrations, to be struck by wonder!

"Indeed, how are social and political systems created?—processes apparently instinctual, by the way, in many species besides man.

"The terms 'swarm intelligence' and 'collective intelligence'—which are similar though not equivalent—and which have been popularized by Hofstadter, Wheeler, Durkheim and others working independently, refer to the study of these effects. Swarm intelligence, or SI, is the collective activity of individual participants who, following very simple rules and without any centralized controlling structure, behave in a manner that appears to be random, or even competitive, but which nonetheless leads to some large, significant result suggesting the emergence of an overall group consensus, or 'intelligent' global behavior.

"As we will show, a remarkable feature of swarm intelligence is that—*with the unique exception of man*—an extensive search through the literature will discover no report of the grand plan going awry under normal conditions. Once a critical mass of individuals congregates, and while the colony is viable, the project *always comes together correctly*. There are no known failures where, for example, the puzzle-pieces of mud lie about in a useless heap because the insects can't figure out how to make the ends join up to make a tower.

"Our studies suggest that each insect has—not an isolated piece of the puzzle in its tiny brain—but a miniature matrix of the whole plan, such that once a critical mass assembles the job of building begins. No one insect is essential, hundreds may die before the structure is half-done. But while the swarm survives, the building goes on. It is an effect remarkably evocative of Aristotle's conundrum of the soul, in which he suggests that the soul is a single force, like a great river that may flow as *separate streams* into each living being, but these separate streams *cannot diverge* from the general movement, direction, and pattern of the whole...."

...And yet the Conference too leaves a bitter taste in Samiel's mouth as he thinks about it now, three years later. For even his appearance there had been a ploy designed by Badat as an inducement to draw him into all the squalid business of the trial that followed. But he has no one to blame other than himself. He'd foreseen Badat's intentions from the beginning. And by the time the PM had shown up at his home in Mudharris, he had already made his decision:

"...It's our new Citizen Participation Kiosk," Badat said. "Wait, wait, I want to show you how it works. It's really quite brilliant!"

Samiel watched, as Badat pressed the Enter key, and the screen changed from the crest of the Qarmatian Constitutional Monarchy to an input form requesting one's name, address, tribal affiliation, email address (optional), and a password. For the sake of the demonstration Badat entered a sample of the necessary information, hit Enter again, and the new screen offered a menu of options:

    a. Vote for a Candidate

    b. Vote on an Issue

    c. Make a Suggestion

d. Register a Complaint

"Most of the people don't yet have computers, of course, and can't even afford one," Badat continued. "So we've installed terminals in the kiosks in local government offices and in the larger souks of every province in the country!" He clicked on "d. Register a Complaint," and proceeded to input some imaginary official misconduct to demonstrate the application. "There's even one in your little town hall here in Mudharris—did you notice?"

Samiel shook his head, no.

"Well, anyway," the PM continued, "we're very proud of this project. It provides ready access to the ballot box, and allows any citizen to report an instance of police brutality or official lapse of duty without having to go through the endlessly indirect earlier process of complaining to the village elder, who passes it on to the sheikh, who passes it on to the local emir, etc., etc. Naturally, the village elders oppose it, they feel they will be by-passed and lose their influence. That's true, of course, but it's no matter. And we've had some criticism from the international human rights people, but that's typical with them. They badger you to make democratic changes, and then criticize the way you do it! But I mean, all these freedom-weirdos in Boston, New York, London, or wherever, don't understand anything about the desert, Arabic culture, or how our people think. This has really been a great boon in our fight against corruption and malfeasance here."

But as the Prime Minister proceeded with his demonstration, Samiel could perceive some of the difficulties that might have been subject to criticism by human rights organizations. The online form had restrictions. There were long, tortuous, repetitive questions requiring excruciating details of the abuse in question, including the name, rank, department, and command post superintendent of the official(s) involved; character limits for answer length, and software anomalies. One, which Samiel witnessed during Badat's demonstration, was the software's tendency to truncate answers to questions in mid-word or mid-sentence at the right- and left-hand margins, confounding attempts to give coherent answers. Another was the automatic time-out. In each instance, the time-out shut down access to the system after five minutes without a keystroke and blanked out all answers. Badat, laughing at one such incident occurring under his own hand as he paused to digress, said that the time-out was imposed purposely for security reasons, to protect the complainant's privacy. But it required the applicant to begin the whole process all over again. And the fee charged for the privilege of filing the application, which was nonrefundable, covered only a maximum of three time-outs.

"Absolutely brilliant!" Badat said, slapping the lid down on his laptop with a final chortle. "No one reads the reports, of course—or counts the ballots either, for that matter. They're saved on disk for a year or two and then discarded. So nothing really changes—but that's the point, isn't it. It does, however, permit us to get an early handle on possible future troublemakers before they wise up and go underground. And the beauty is that the people love it! They have the satisfaction of having somebody—albeit, only a machine—to tell their troubles to. And as for us," he added, turning his fingers inward toward himself as the head of the government, "I can't tell you how much trouble it's already saved us!"

Samiel could not help noticing how fat and prosperous and official Badat looked, nattily dressed in an expensive Savile Row suit of clothes and bedecked with the gold chain and badge of the Prime Minister draped across his chest. "Excuse me," he said, with a smile, and stepped away for a moment.

"Ah, but I'm boring you with my new toy," Badat said, as Samiel returned with a kettle of fresh mint tea. "I apologize, Amal Koraoun. That's not what I came to see you about, obviously. Oh, I'm sorry!" he added, as he saw Samiel suddenly look at him sharply, "I just forgot for the moment that you prefer to be known now as Samiel. I'm curious about that, by the way—but!" he raised a hand to ward off a response, "no need to explain, certainly not to me! If that's your choice, I accept it, of course! It's just that it makes it a little confusing, d'you see, for another reason—but we'll get to that later. No problem! So, um...."

He paused to glance around at the sparse, functional furnishings in the little sitting room of the modest concrete house that Samiel now called home, and pursed his lips in silent disdain. After a moment, he said, "I've known for some time that you were back, of course." And with a wave of his hand, as if to gesture toward the obvious, he added, "But I assumed, since you'd returned so...*quietly*, that you wanted your privacy. I didn't wish to disturb you. It'd been my hope, as I'm sure, it was yours, that you live out the rest of your days in peace and quiet here in your ancestral home."

Samiel nodded patiently, but said nothing.

Badat took a sip of tea, smiled and smacked his lips, "Excellent! Most excellent!"

They fell silent for a moment, and Samiel's thoughts

turned ironically to the revolutionary struggle they'd shared, the curious ways times had changed, and the details that had gone unmentioned in the laconic responses each had given the other earlier in the visit regarding the turn their lives had taken in the twenty-five years since they'd last met.

Samiel had, in fact, been living in Qarmat again for some time. Initially, there'd been some signs of sullenness among his neighbors, but that had passed, and a large percentage of the population was too young to know him or remember the Revolution. Meanwhile, in the past twenty-five years the country had experienced violent changes. The government of the Qarmatian People's Republic had fallen after only five years, when King Saddahi, having fled the country to save his own skin, had succeeded in inducing both Dar el-Nar and Libya to invade his own country and put him back on the throne by promising them a share in the future profits anticipated from the development of Qarmat's oil reserves. The QPR was at a disadvantage at the time. The war that had brought them to power had devastated the country and drained the Treasury. The fledgling government was still in the process of rebuilding, but the Qarmatians had to do everything from scratch themselves, because the French were gone and other developed countries were hanging back, waiting to learn if the new QPR government would be stable and amenable to trade and other diplomatic niceties.

Notwithstanding, they might still have beaten back the invaders, had the country not been struck at the time by a flare-up of endemic malaria—and had the enterprising General Karim el-Akhmeinie, who'd initially abandoned the old monarchy to lead the Army of the Revolution to victory, not deserted again. He crossed the line to lead Dar el-Nar's forces under the flag of the King and took the best-equipped regiments with him. But when the General discovered that Saddahi had been assassinated, he had another change of heart. Ironically, Samiel reflected, it was Badat, Saddahi's distant cousin, who'd sent one of his adjutants, a scoundrel named Hamid bin Assad, on a secret mission to Dar el-Nar to assassinate Saddahi. In the event, when the General, who by that time had led the Dar el-Nar forces to victory over the QPR, heard the King was dead, he realized that Libya and the megalomaniacal ruler of Dar el-Nar would divide up his own country and exploit it even more voraciously than the French had. So el-Akhmeinie decided to gather up the remnants of his old Qarmatian Army and drive the invaders out again. He then set up Saddahi's infant nephew, Essid el-Roweed, as heir to the throne under a new Constitution, which created a constitutional monarchy—but the General retained the powers of regent, until the boy came of age.

Now, however, the illustrious, ingenious, and dou-ble-dealing General Karim el-Akhmeinie had finally gone to his reward, and the government was in trouble again. The boy he'd left on the throne was of little use. The el-Roweed blood had run thin two generations before, and Essid—though King and a man in age now, was still thought of as a boy, a figurehead and a fool, ignored or manipulated by his own ministers and unaware the country was verging again on collapse. The economy was a shambles, political corruption once more rampant, and the population, hun-gry and impatient, was becoming restive. Local violence was resurgent, but the police did nothing because they were not being paid regularly. And Dar el-Nar was back to making aggressive noises, lusting after the oil-rich deposits in the southern border provinces. But in the absence of the old General, the new Army, under inexperienced officers who'd been appointed by patronage, was sitting out the crisis, possibly hoping for an opportunity to institute a coup. Ahmed Ruhani, the Minister of the Interior and the most intelligent and capable of the current roster of politicians, refused for his own reasons to step into the leadership role, leaving it to Badat, ironically enough, to emerge as the new political force amid this chaos. But Badat had his hands full. How would he manage, Samiel wondered?

He was roused from his reverie by an ear-splitting roar that suddenly broke the quiet, as a swarm of young men raced their motorcycles past the house, raising a small dust storm that drifted in through the windows.

He glanced over to see Badat leaning forward and addressing him confidentially. The PM had apparently said something he hadn't heard, and was inching closer to speak over the noise outside.

"Actually, Amal—I mean, Samiel—excuse me—this human rights thing has become a big headache for us...." Badat paused, as if considering how to continue. Then said, "Well, fortunately, the solution is imminent! Russia, China and almost every country in the West are beating down our door for the rights to drill our oil. They're offering money, arms, food, medical assistance, favorable trading status, anything we want. We're going to have everything we need to give Dar el-Nar second thoughts about trying another invasion, and to keep order at home.

"There's only one small hitch," he added, with a sardonic twist to his mouth, "Public opinion! The U.N. has put everything on hold, until they can bring someone to trial for what they call 'crimes against humanity' committed during the Revolution—I know!" he said, as if anticipating a protest from Samiel, "It's absurd! Ridiculous! What business is it of theirs, if some small, out-of-the-way country like Qarmat experiences an occasional internal upheaval and sheds a little local blood along the way? None! It's none of their business! They've ignored us or exploited us for a hundred and fifty years, and now all of a sudden they want to put *us* on trial for 'crimes of humanity!'"

Samiel understood that Badat had meant to say "crimes *against* humanity" again, but let the error pass. Meanwhile, seeing through the histrionics, he waited impassively to hear the proposition that he'd anticipated all along that Badat had come to make.

As Badat went on to explain, he'd urged the King to hire a couple of American political hacks—ex-White House staff members, one a former agriculture secretary and the other a former chief counsel to a previous U.S. president—as lobbyists to spin up a positive image of Qarmat in order to gain sympathy in Washington and U.S. support to put pressure on the U.N. to drop the injunction. But so far, this had had little success. The U.N. was insisting on setting up a court of inquiry into the "oppressive and murderous rule" of the deposed Qarmatian People's Republic.

"…And," Badat continued, flapping his arms in frustration, "they say they want to punish the 'responsible' people! They're particularly insistent on trying the person who—as *they* put it—was the QPR's 'head of security and highest authority for military operations, torture and executions'—whose identity they know—and whose whereabouts, unfortunately, they also know—although how they found out you were back here, I haven't the faintest idea! I thought it was a well-kept secret, until now!"

He paused, and looked at Samiel, as though wanting to gauge his reaction before making his pitch.

But Samiel gave him no help. He sat in silence, showing no outward expression, calmly waiting for Badat to continue.

The PM flushed after a moment, and murmured, "Must I say it, Samiel?"

"Yes."

Badat took a deep breath, and then said, "You have given so much to this country already, Samiel. No one questions your devotion and patriotism and your selfless sacrifice over the years. And more than this, the government is fully cognizant and deeply appreciative of the glory that redounds to Qarmat for the magnificent scientific work done by you, as her native son. To Qarmat, you will always be a national hero. It would be beyond reason and conscience to ask, or expect, more of you—under any *normal* circumstance. However, in this extraordinary moment, we find that our hands are tied. The time is grave, the wolves are at the door, so to speak, and the fate of your country now hangs in the balance. With all due respect, and in deepest humility, your King has sent me as his messenger to ask you for this one last favor."

As Badat spoke, it passed through Samiel's mind that Mumi Malagawi el-Hawhza, the spiritual leader and inspiration for the Revolution, had died years earlier, and the mullah's son, Mumi Ahmed el-Hawhza, who'd been only a boy at the time of the Revolution, was now a respected imam in the community who extolled the virtues of peace. That left only Badat and himself as parties who might be held "responsible" for actions taken by the QPR. The other senior officers of the QPR were dead, in hiding, or fled into exile.

"If I had my way," Badat was saying, "I'd like to put that retromingent old bastard, Saddahi, in the dock! That would be something, eh? Well, at least we had the satisfaction of assassinating him! Meanwhile, the World Court at the Hague insists we find someone now living to put on trial. They know, of course, about me, that I was only a spy posing as a midlevel lieutenant—"

"Excuse me, Marwan," Samiel said, interrupting him, "did I hear you say you were *posing* as a midlevel lieutenant in the QPR?"

"Why, yes!" Badat said, looking at him as though surprised by the question. "You must have realized that yourself, toward the end. I was actually acting as a spy for the Crown!"

"Oh?" Samiel said, mildly, looking at the PM as an entomologist might have looked at a dung beetle that had suddenly sprouted a butterfly's wings.

"Of course!" Badat insisted. "Don't tell me you never realized that, Samiel! My goodness, for that whole five years I was a nervous wreck, thinking you were about to discover the truth and have me executed! I mean, after all, when you approached me to join, I was the Deputy Commander of the Qarmatian Security and Intelligence Service, was I not? I was surprised that you thought I might stoop to treachery against my own government! I only went along, d'you see, in the hope of taking advantage of the opportunity to gain intelligence against you—nothing personal, of course—but we were political enemies! The arrangement we made, as you remember, was that I would remain in my post with the government as a spy for the QPR—but this is twenty-five years later, Samiel, I think we can be frank with each other now, eh? And of course, the Hague has been made aware of all that, so, there'll be no question of my name coming up in the prosecution. In fact, perhaps I should warn you that any comments you might make in an attempt to incriminate me would only be interpreted as a ploy to evade your own responsibility and be turned against you! I'm sure you understand me, Samiel," he added, looking at him meaningfully.

"You've been uncharacteristically clear, Marwan," Samiel said, sardonically.

Badat smiled again, "Excellent! Excellent! But it's amazing, you know, because I never flattered myself that I could have kept such a brilliant man fooled for so long!"

Samiel merely nodded and let that too pass. He hadn't been fooled at all, then or now. And Badat's warning, as far as Samiel was concerned, was superfluous. At this stage in his life, he had nothing to fear from Badat or from any sentence a court might impose. If he were to agree to go to trial, his willingness would rest entirely on the opportunity to explain, for the sake of history, the larger causes and dynamics of the Revolution. He felt no guilt, and had no interest in spreading the blame—or for that matter in sharing the credit—for what he'd done, certainly not with the likes of Marwan Badat. And for all his shallow self-regard and predisposition to suspiciousness, the Prime Minister, Samiel knew, was shrewd enough to perceive that, otherwise he would never risk letting him go to trial. During the Revolution of course he had realized that Badat was a mere opportunist and would pass intelligence both ways, as he saw the advantage. Samiel had had little doubt that he would be able to distinguish truth from falsehood in Badat's reports to him, and had used those reports as mere possibilities in his own calculations. Meanwhile, he had used Badat to convey misleading information back to the Crown when it had served his purpose, so that Badat, frequently given real intelligence as well, never suspected he was being played. Badat had been a mere tool of the QPR—despite whatever delusions of grandeur he'd had at the time. Nevertheless, Samiel reflected ironically, Badat was a survivor, and had only proven once again his agility and resourcefulness in setting himself up as the hero in the scenario he was now proposing.

"…You know how these institutions work," Badat was saying, "they want someone of high rank to take responsibility. And hell, where can you find a responsible person when you need him, eh?" he laughed and slapped Samiel chummily on the knee, then instantly sobered and apologized, "Ah, please excuse me, Samiel, it was just a silly, impulsive gesture, I meant no disrespect."

Samiel dismissed it with a glance.

"Anyhow," Badat went on, "they know you're here, in Mudharris, and they threaten—*Allah karim!*" he shook his head at the outrageousness of it, "They have no sense of respect! They have the fucking balls to threaten to hunt you down themselves, if we don't produce you! In a way, I suppose, you've left yourself open to that by insisting on using your nom de guerre. I can't imagine why you do that, myself, but it probably made it easier for them to find you! Anyway, rest assured, *we*—I mean the Qarmatian Government—have absolutely no intention—let me repeat: *no intention*—of arresting you, *inshallah*! It was our hope that, once you understood the situation the country was in, you'd offer to come forward on your own." He hesitated, then added, "I know you're ill, Samiel, I've heard the rumors. But at least I'm in a position now to be of some help to you. And I can promise you that the court will be lenient with you. After all, it's just a public relations game they'll be playing. They'll delve into a few gory details, make a few speeches for the benefit of the press, and it'll all be over in a trice! Maybe they'll sentence you to a few days' community service—with time off for good behavior, who knows? Rest assured, I'll certainly put in a good word for you! But after that, I promise you, you'll be able to spend the rest of your days at home here in peace and quiet."

The Prime Minister heaved a sigh, as though he'd gotten a great weight off his chest, then laughed, "We've been through a lot together, you and I, over the years, eh? Hopefully, we'll all quietly fade away into *ghaybah* when this is all over, *inshallah!*" he said, referring, ironically, to the Islamic version of apotheosis available to saints and holy men only.

They were silent a moment, as Badat awaited Samiel's consideration of the proposal.

"No welcoming palm fronds, then!" Samiel said, finally, matching Badat's sarcasm. "I'm to be *dhabîhah?*"

Badat appeared to be taken aback by the harshness of the term, which referred to a sacrificial animal especially chosen and prepared for ritual slaughter. "Samiel! For Heaven's sake, you do us an injustice—and a dishonor to yourself, as well! I am deeply hurt! I—we did not mean to—"

"No matter," Samiel said, cutting him off with a gesture. And then, to bring the conversation to a close—for it had gone on too long already for his taste—he rose and added, "Thank you for your time, Your Excellency. I will give your proposal due consideration."

But of course he'd already thought about it. Rumors travelled both ways between the Capital and the little medina of Mudharris, and Samiel had been expecting this visit. He would be arrested—Badat's protestations were merely spurious—and put on trial in any case. Badat was right too, that he was ill, and at his age he had neither the reason nor the will to escape again into exile. In fact, it was even odds whether he might even live long enough to see the end of such a trial. Suicide might be something he'd consider toward the end, should the physical symptoms reach that point, but otherwise it would only give the wrong impression, that he felt overcome by guilt or was reluctant to present his own argument to the world. For neither was the case. He did not feel guilty for what he had done, he had merely done what had been necessary at the time to implement a decision of conscience, and he actually welcomed the opportunity to make that clear. He was not really sanguine that the prosecution would be interested in undertaking the probing investigation he would prefer, which would give him the chance to guide the Court through the history of abuses, corruption, exploitation, cultural debasement, and national shame that had led to the Revolution—factors that were common to all such violent revolutions—but it might be worth the try, he had nothing to lose. And there was also the possible side-benefit that the trial would offer the survivors some closure. They deserved at least that, after all these years. So there was nothing now to consider, he'd made up his mind before Badat had come through the door.

Badat, however, seemed nonplussed by the philosophical imperturbability of the man before him. He stumbled to his feet, his urge to exit an uncomfortable situation apparently at odds with his reluctance to leave without nailing his prey to the wall. "I hope you will—" he began, but stopped as he saw Samiel showing him out. "We have only a little time," he prompted, walking toward the door. Then, he turned back, his eyes alight with a sudden inspiration. "Ah! What an idiot!" he said, slapping his own temple. "I completely forgot to mention the Conference! As you know, the bi-annual World Conference of Theoretical Mathematics is being held here—in el-Rawi, I mean—next month. And the King—well, this was the little problem I mentioned earlier," he said, blushing. "You see, the King made a special request that you attend—but you see, the invitation is extended to you as Amal Koraoun, because, after all, that's the name you are famous under as a mathematician, am I correct?"

Samiel nodded and pursed his lips ironically at Badat's confusion.

Badat smiled, "Yes, correct! So, hopefully, this will be no problem, I mean, certainly no offense was intended…!" He was rummaging in the inside breast pocket of his pin-striped suit, and finally pulled out a large deckle-edged envelope embossed with the royal crest and printed with the name, "Dr. Amal Koraoun el-Mudharrisi" in gold-leaf Arabic script.

"The King would be most pleased," he continued, pressing the envelope into Samiel's hand, "to have you attend as the guest of honor, and would be most grateful if you would be so kind as to consider delivering the keynote address for the occasion."

19.

"We submit," Samiel said, concluding his lecture at the Mathematics Conference in the Royal Palace Hall, a month after that visit from Badat, "that these miniature matrices that we have proposed to exist in the brains of birds, animals and insects—for termites building towers, for instance, for ants herding aphids, or the choreography of bird flight—we submit that these matrices and the matrix for language that Mr. Noam Chomsky has proposed as being innate in every human infant, are essentially of the same nature, although, in the human brain, different areas of neuronal systems may be involved. It's even possible that this complex and species-wide matrix of latent ability in humans also accounts, on the larger scale, for Jung's archetypal patterns of human cultural development, although Jung would've had no way of anticipating that, given the state of neuroscience in his time. It would seem to be the common tendency of peoples across cultures to invent narratives to explain phenomena not otherwise immediately comprehensible: Who are we? Where did we come from? Why does day follow night? And, what follows death? The neuroscientist Michael Gazzaniga has identified an area in the left forebrain which he calls 'the interpreter,' which seems to collate and make sense of our diverse, separate neural input and output systems, explains our own actions to us, and gives the brain a sense of unity—and ourselves a sense of identity. Further study might show that this 'interpreter' could prove to be instrumental in fabricating these larger cultural narratives, suggesting a common neurological basis underlying all social, cultural and political constructs of man. For in all these cases, socialization is necessary to elicit the expression of these tendencies. Indeed, Émile Durkheim has argued that society is the sole source of human logical thought.

"The current fascination—and skill—of our youth, wherever the facilities are available, with video games, computer programming, and social media would seem to be an illustration of this. Political and social ideas seem to spread at a greater rate with each generation. Through the Internet they now spread all around the globe in the blink of an eye. Governments, once secure within the walls of their ideologies, must now scramble to wall out this deluge. Whether you want to call it Lamarckian revisionism, phenotypic plasticity, or some other Darwinian heresy, it cannot be denied that historically, among Hominids at least, whatever new technology one generation has to invent the next generation seems to the manner born, to take it in with the air it breathes, as if the expertise to operate and elaborate these new technologies was already innate. Within a single modern generation the intelligence of the species seems dramatically enhanced.

"As our research suggests," he added then, turning and gesturing toward the mathematical graph and notations on the final slide projected on the screen behind him, "the unfolding of swarm intelligence in a species collective might be said to be of the order of $(ni)^x$ in all dimensions, where *n* equals the matrices of neuronal subsystems per individual, *i* equals the number of individuals of the same species within the community (that is, in communication with one another), and *x* equals the unpredictable power of environmental influences."

Samiel paused as if he'd come to the end of his lecture. Then he tilted his head, deliberating on whether to express an afterthought. He said, "We've been speaking here of *technical* intelligence. Swarm intelligence necessarily involves another capacity, which might be called *cooperative* intelligence. It has been suggested, by the mathematician Yuri Manin, among others, that sentience developed as an evolutionary strategy for constraint, to protect the organism against its own self-destructive impulses. This can be extrapolated to the *con*structive impulse of the swarm. Obviously, the tendency of swarms to build things would be pointless if the individual organisms could not cooperate, could not resist the temptation to destroy one another—as they might, say, if they followed the blind impulse to compete for food. So, here, it must be said, we have a tension between what seem contradictory innate impulses: swarm-negative individual self-preservation on one hand—*competition*, in other words—and self-sacrificing swarm *cooperation* on the other. This is a tension operating on the most rudimentary levels extending across numerous species in diverse phyla."

He paused again, choosing his words carefully, before continuing, "Certain commentators have construed this tension, at least on the human scale, as a *moral* tension. Some have even posited it to be an existential dilemma that civilizations over time have sought to resolve in the form of civil laws or moral codes. Whether there has been any progress in this area, however, remains uncertain. I said, earlier, that man provides the only known exception to the grand plan of swarm intelligence succeeding under normal conditions. History provides countless instances in which the technical intelligence of the species seems enhanced with succeeding generations, while evidence of comparable advances in *moral* intelligence seem transitory at best. Apparent advancements seem continually to experience setbacks. And yet there seems to persist in our species a paradoxical desire to rise above our nature. As one neuroscientist, V. S. Ramachandran, has put it, we seem to "want to be more than merely human…. We feel like angels trapped inside the bodies of beasts, forever craving transcendence…."

"But that is a matter for another discussion," he added. "Thank you."

He turned abruptly from the microphone, and without pausing to acknowledge the standing ovation, left the stage. He continued up the side aisle to the massive brass doors of the hall, which the guards swung open before him, stepped out into the vestibule and presented his wrists to be hand-cuffed by the waiting police.

20.

"In addition to the defendant's admissions on the witness stand," the prosecutor is saying now, the week following Samiel's MRI, "admissions to participating in torture, genocide, and—"

"Objection! The interrogation procedures, as described by the prosecution, that these victims may have been subjected to, however unpleasant, have not specifically been included under the definition of torture as it appears in the Treaty document—"

"Excuse me! Your Honor, the prosecution wishes to have the Court note that in addition to the defendant's admissions on the witness stand to participating in torture, genocide, and mass murder—if not by direct commission, then indirectly by virtue of the fact that they occurred under his command and with his full knowledge—"

"Objection! The Treaty document does *not*—"

"What? It's absurd for the defense to question the nature, or rather, the definition of torture in these cases, when—"

"Order!"

"Objection! The defendant has not made any admission of committing *genocide* in these proceedings! And as regards to torture—"

"He most certainly *has!*—at least, by implication! But irrespective of that fine point, the prosecution will prove his responsible role in the genocide that was committed—"

"Order!"

"Objection! Firstly, the U.N. Treaty does not include political groups among those eligible for protection under the definition of genocide. This was the reason given why the International Court of Justice has not brought charges against the Khmer Rouge in Cambodia. Secondly, regarding the numbers of individuals that must be affected in order to satisfy the definition of mass murder—"

"If the Court please, the prosecution intends to show that among the nearly two million people killed by the QPR, in addition to purely political victims—"

"—Thirdly—excuse me, Your Honor, but thirdly, and most significantly, there remains the question of proof of *intent*—"

"—the numbers of those slain among certain tribes will be shown to have nearly resulted in complete decimation of those tribes—and we will make a special case for certain religious groups, as well, most especially, the Maturidist Sunni—"

"Order!"

"—congregation in the Department of Bi'r Tareekh, of whom a mere handful remained by the time—"

"—The question of *proof of intent* is paramount and critical to the prosecution's case, and so far, the prosecution has not—"

"Order!"

"If the Court please, we maintain that Samiel has admitted to playing a significant role—'second in command,' to quote his own words—in the terror, torture, and mass murders...."

"Order!" the Chief Magistrate repeats, striking the bench with his gavel. "Come to order at once, or I'll have the courtroom cleared!"

"Excuse me! Your Honor? Excuse me!" the defense counsel calls out with sudden urgency. "With apologies to the prosecuting attorney," he continues, turning to the judges, "the defense requests the Court grant permission for us to approach the bench." And waving a document in the air that he's just been handed by an aid, he adds, "Defense would like a brief conference in anticipation of making a motion."

"Permission granted," the Chief Magistrate says. Counselors may come forward."

"Your Honor, if you please," the defense counsel says, as the two attorneys reach the bench, "we've just received a joint statement from the medical doctors, the psychiatrists, and the internist, assigned by the Court to evaluate our client's physical and mental status. The defense feels it reveals new information that is extremely pertinent to the case, and we request to submit it for the Court's evaluation before continuing with these proceedings."

Chief Magistrate Abul-Abbas glances briefly at the young prosecuting attorney, whose face betrays his bewilderment, then turns a shrewd eye on the defense counsel, before gesturing for him to hand up the document. After studying it for a long moment, he looks up, his expression a mask of impassivity, and hands it to the prosecutor for his perusal.

The document consists of three short paragraphs of text on a single typed page, but the prosecutor reads it over several times, his face flushing with growing disbelief, before handing it back across the bench.

The Chief Magistrate passes it along to his associate

judges, then hands it to the court clerk to be entered into the record, before turning back to address the defending attorney.

"Defense counsel wishes to make a motion?"

"Yes, Your Honor. According to the statement you've just read, our client experienced 'cruel and unusual treatment' at the hands of the medical technicians at the hospital last week, where he was subjected, against his wishes, to Magnetic Resonance Imaging. He experienced a nervous attack of claustrophobia when he was inserted into the tube, and he had so violent a reaction that he bruised both hands badly and actually fractured the knuckle of one hand. We all saw him in the witness box on the days following that experience with his hands bandaged as he, nevertheless, patiently gave testimony. Further, the medicine he is required to take as treatment for his gastro-intestinal disease was taken away from him at the hospital and not returned until several days later, during which time he experienced severe discomfort and pain preventing him from sleeping, in addition to incontinence, vomiting, rectal bleeding, loss of appetite, weight loss, severe psychological stress—"

"We've read the medical report," the Chief Magistrate says, interrupting him. "Your point, counselor?"

"The point, Your Honor, is that, according to Article Fifteen of the International Convention Against Torture, statements made as a result of torture cannot be invoked as evidence, except against a person accused of torture as evidence that the statement was made. This means that the fact that a confession was made as a result of torture is an admissible fact, but the contents of such confessions cannot be accepted for their truthfulness."

"We are aware of the articles of the Convention," the Chief Magistrate says, "kindly state your motion."

The defense counsel draws a breath, then says, "Based on the fact that, however inadvertently, the defendant was subjected to torture, and according to Article Fifteen, any confessions or admissions he may have made under the conditions of torture are not admissible evidence against him in the International Court, defense moves to declare a mistrial!"

———

That same night, Samiel is startled when he looks up from the book of Hafez's poems he's reading in his cell and sees Ibrahim walking down the corridor toward him—alone! He blinks his eyes to be sure he isn't hallucinating. It's been at least three years since he's last seen the boy. Ibrahim is taller now, his youthful angularity filling out, and his features prematurely aged by the shadows of the overhead lights in the prison corridor. But for Samiel to see him there, in the flesh, is an entirely unexpected pleasure. But wait, Samiel thinks, it's the middle of the night. And other than that abortive meeting with the handful of torture survivors—and the one visit from his old Revolutionary comrades, who'd bribed the guard—he's had no visitors. He had been explicitly told he would not be allowed any. But here is Ibrahim—alone, no guard accompanying him. He can't have simply slipped past the guards…has somebody "arranged" this visit?

The boy's expression has also gained some hardness, Samiel sees as he approaches, but in that handsome, hawklike face the same dark eyes hunted restlessly. And despite his initial pleasure in seeing Ibrahim there, Samiel begins to sense the tension coiled inside the boy, and soon guesses his reason for coming. As Ibrahim stands there staring at him without speaking, Samiel can well imagine what he may be thinking. And yet curiously, Ibrahim seems like an image carved out of sand, the relic of a past of which the boy has no consciousness, shaped by a present he doesn't understand, and propelled toward a future without clear purpose. Until he confronted Ibrahim the first time, in Abul-Abbas's courtyard, the boy's one guiding principle had seemed to be making mischief—by way of avoiding boredom. He'd acted as if he'd been born of disillusionment. But at that moment in the courtyard, when Ibrahim had taken el-Aqrab's knife in his hand, Samiel had seen a new fervor shine in his eyes. Now only fourteen and standing on the other side of the bars, he is already, Samiel feels, a formidable psychological presence. Even in shadow, his eyes are compelling. As he stands there, unmoving and without saying a word, his energy is palpable. A strange light seems to emanate from the air about him. He has intelligence and will— and, Samiel perceives, a purpose now. Samiel smiles at the irony, thinking he can almost admire the boy's focus and passion—except for the fact that he fears they are ephemeral and may only lead him into self-destructive tantrums later. Will the vengeance Ibrahim seeks now bring him any peace, Samiel wonders? Or will the fire, once released, only rage on until the boy himself is eventually consumed by it? He can't blame the boy, he realizes, because Ibrahim's wild, resentful nature is largely due to an inevitable feeling of abandonment—for which he must accept the blame. Ibrahim, he suddenly thinks, is like the man in the poem who wandered in the desert without a shade in his soul.

A man like me? Samiel wonders, as he rises to meet him. Ibrahim is only a boy, after all, still a child. Is it the children, in the end, who'll be our judges? The old cloth merchant, the boy's grandfather, has most likely poisoned Ibrahim's mind against him. But the old man had his reasons....

As Samiel rests his hands on the cell door, it swings open and he steps back, surprised. It isn't locked! The guard must have forgotten to lock it behind him when he'd been brought back from court earlier that afternoon.

He sees Ibrahim hesitate, apparently equally surprised to find the door opening before him. But as he steps back, Ibrahim steps into the cell toward him, his hand sliding against his thigh.

Samiel studies the boy for a moment, and suddenly it's almost as if he can read Ibrahim's mind, and even hear the voice of the boy's grandfather echoing in his ear:

"Samiel! His name is Samiel! He cut their throats. He beheaded them. I saved you! I saved you!"

Samiel has been aware that from the time Ibrahim was a small child his grandfather had been poisoning the boy's image of him, depicting him as a monster, saying that he, Samiel, was a killer and had murdered millions of people. And now, with the boy having reached his fourteenth birthday, the grandfather would probably have told him that he was old enough now to know the whole truth. He would have embellished the story, of course, painting the scene over and over so vividly into the child's mind that by now Ibrahim would probably think he was there and remembered it himself:

They'd come in the dark before dawn. He'd been asleep inside. Something had awakened him and when he'd gotten out of bed and gone to the door, all he'd been able to make out in the starlight were the dogs, they were running among the shadows of the stucco houses, running away from the village with their tails between their legs. Then he'd heard the camels, or actually felt them, felt their hooves drumming in the sand beneath his bare feet. When he'd looked to the east where the sky over the desert was just graying into light, there against the pale rim of the false dawn he'd seen the riders, still only gray ribbons of movement like heat waves shimmering against the paler gray of the sky, as they'd drifted toward him, slow and timeless like forever. He'd turned and run back inside to tell his mother and father—

"But it was too late," the old man would've said. "Samiel was the leader of those raiders. It was Samiel who beheaded your parents! But you're a man now, and the shame of it is upon your head. You must avenge them. You're a man now, and it's time you avenged them. This is the way it happened!"

Meanwhile, Samiel is aware that Ibrahim has taken another step toward him with the jade-handled knife, previously hidden in the boy's clothes, now raised in his hand.

But he doesn't react. He's thinking of when he'd first returned from his voluntary exile in Russia. He finds it hard to believe that it was so long ago. He'd started teaching elementary arithmetic again at a *mektaba,* a local primary school in the little *qarya* of Bi'r Tareekh, a very ancient settlement that even predated the coming of the Romans. After the first few years he taught there, among the parents and older siblings who brought the children to class was a young widow. She had had no schooling, but she was intelligent and curious. Some months into the school term, she asked him to teach her to read so that she might help her son with his homework. The reading lessons had to be very short because even though she was a widow, her husband had left her with nothing and she'd had to return to her father's house. Her father, the headman of the village who'd taken upon himself the title of Sheikh el-Bi'r Tareekh, eked out a living as a peripatetic cloth merchant. But he was the imam of a very conservative sect of Maturidist Sunni, she said, and would not approve of her getting schooling. And if she returned home as much as an hour later than expected, he would beat her. It didn't matter that she was a widow and a mother, she said, he would beat her anyway.

Halfway through the school term, her son took sick with malaria and died. But one afternoon, a month or so later, he found the young widow sitting outside the classroom. She wanted to continue her lessons. She said her name was Manât and she wanted to learn. So, they began again. But she was still distraught about the loss of her little boy, and she would sometimes have to beg his pardon and draw aside to grieve. He tried to comfort her. They were both lonely. They became lovers. It was never meant to be anything more than that. But even that was difficult in a small, strict Maturidist community, and they had to hide their affection from others. But he remembered that she used to wear a perfume she made herself from the crushed petals of orange blossoms. He began to look forward to that scent as he anticipated her coming on each of their appointed days. She was very beautiful.

And then, a little more than a year later, with great trepidation, Manât told him she was pregnant. She must have thought his reaction idiotic. He simply gaped at her in perplexity, as if she'd just spoken to him in a language he didn't know.

And in truth, he didn't know how to respond.

As a young man, he'd had affairs, but only two passions: mathematics and the Revolution. And once the Revolution had become a reality, all else had been put aside. He'd never been very close to anyone. Despite being well-aware of his intellectual and psychological powers—the latter evidenced time and again in his ability to anticipate and manipulate others—he'd always been extremely shy, self-critical and conscious of his own strangeness, almost as if he were of a species apart. To open himself to others, he felt, would risk their discovering this inner strangeness only to be driven off by it—leaving him feeling even more alienated than before. Yet he relished the high opinion of others and kept alert for overheard or unprompted observations about him, in his ongoing effort to ascertain what sort of creature he might actually be. Still, he took pride in his self-sufficiency and realized that he possessed an extraordinary ease and agility in outward behavior. But this often left him feeling like a fraud and puzzled him. In odd moments, he'd run his finger along the line of his jaw or press at his temples, as if feeling for the edges of a mask—doing this with an urge like that of the painter who peeked impulsively under his own finished canvases to see what it was they'd come into existence to hide. In his associations with others there were few with whom he shared a common interest, and none with a commensurable ambition. He was immoderately ambitious, and at the same time contemptuous of the public trappings of honor and repulsed by the confidence games this ambivalence led him to play, time and again, with his own conscience. It made him particularly sensitive to the duplicity and presumption of others, and dismissive of all those international programs sponsored by public or private institutions under the guise of promoting some ideal or other, for what they called benevolence and patronage he understood to be nothing more than vanity and co-optation.

Beyond this, he'd always chosen to live simply. He'd never cared to own anything and had no keepsakes. Whenever he'd travelled, whether crossing the desert or the sea, he'd carried little or nothing with him. All he'd ever needed was in his head. Even among the hardened desert nomads beside whom he'd fought in the Revolution, he'd been known as the one who could outpace and outlast anyone among them when it came to crossing miles of desolate wasteland without a pause for rest, food or water. More than once, under the pressures of sheer necessity, he'd ridden horses and camels into the ground. It was his soldiers who'd given him the name "Samiel."

But he hadn't always felt so centered within himself. As a youth, he'd sought earnestly for a model, a living ideal of the man he wished to become, one before whom he could willingly bow down and strive to emulate. His father, a good man but weak in spirit, had died young. And afterward, he'd found no viable candidates. Of two whose historical vision and depth of perception he'd found arresting, Mumi Malagawi el-Hawhza had proven to be vain, politically inept, slow to map concept to action, and lacking the psychological edge to lead the Revolution he'd inspired—having to pass that mantle on to him. And the other was the brilliant German-born French mathematician Alexander

Grothendieck, whose originality, independence of spirit, and boldness of intellect had so impressed him in his published papers and in their conversations during that mathematics conference so many years ago in Heidelberg. But in their correspondence over the following years he came to realize that Grothendieck was growing increasingly withdrawn, self-conflicted, quixotic and unstable. As for the rest, he was distanced from most other men—if not by their preoccupation with animal appetites, then by the limits of their perception and judgment. Women he'd regarded as too influenced by their carnal and maternal natures to be taken seriously. The fact that many of those he'd met had been attracted to him only seemed to underscore this assessment, for he considered carnal pleasure even lower on the scale of bestial indulgences than the need to seek comfort in another's arms out of weakness, hunger, or loneliness—a need he'd never experienced. And yet, although he'd taken little pleasure in sensual experience and usually shunned it, he had to admit to an inner conflict, because he'd also craved it in a way. He'd envied other men for their serene superficiality, for many of those same animal affinities he despised in himself. He had sometimes wished he could have enjoyed the interplay with women, the physicality of male bonding, and the tactile affection for animals that seemed to come to other men so naturally. But he was a creature apart.

And so, when he'd returned to Qarmat from his university studies abroad, he'd put his heart and soul into the Revolution. Later, when he'd gone into exile in Russia after the collapse of the Revolution, psychologists and journalists would seek to interview him and ask him why an academic, a man of science with his intellectual abilities, would have wanted to soil his hands with the sordid, bloody business of a popular insurrection. But as he told them, the challenging possibility of a momentous political endeavor was a form of seduction he could appreciate. It demanded deep insight, historical vision, a prescient sense of the exigencies of time, and a profound understanding of how to orchestrate the potential strengths of a huge collective effort irrespective of the individual weaknesses of men. It required an informed intelligence to set realistic goals, creative abilities of dissimulation and misdirection to motivate the hungry spirits of a confused population without alienating its more selfish impulses, an iron will to drive the necessary forces, a distant and devious nature with sufficient clarity of focus to manipulate others—attendant on an innate asceticism impervious to the temptations that distracted lesser men, an instinct for winning, and an imaginative and agile mind to anticipate and respond to countless contingencies and set-backs along the way. It would always be a grand gamble, for you would be playing spiritual reach against animal instinct, the longing of the soul against the lethargy of habit.

It was something he was born to do.

Nevertheless, he felt it was his role to serve as a caution to others, and this had both exhilarated and dismayed him. It had given him range and power to effect consequential changes in the country, but it had also left too many at his mercy. It was a great burden, and in the end, perhaps, it was too dangerous for one such as he to have had so much power. But he'd never found another whom he would have trusted with it. And so, if not he, then who?

All such questions had been mooted by the time of that April afternoon, when Manât walked into his classroom. He was already in middle age, his best work in mathematics was behind him, and the Revolution was a dream lost in time. His feeling about the future, then, was simply to walk through one day after another until the disappointments of the past and what seemed to be a prolonged and rather pointless present simply collided at the end. And while meeting her had offered a pleasant, unexpected interlude, it had seemed to him to be only that, a last, momentary indulgence in the lower appetites of his nature.

So that when Manât told him she was pregnant, he was caught completely off-guard. His instinctive response was simply to withdraw and dismiss her from his life—and yet, he found this instinct suddenly and inexplicably inhibited. Out of the blue, this charming, unaffected country girl had presented him with complications. He resented it. How could he not resent it—and resent her—if not so much because of her pregnancy, then because of how the astonishing clarity of her temperament had crept up on him unawares over so short a period of time that it could have elicited a reaction which, for him, was the strangest of all experiences: *confusion?* He smiled inwardly, now, at his own expense, thinking that although he'd been one who'd always intellectualized everything, at the time he'd given the possibility of such a development no thought whatsoever. It was as if she'd suddenly presented him with a problem for which he had no conceptual framework. That she might one day become pregnant was a known risk, although neither of them had wanted to think about it. But that he would be ambivalent about how to respond to the situation when it arose was something he could not have anticipated. He'd never before faced a situation he'd neither anticipated nor knew instinctively and immediately how to respond to. But now suddenly, standing against his natural impulse to get out of the relationship and throw her over, he'd discovered an incomprehensible wall of resistance: he did not want to throw her over, he wanted to keep her!

And while pondering this, he'd realized, in the next moment, that she'd told him he was about to be a father. But how could he be a father? He'd never considered being a father, he hadn't planned for that. Of course, he hadn't planned on meeting someone like Manât, either—but then he hadn't even realized how important to him she'd become until that moment. All at once, he felt foolish and inept, like a child out of school.

Finally, after he'd managed to overcome his momentary witlessness enough to calm her fears, they made a plan. First, as Manât's father was a very religious man, Samiel would begin attending regular prayer services at the small Maturidist mosque in the village. After a few weeks, he would approach the old Sheikh with a made-up story. Samiel would tell him that he was a well-to-do spice merchant from Thrace who was looking for a wife—but as he was getting older, he would prefer one who was not too young and frivolous. He would ask whether, for a small gratuity, the Sheikh would be good enough to accept an arrangement for the hand of a certain widow he'd heard of who'd recently lost a child— possibly the Sheikhs' own daughter, as he'd been told?—and then hint that he could afford to make it well worth the old man's while.

So one Friday, in the vestibule of the mosque, after *salat al-maghrib,* the sunset prayer, he approached the old man. But before he could tender his proposal, the old Sheikh suddenly jumped up and down, shouting and gesticulating wildly. And then the worshipers crowded around Samiel threateningly, as the old man cursed him, yelling that he was an apostate and a murderer and demanding he be thrown out of the prayer hall. It was all going wrong. Samiel wasn't concerned about any possible violence toward himself at the time. He knew that, even so long after the fall of the QPR, the simple country people there still feared him, as one might fear the Devil himself, and while they might hate him, they wouldn't touch him. But under the circumstances, he realized his cause was lost, and he withdrew.

He hadn't understood the old man's reaction until later. But in the effort to mollify Manât he'd been stupid. Over time, since the fall of the Revolution, he had forgotten the particulars of many of the victims—if, indeed, he'd ever known them, because he'd left the responsibility of prisoners largely to others—in fact, to Badat, mostly. And so, he didn't know, when he'd approached the Sheikh in the mosque, that the old man had been such a victim—one of the few lucky enough to escape—or that his three brothers and father had died in a QPR prison. He hadn't known, and so he hadn't expected to be recognized.

Then Manât, realizing she couldn't hide her pregnancy for long, fled. But she disappeared without telling him, or even giving him the chance to come up with another solution. He had means—they could simply have left the country. Now, she was gone, and he didn't know where.

He immediately set out to find her. Conflicting rumors had her in Qued Seenib, or in Sennai, or still hiding somewhere in Bi'r Tareekh. In desperation, he even sought out an old comrade, Muhammad el-Beghal, who'd been his most trusted lieutenant in the Revolution, to help to search for her. He'd heard that Muhammad had gone into hiding and was living under an assumed name. He didn't know where, but he didn't think the one-eyed, garrulous giant, whom he knew happened to be a native of Bi'r Tareekh, would be too hard to find. And he did find him, although it took a few days because el-Beghal had gone through several disguises since they'd parted. But he eventually discovered his trusted ex-lieutenant masquerading as an old woman in a ramshackle house overlooking a drainage ditch on the wrong side of town. The disguise was a little absurd, he reflected, as he finally stood facing the man. Despite the real stoop of age and the *niqab* covering el-Beghal's face, as soon as he opened his mouth, one heard his heavy bass voice, nor could one ignore the fact that there probably wasn't an *abaya* in all of Qarmat large enough to conceal those broad shoulders. Still, Samiel thought with a wry smile, it was a *likely* choice. El-Beghal had been a notorious womanizer in the old days, and so it was not so far-fetched to find him posing as the madam of a bordello.

Muhammad was happy to see him again, but hesitated at first to help, for fear of exposing himself to prosecution for his activities in the Revolution. But on seeing his old captain going freely about the country, he put aside his disguise for the sake of loyalty. Muhammad still had many contacts in the country, which they thought might be helpful in covering more ground. Even more important for Samiel, Muhammad was the one person at the time he thought he could entrust with his secret. And so he and Muhammad scoured the towns and countless desert communities along the way searching for Manât. At one point, they were given reason to believe that she might have been living hand-to-mouth on her own somewhere in el-Rawi. But they couldn't find her there. The search went on for over a year. And all during that time, Samiel felt his body physically clenching, as if readying for impact with some rushing blow that never came. It was during that period, the first and only time, that he felt fear.

He never found Manât, and never heard from her again.

For him, the months following her disappearance were fraught with emotional conflict. He felt disoriented, angry, and deceived, imposed upon by a sudden crowding confusion where there'd always previously been clarity and space. He felt put upon, taken advantage of, betrayed, and disillusioned. He'd never felt hate before, but now he hated himself for being weak enough to have been taken in by a little show of tenderness, and he hated Manât as the instrument of his vulnerability. But most of all, he felt deeply saddened and missed her terribly. He realized of course that without conscious intention on either side, he and Manât had become more deeply involved than they knew. And this had only happened in the short time they were together because they'd met at the one moment in each of their lives when this was possible. As for him, whether because of age or weariness, he'd simply let his guard down. Water under the bridge. Afterward, he'd keep an eye out whenever he had occasion to journey through the country, hoping against hope that he'd find her again. In the meantime, there was little else he could do but return to his work in mathematics.

It wasn't until years later that he learned her father had had people looking for her too, and someone had eventually found her in el-Rawi after all. The old man had had her brought back to Bi'r Tareekh, where he then vilified her, accused her of *zina*, the mortal sin of harlotry, and taken the child away from her. And then he'd had her—his own daughter—stoned to death in the village square.

Samiel was horrified when he heard—and oppressed by the sense of inevitability. It was *Sharî'ah*. *Sharî'ah* was her people's way of life. It was always the woman they accused, the woman they stoned. Except in the rarest of instances, the man was considered innocent, an honest soul seduced by an evil woman. He knew that. But she was a *widow*, he said, arguing with himself. Widows were no longer virgins, and normally shouldn't be held to so dire a standard. Her father was a monster! It was horrible, and unfair—and yet, it had always been this way. Traditionally, the father, or patriarch, was the sole arbiter of all virtue and sin within the family. He knew that, he'd grown up in the midst of it, and truth to say, he'd never given it much thought—until then. He could only blame himself.

But there was still the boy, his son. He determined that in the time he had remaining, he would watch out for Ibrahim. He'd keep a respectful distance while the child was in his grandfather's house, but he'd intervene, if necessary, to see that he was never in want, and when the time came, he would make sure that Ibrahim received a good education.

But the old man had later moved to the Capital and taken Ibrahim with him, and whenever he journeyed there to look in on the boy, Ibrahim would run away if he spotted him. But then, of course, he realized why. Ibrahim didn't know who he was, and the old man had been tortured by the QPR and he must have told the boy this, told him that

Samiel, had tortured and killed people. Hearing this almost from infancy, the boy had apparently accepted it, probably even internalized it as a memory of his own, imagining that he'd seen it happening with his own eyes—without stopping to reflect that the Revolution had ended thirteen years before he was born—

"*Allahu akbar!*"

— Samiel reaches out—and as the knife enters his heart—embraces his son.

The End

Other Books by Paul Hastings Wilson

Hunger's Season

Blues By the Numbers…And Other Numbers

A Son of the Wind, volume II of *Ibrahim's Eyes*
(forthcoming)